Ford
A bride for Bedivere

WITHDRAWN

WITHDRAWN

Baldwinsville Public Library
Baldwinsville, New York

First U.S. ed. ED. F

A BRIDE FOR BEDIVERE

By the same author

SARNIA
CASTLE MALINDINE

A BRIDE FOR BEDIVERE

by

Hilary Ford

WITHDRAWN

1817

HARPER & ROW, PUBLISHERS

New York, Hagerstown, San Francisco, London

This book was first published in Great Britain by Hamish Hamilton Ltd.

A BRIDE FOR BEDIVERE. Copyright © 1976 by Hilary Ford. All rights reserved. Printed in the United States of America. No part of this book may be used or reproduced in any manner whatsoever without written permission except in the case of brief quotations embodied in critical articles and reviews. For information address Harper & Row, Publishers, Inc., 10 East 53rd Street, New York, N.Y. 10022.

FIRST U.S. EDITION

ISBN: 0-06-011306-5

LIBRARY OF CONGRESS CATALOG CARD NUMBER: 76-26267

A BRIDE FOR
BEDIVERE

APR 2 5 1977

1

I cried the day my father died; but from joy.

They brought him back from the dockyard on a cart. It was a cold day, with drizzling rain, and the men who accompanied the body were wet and bedraggled. They had covered him with a tarpaulin, but one hand was exposed and rain had made a small puddle in the upturned palm. I did not need the halting and confused explanation from his fellow exciseman, Jos Larrimer: the hand, with the heavy gold ring on its little finger, told me everything. I put my own hand to my face, and touched the spot where, only a few days before, it had struck me.

From inside the house, Mama called: 'What is it, Jenny?', as Larrimer stumbled on: a fall from a ship's side ... dead instanter ... no pain ... no one's fault ... a sad accident.

I could smell the rum on his breath. Although it was morning, scarcely past eleven of the clock, he was well in liquor; and my father, I could be certain, would have been drunk. The excisemen, well supplied by their calling with the instruments of intoxication, started their drinking early. Drunkenness was one of the things I had loathed in him, but I blessed it now. I stared at the stiff white hand, realizing that never again would it clench into a fist.

My mother, getting no answer, came to the door. She was longer than I had been in grasping the situation. She stared at Larrimer and at the cart, at the drenched figures of the other two men, but somehow her eyes avoided the out-stretched hand and the bulge under the tarpaulin. It was only as Larrimer launched, even less coherently, a second time into his explanation, that she took it in. Then with a scream of pain and despair she rushed out to the cart, dragged down the top edge of the tarpaulin, and flung herself on the corpse, embracing it. I went after her to hold the frail body, racked with sobs of passionate grief for this man who, as long as I could remember, had brutalized and bullied and made a slave of her. I cried with her, but my heart sang.

There were only the two of us in the house—Harry was away at his job as errand-boy to Seddon's the grocers, and the little ones were at school. The men carried the body through into the front parlour, and laid it on the sofa. The clock ticked drily on the wall as it had done on so many occasions when I had come into here, a room used by the family only on special occasions, to escape him and to count the beads of my hate. My mother knelt beside the sofa, weeping for her loss.

Larrimer shuffled his feet and spoke to me. There would be a whip-round among the lads ... he'd be coming to see us again about that ... if there was anything else he could do. ... I thanked him, and said we should be all right. He nodded, tugging at a button on his uniform, and gave a sign to the men. They clumped out of the house, and I heard the creak and rattle of the cart-wheels on the cobbles, going away.

I left her to set the kettle on the fire : a cup of tea might help. She was shaking but had stopped crying when I returned. I put a hand gently on her shoulder and helped her to her feet. I urged her to sit down, but she shook her head. Things needed to be done, she said. She must go and get Mrs Tyrer, before he stiffened up.

Mrs Tyrer, in the next street, was the woman who laid out the dead. She had done that service for my sister and brother who died in infancy, charging only sixpence instead of the customary shilling. I said I would go for her, but my mother refused. I was to stay by my father, and see to making the tea. Mrs Tyrer would need a cup before she started on her work.

So I was left alone with him. Against the green gloom of aspidistras, which seemed to fill the room on this dark grey morning, his face was very white. I stared at it, almost as though seeing it for the first time; and it was true that for years now I had as far as possible averted my gaze from him.

He had been fifty the previous November, an occasion for even greater drunkenness than usual, culminating in yet another beating for my mother. He was a big man, six feet tall, broad of chest and shoulder, who had glorified in his physical strength. And he had been, I saw now with surprise, good-looking for his years. The dissoluteness of his life had done little to mar the handsome lines of his face. His moustache, brown flecked with white, was luxuriant over lips parted to show strong teeth and a firm chin dimpled in the middle. There was no sign of the violence either of his death or his life. He looked peacefully asleep. I touched my cheek again. A handsome man, and a brute.

My earliest memory was of watching, wide-eyed and sick with fear, as he beat my mother. It was a scene that was to be repeated times far beyond counting. Later I had been beaten myself, with the strap hanging inside the wash-house door on which he honed his razor. As the other children came, the same senseless cruelty had been enacted on them—right up to the occasion of last Sunday afternoon.

He had been drinking that day, not on duty, but at the pub. We had kept dinner for him until nearly three o'clock and then, with the children ravenously hungry, I had insisted that we sit down to eat. Mama had been nervous and uncertain—although he sometimes cursed the children and insisted on eating alone, there were other times when he liked them to be there, begging titbits off his plate—but I out-argued her, as I had often felt obliged to do in recent years.

3

I covered his plate and put it in the oven, checked the children's hands for cleanliness, and served them.

He came in when we were half-way through the meat, and a single look was enough to tell the blackness of his mood. Mama scurried to bring out his plate and put it in front of the carver chair. He said nothing until she had taken off the cover. It was roast beef with horse-radish sauce, of which he was particularly fond, with Yorkshire pudding, roast potatoes and cabbage. He stared at it, but did not take his seat. His gaze went to my mother, standing anxiously at his elbow.

'Dried-up muck.' His voice was slurred and heavy. 'What sort of a dinner is that to set before a man of a Sunday?'

She began a cringing apology. It might be enough, I thought: it sometimes was. Providing she was sufficiently abject, he might condescend to sit down and eat. But this time his belly was too swollen with ale. He put his hand to the plate, picked it up, and sent it crashing against the wall. The plate splintered, and gravy and scraps of food stuck there or trickled down to the skirting board. The paper was new: we had papered the room—all of us except him, of course—the previous weekend.

Harry's place at table was immediately to his right. I saw his look and willed him not to speak, but in vain. He started to protest, but before more than a word or two had left his mouth it was closed by a savage back-hand blow from my father's fist. It sprawled Harry back in his chair, and while he was off balance Father grabbed him by the shirt, and lifted him to punch again.

Mother and the little ones were crying. Harry struggled helplessly. Although fourteen and at work, he was no match for Father's strength. The arm was drawn back, the fist clenched to smash into his face, and I would not bear it. I got up and threw myself at him. But he was not enough befuddled by drink for me to get to him. He let go Harry's

4

shirt and the fist struck me instead, high on the cheek, knocking me to the floor.

Dazed by the blow I looked up, and saw him grinning down at me.

'Go for your father, would you? I'll tell you, missy, you've been getting above yourself lately. You're still a brat, and saucy brats are best served with a whipping.' He nodded to my sister Mary. 'Go to the wash-house, and fetch me my strap.'

I shook my head. 'No. . . .'

'No, is it? You'll defy me, will you? Has your mother been telling you more tales of your grand relations in the nobility?' He spoke thickly, but with withering sarcasm. 'You may be seventeen, and think yourself a lady, but I'll make that blue blood your mother boasts of run, before I've finished with you. And after I'll see to that brother of yours, who fancies himself a man.'

Mary had risen from her chair, but stood irresolute. He gestured angrily to her, and she hurried from the room. It was a couple of years since he last strapped me, and I had not thought he would attempt it again. I knew suddenly that I would not stand for the humiliation, that anything was better than surrendering to it. Mother and the two other girls, Liza and Maud, were crying quietly. I backed away, in the direction of the fire. He watched me, with an ugly smile.

'Think you'll run off, do you?' He was between me and the door to the outside. 'You're only making things worse for yourself.'

The remains of the joint were on a plate on top of the black-leaded oven. The carving knife and fork were there, too, where I had left them. I took another step back, and reached out for the knife.

'Would you, then?' His tone was low and vicious. 'Do you think you'll frighten me, my girl? You've asked for it, and you'll get it—the finest hiding you've ever had.'

He moved forward. I lifted the knife, and he stopped.

'Drop it, before I take it off you. Because when I do ...'

I had no doubt that he could do what he said. He had been in the Navy before becoming an exciseman, and was famous throughout Portsmouth as a fighting man. I looked at him and the frightened children, at my sobbing mother, at the brother I loved so dearly. I was very frightened myself, but I said:

'Then you'd better kill me. Because if you don't—if you strap me—I swear I'll not rest until I've killed you. You may take the knife off me now, but I'll get it again. I'll kill you while you sleep.'

My mother moaned. My father and I stared into each other's faces. I hated him and feared him, and I knew that if my eyes dropped I was finished. He would beat me and degrade me and I would become what my mother had been for so long: his victim, to be tortured at will.

But I kept my eyes up, my fine-honed hatred stronger than my fear, and he did not advance on me. Mary had come back into the room and stood by the door, the leather strap in her hands.

'You vicious little bitch.' There was anger in his voice, but also a grudging respect. 'I believe you might, at that.'

My grip was tight on the handle of the knife. He said: 'I'll tell you what you *can* do, missy—you can get out of this house as soon as you like. You've been long enough idling on my hard-earned money. I don't suppose you'll do much in the way of work yourself, but you're not bad-looking and you'll probably find sailors who'll give you a shilling or two. It's the kind of thing you're fit for.'

I still stared, still silent. It was he who looked away. He said roughly to my mother:

'I'm off up to bed. You can come and rub my shoulder for me. I've had the rheumatics in it again.'

That had been three days ago. He had spoken only once to me since. On Monday morning, when I brought him the boots I had polished to the high gloss he liked, he said:

'The end of this week.' His voice was cold and sober. 'Do you understand me? I want you out of here by Saturday.'

I had known he meant it. And I would have been glad to go, happy to earn my keep as a skivvy if it meant seeing no more of him. But it also meant leaving Mama to his mercy— Mama and the girls and Harry—who was the one person in the world I loved, and loved as strongly as I hated my father. I tried to think what I could do, and found no answer. Yet here the solution was. I had not prayed for his death because I had thought him indestructible, but my unframed prayer had been answered. Larrimer, before he left, had put pennies on his eyes and folded his arms across his breast. The big hands rested, one over the other, helpless and innocent. They would never strike Mama again, I thought with fierce joy—never lift a leather strap.

My ear caught the hiss of steam as the kettle boiled, and I went through to the kitchen to brew the tea. Leaving it to draw, I went back to the parlour. I had an irrational fear that he was not dead after all—that I would find him sitting up, his cold grey eyes open and watchful. But he lay there still.

I heard his voice echoing in my mind. 'You're not bad-looking....' It was the only compliment I remembered him paying me; and even despite the filthy jibe which accompanied it, it *had* been a compliment. I looked into the glass above the mantel, and saw myself reflected, with the green potted plants behind me.

Not bad-looking.... And from him, of all men. I stared at my mirrored image. I had always imagined myself plain: small, dark, a brown insignificant creature, sharp of feature and bony of figure. Believing this, I had not been given to studying myself in looking-glasses. Their value for me had been practical, their use confined to hurried toilettes.

But in the last year or two I had grown, and almost without my realizing it my figure had acquired curves as well

7

as a reasonable height. I stood several inches taller than my mother, though it was true she was a small woman. And my body's curves, I saw now, were matched by a more pleasing roundness in the face. My cheekbones, high and prominent, looked better for the fulness of flesh beneath them, and though my colouring was more brown than I might wish, the brown was delicately tinged with rose. My teeth had always been, like my father's, strong and white; and my black hair, which I had disliked for its wiriness, offered a new suggestion of luxuriance.

Had anyone but my father said it, I should not have heeded it. From him, whom I hated, it was startling enough for me to think it might be true. Not pretty, perhaps, but ... not bad-looking.

I heard a chink of metal as the outside door latch lifted, and the sound of voices—Mama's soft and broken, Mrs Tyrer's strident and assured. Hastily I left off looking at myself, and went to pour the tea.

It took a day or two for relief over my father's death to give way to a different apprehension. I felt it first after the funeral, when Joe Larrimer came to the house to hand over to Mama the fruits of the collection that had been made. It amounted to seven pounds, eleven shillings and a few pence, which was generous in view of the fact that, except for his close drinking cronies, he had been disliked in the dockyard, too, for his bullying ways. My mother thanked Larrimer and put the money away in her purse, and I suddenly realized how precarious our situation was.

Although brutalized, we had not lived in poverty. The post of exciseman was not badly paid, and much of the drink he consumed came free. In his good moods, Father could be reasonably liberal: he gave her two pounds a week for housekeeping, and now and then a few shillings more. We had been kept in clothes and stout boots, and adequately fed. Our schooling had been paid for at the dame school kept by the Misses Tranny. All of us bar six-year-old Maud could read and write, and I had even learned a little French before I left.

Until then we had also kept a maid, and I guessed she had only been given notice because of my father's attitude towards me. I was big enough, he said, to give all necessary help: a house provided little enough work for two able women. What he wanted in fact was to have me at home, serving him rather than anyone else, getting no wage and dependent on his whims, subject to the power of his pocket. I had not minded it. I could have been sent into service and so lost Harry, and though my feelings for my mother and my sisters were more detached, I felt by being there I could protect them.

Now all that was changed. The provision he had made for us ended with his death. He had put nothing by—he was not a man to exercise prudence, especially in the interest of others—and the money Larrimer had handed over represented, apart from the half-crown Harry collected each Friday evening from Seddon, almost the sum of our resources. Our house was a modest terraced one, but the rent took up four shillings and sixpence a week. Apart from that, there was food for six hungry mouths, coal for the fire, paraffin for the lamps—all the things a family must have in order to go on living. My mother had never been very good at handling money, but the wisest and most frugal housekeeper in the world could not make something out of nothing.

She answered vaguely when I spoke to her about it. Something would turn up, she said. She had seven pounds in her purse, a larger sum than she had had for many years, if ever, and I guessed she was simply refusing to think of the future. When she was not crying in a corner, she seemed to go about in a daze. I tried to argue with her, but it was no good. She just shook her head, not listening.

I decided I must do what I could myself. I was old for going into service but might nevertheless have found a post,

9

except that it meant abandoning Harry and the others. To a lesser extent the same applied to taking a job as a shop assistant; work which in any case was not easily come by in Portsmouth at that time. In the end I approached a shirt-maker for work which I could do at home: I had some skill with a needle. He would pay no more than tuppence for finishing a shirt, and as I could not complete one in much less than two and a half hours the return was meagre. But it was something. I sat up late into the night, stitching by candle-light; then fell for a few hours into exhausted sleep. At least weariness blurred the edges of my anxiety for the future.

On the second Sunday following Father's death, I took Harry and the girls for a walk into the country. Mama was finding the young ones more trying than she had done in the past, and had hinted that she would be glad of some relief. And the day, though cold and blustery, was fine. I made sure they were wrapped up warmly—with a pang of worry as to where the next new clothing might be coming from—and we set out, toiling up the winding roads that led to the green fields above the city. It was tiring, but I felt the fresh air did us good after the town's confinement.

In the end, though, Maud and Liza complained, and I realized how weary their small legs were getting. I made them go on a little further, to be out of sight of a shop selling lemonade and sarsaparilla and sweets and buns at which they had cast longing eyes. Then I settled them in a spot sheltered from the wind, and handed out the slices of bread and dripping I had brought, to be washed down from a ginger ale bottle that now held water. The exercise had sharpened their appetites. They ate hungrily, and afterwards played in the ruins of a cottage that stood close by, while Harry and I sat on a grassy bank and talked.

One of my reasons for choosing this place to bring them to had been that from here one could look down not merely over the city but, with a bird's eye view almost, down into the harbour. The harbour, since he had been a toddler, had been Harry's preoccupation and joy. The ships, anchored so far below, were tiny, but he numbered them and named them. The naval vessels, at least, because it was on the Royal Navy that his true longing was fixed.

His single ambition was to join that service. My father, of course, had known of it, and had connections that could have procured him admission, but he had preferred to send him out to be a grocer's errand-boy. I had recognized it as just another aspect of the possessiveness, jealous and unloving, which he had shown towards me.

Harry had not complained of his disappointment but now, talking of the ships, of the Navy, of the seas and shores into which those lucky enough to wear the bell-bottoms might venture, it all came out. I said, half chaffing, half regretful:

'So you'd leave me, Harry, if you could.'

He looked at me. His cheeks were pink from the wind and the walking, his face altogether so open and fresh, with its snub nose and quick brown eyes that I wanted to kiss him, but knew I must not. He said:

'I'd come back bringing you presents. A tortoise-shell comb, silk scarves. A cockatoo, maybe. Would you not like to have a cockatoo? Or perhaps a monkey!'

I smiled. 'I've monkeys enough, with the girls.'

His gaze returned to the harbour. He did not speak for some moments; then said:

'They're commissioning the new turret ship, the *Belphoebe*, soon. She's coming down from the shipyard next month. I've heard tell they're taking on cabin-boys. Mr Larrimer was saying I might find a place.'

I was silent. From the practical consideration of keeping the family's bodies and souls together it made little difference —would even offer an advantage. The weekly half-crown, even now that he refused to keep back the tuppence which previously had been his pocket-money—did not really support him, let alone the others. In the Navy he would be fed and cared for, which would surely be one worry off my mind.

11

But my spirit quailed at the prospect of losing him, of being left to cope on my own.

The wind blew up the hillside, bringing the smell of the sea. I must say something; and he would be secure and cared for, and possessed of his heart's desire. I said at last:

'It might be a good thing, Harry. Did Mr Larrimer say he would speak on your behalf?'

He chewed a blade of grass without answering. A single magpie flew across, calling harshly, and I thought of the rhyme, and licked my finger, and under my breath placatingly inquired after his wife and children; but I did not believe sorrow could be put off so easily. Harry said:

'I've given my notice in to Mr Seddon.'

In alarm I asked: 'Is that wise, Harry, before you know for certain the Navy will have you?'

'I'm starting work with Mangan's, on Monday.' Mangan's was a family butcher's. 'I'm to get three shillings instead of half a crown, and he says there may be a chance of bringing some meat home. Scraps and bones, but he says they will make a stew. Old Seddon would never have parted with a biscuit crumb.'

'Harry....'

'I was awake in the night,' he said. 'I saw the candle-light beneath your door, and heard the snip of your scissors. I don't know what time it was, except that it was late. You must not work too hard, Jenny. If you should take ill, what would we do?'

I started to cry. He gave me his handkerchief, and looked away. He looked down the slope, towards the harbour and his beloved ships. After a time, when I had controlled myself, he said awkwardly:

'We shall manage somehow, Jenny. Try not to worry about things.'

My mother resembled a bird, though so often a bruised

12

and wretched one. She was small in body, quick and darting of gesture, fluttering in her motions. Her eyes were brown like Harry's, but looked too big for her little face. She had been bright like a bird, too, in times of freedom from my father's oppression; and as the days passed the dazed numbness which had succeeded her first grief itself gave way to a rediscovered lightness. At the beginning I was glad of it, then doubtful, in the end impatient. I heard her trilling a song, a ditty of Moore's about a colleen and her plough-boy lover, and thought of how the little store of money was dwindling, and wondered what we should do for next week's rent.

Impatience turned to bitterness the day she bought the snowdrops. I had been out, taking finished shirts and bringing more work back, and I came into the kitchen to see them standing in a vase on the table. They looked white and delicate, beautiful in their purity and daintiness. I loved flowers, too, but these must have cost at least a penny, and we could not afford it. I told her so, and she smiled, untroubled. I was too much of a worrier, she said.

I was angry with her then. I told her the few shillings a week Harry and I earned were not enough to keep us. If we could not pay the rent we should lose our home, and the girls, if they were lucky, would be taken into an orphanage. How could one do anything else but worry?

'It is all right,' she said simply. 'I have written to the family.'

In the early days she had chattered about the family, though not latterly. My father's taunts had put an end to that, even in his absence. Mama's father had been an attorney, and her mother the cousin to a baronet. She was their only surviving child but even so they had disowned her when she married so far beneath her class, swept off her feet by strong arms and a handsome face. There had been only one communication since. She had written to them when Harry arrived, her first-born son. She had kept the letter she got in

13

return, from her father's brother, and I had seen it. It gave cold report of her parents' deaths; both, it implied, due to hearts broken by a daughter's undutifulness. Its tone forbade response, and she had not attempted any.

Grief had perhaps unhinged her. I wondered if what I had taken for brightness might instead be some derangement of the mind—a refusal to contemplate a future that was too fearful to be borne. I resolved to be more patient with her, and patiently now tried to explain the folly of seeking help in that quarter. Her uncle's letter had shown him to be a man as rigid and implacable as her father.

'Indeed, yes.' She nodded quick agreement. 'But I have not written to Uncle Matthias.'

'You said ...'

'It would do no good. It is to my cousin, once removed, that I have applied. To Sir Donald Bedivere, of Carmaliot.'

It was hopeless. I remembered what she had told me of the Bediveres of Carmaliot. Her mother's marriage, even before her own, had been regarded as a misalliance. If there had not been quite the brutality of rejection which she had experienced, there had been a subtler but equally effective one. Her mother had never visited the great house at Carmaliot of which her sister was mistress, and after the sister died, in childbirth, all communication ceased.

As gently as I could, I tried to put this to her. The Bediveres, having refused to acknowledge the wife of an attorney, would scarcely do better for an exciseman's widow. I could see what had impelled her to write, but it was no good building hopes. We had nothing to rely on but our own resources, desperately thin as they were.

She touched the white bell of a snowdrop, humming under her breath. Looking up, she darted a smile at me.

'But he has written back.'

'I don't ... Who? Who has written?'

It was a delusion, perhaps. I had seen no letter.

'Sir Donald.' She brought out an envelope from her apron pocket. 'It came while you were out.' She smiled again. 'He promises he will help us.'

2

I took the envelope from my mother's hand. It was long, creamy in colour, made of heavy paper, and had a crest blackly embossed on the back: of a ship sitting among curly waves. The same crest appeared on the writing paper inside: beneath it the address was simply Carmaliot, Cornwall. The script was thickly inked, in a bold and upright hand, with a bolder flourishing signature at the foot. I looked there first and read: Donald Bedivere, Bart. I turned back to the text of the letter.

Dear Madam,
    I have received your letter of the 7th, and sympathize with you in your loss. Our cousinship is distant but has its claims, and rank has its obligations. I propose calling on you at an early date. You speak of your children, and their needs. It is possible—I undertake nothing at this stage —that I may be willing to take on one of them, and provide you with assistance in maintaining the rest.

I refolded the letter and returned it to her, still trying to grasp its significance.
    'What does he mean—take on one of them?'
    'His own children will be now grown up. Men in their later years often feel a need for a child's company. And it is not usual for a rich family to adopt a child from one whose conditions are straitened but who have a tie of blood.'

What she said was true enough, but I was unhappy. I did not feel for my sisters anything like the affection I had for Harry, but I was fond of them, and caring for them was something which long practice had engrained in me. I asked:

'Which one? Whom are we to give him? Liza or Maud? Mary?'

She shrugged, untroubled. 'It would be whichever one he fancies.'

'Like choosing a puppy?' A thought horrified me. I cried: 'Not Harry!'

'I should not think so.' She saw my look; my partiality was no secret to her. 'No, of course not. Sir Donald has sons of his own, and besides Harry is no longer a child. It would be Maud, most likely.'

Maud, apart from being the youngest, was undoubtedly the prettiest—fair in complexion with curling yellow hair and blue eyes. I did not speak, and Mama went on:

'It would be a wonderful thing for her. To be brought up at Carmaliot, as a lady.'

She spoke with a wistfulness that was heartfelt. I could imagine that it might have been a childhood dream of her own, fed by the occasional reference to the great house and the haughty relations who lived there. I said:

'Perhaps it will not come to anything. He does not promise, you know. He says he undertakes nothing.'

'Oh, he will do it.' Her chin jerked up confidently. 'Our troubles will soon be at an end.'

In fact a further letter followed shortly, naming a day in the ensuing week for the momentous visit. The letter also asked that the family should be present in its entirety. As far as the girls were concerned, that simply meant keeping them from the dame school for the afternoon, but for Harry it would mean getting time off from his duties as a butcher's boy. I argued that his presence was not really necessary, citing Mama's remark that he was no longer a child and so

17

ineligible for Sir Donald's selection. (My true reason, as I admitted to myself, was that I was uneasy still—and if he were not there he could not be chosen.) But Mama was determined that we should follow her noble cousin's instructions to the letter; and Harry himself took the wind out of my sails by supporting her. He had already spoken to Mr Mangan, and obtained the necessary leave of absence. In fact, I realized, he was thrilled at the prospect of meeting so grand a person.

Accordingly on the appointed day, Mama and I set to work dressing the girls in their Sunday best, scrubbing and primping and prettying them for the crucial interview. I worked at it with a will. Whatever my private misgivings, it was only fair that the chances should be equal, and I spent a long time plaiting and ribboning the brown hair of the elder two to enable them to compete with Maud's golden curls.

He would call in the afternoon, his letter had said, so we had our mid-day meal at noon precisely. From a quarter to one we were ready and waiting; in anticipation at first, then more fretfully, eventually in boredom and with a growing sense of disillusion.

Perhaps after all he would not come. I had mixed feelings about that. I was not eager either for the visit or the choice he might make but the others would be disappointed; and one could not ignore the fact that our financial state was becoming desperate. The rent-man had been sent away the day before with a promise to pay double next week; and I had not cared for the look in his eye, nor for his remark that he had a long list of people waiting for houses.

It was just after four o'clock that Sir Donald arrived, by growler and unaccompanied. I had expected something more impressive: a private carriage and a retinue of servants. But it was a rare occasion even for a hansom to come into our street, and I saw curtains being twitched aside as I let him in.

And he himself, though at least sixty years of age, was

18

a fine figure of a man. He was as tall as my father, with a silver and black spade beard, thick silvery eyebrows, grey eyes that rested with calm assurance on the person he was viewing, a long straight nose that was slightly hooked.

He wore a black cape over a double-breasted black frock coat, hanging unbuttoned to knee level. Beneath it he had a waistcoat of grey and white striped silk, showing a heavy gold watch chain, and dark grey trousers with a braided side seam. On his head was a black silk top hat with a broad ribbon, and at his neck a black silk neckcloth fastened by a gold pin with a black pearl as its head. He wore grey kid gloves and carried a silver-topped cane. His appearance was that of a fine gentleman, to the last inch.

He doffed his hat as I nervously greeted him, and yielded it to my care when I ushered him in. Mother had hurried the children into the parlour at the sound of the cabbie's ratta-tatting on the door, and I led him through the kitchen to meet them. The parlour, in his presence, looked suddenly small and poky, but he himself seemed quite at ease, though in a grand and somewhat forbidding way.

I feared him again, and more sharply, for what he was—the power he held. As he put a hand out to Mama, I saw his glance take in Harry who stood at the end of the little line—plainly nervous, but scrubbed and brushed and glowing with rosy health. My nails squeezed into my palms. That could not happen—must not!

And yet, I asked myself as Sir Donald made grave response to Mama's breathless chatter, was I being selfish in thinking so? Mama had said, of Maud, that it would be wonderful for her to be brought up as a lady. Would it not equally be the case with Harry being brought up to be a gentleman? I should lose him, of course. His future life would be much more separated from mine than if he had fulfilled his ambition to become a sailor. There would be no bringing combs or scarves or cockatoos on leave from Carmaliot. But if it were to his advantage ... I made an end to my silent prayer, but my

19

fingernails did not give up digging into my flesh.

From Mama, Sir Donald turned his attention to the others. He studied the girls in turn, addressing them solemnly but moderating it somewhat with presents of sugar pigs, which he produced from a bag in the pocket of his coat: he must have had the cabbie stop at a sweet-shop on the way. He came last to Maud, and lingered. She was less nervous than Mary and Liza had been—by nature she was sunnier and more confident—and piped up answers that were ready though not pert, in a small sweet voice. Mama was right, I felt. He must want Maud.

But he passed from her to Harry and, leaning forward slightly, hands clasped behind his back, closely surveyed him. He inquired if he were still attending school and when Harry said 'No, sir', asked what work he did.

'I am a butcher's boy, sir.'

'Indeed.' Sir Donald rocked a little on his heels but did not take his eyes from Harry's face. 'And is it your ambition to become a butcher?'

'No, sir.'

'Then what? Do you have an aim in life?'

'I should like to be a sailor, sir. In the Queen's Navy.'

Sir Donald said, with warm approval: 'A worthy aim, for any English lad. My father served with the Navy, in the great sea battles against Napoleon, fifty years and more ago. Have you heard of Admiral Bedivere?'

'Oh yes, sir!'

'That was he.'

Harry's face showed he was impressed. Sir Donald, for his part, took a step back, but only it seemed to find a better vantage point from which to scrutinize him. He said, nodding his head, and speaking as though to himself:

'A fine boy.' He nodded again. 'Yes, a fine boy, indeed.'

He turned abruptly and addressed Mama.

'Madam, you are to be congratulated on your family. They do you credit.'

She said nervously: 'Why, thank you, Sir Donald.'

'You will recall my first letter to you? In it I said that I might be prepared to take one of your children back to Carmaliot with me, and to help you with the upkeep of the rest. I will tell you at once that having had the opportunity of seeing them, I am ready to make that offer firm.'

Mama fluttered at him, in a confusion of satisfaction and gratitude:

'I cannot tell you, Sir Donald, how deeply in your debt ... the extent of my appreciation ... your kindness quite overwhelms me. ...'

His raised hand commanded silence.

'Enough, ma'am. The fact is established. There is left only the question of election.'

His gaze went from her along the line of my sisters, and wound up at Harry.

'And I would emphasize that to choose one is not to denigrate the rest. They are a goodly quiverful. But choice there must be.'

He paused while I stared, agonized, at my brother. Then Sir Donald turned round and looked at me.

'I have chosen your daughter Jane.'

I said: 'But it is absurd!'

It must be some strange foolery, I thought. He had surveyed me when he entered, but briefly, paying me less attention than he had Mama. And the notion was plainly ridiculous. Perhaps the entire project, starting with his reply to Mama's letter, had been no more than an idiot jest. Being a baronet did not stop a person being mad.

Sir Donald said impassively: 'Your modesty, Jane, does you credit. But I am a man who weighs his words. A man, too, who has little time for uncertainty and delay. Swift decisions are best, where the basis of judgement is sound. I shall take you to Carmaliot with no misgivings.'

'You spoke of children ...'

He inclined his head. 'Yes.'

'And I am not a child! I am seventeen. It is out of the question that I should go to Carmaliot.'

He was unruffled. 'Child or woman—let us not quibble over definitions. The fact is that I have chosen you. There is nothing more to be said.'

'There is everything to be said.' My amazement was beginning to yield to indignation. 'But it can be summed up in a single word: no!'

Mama, who had been staring at me like someone mesmerized, cried suddenly:

'Jenny! Recollect yourself ...'

I made a great effort to be calm. 'Sir Donald, I am aware of the favour you show me, and grateful for it. But ... I cannot accept your generous offer.' I saw Mama's face crumple. 'Choose some other one of my sisters—I beg you.'

He seemed neither surprised nor put out. He said simply:

'No. I do not see an alternative to the decision I have made. If you will not come, you will not, and there's an end of it.'

He produced from his waistcoat pocket a gold hunter, clicked it open, and studied the face. There was a silence I felt I ought to break, but I could not think of what to say. It was Sir Donald who said at last:

'Half past four.' He made a small stiff bow to Mama. 'Thank you, ma'am, for receiving me. I shall not trouble you further, but take my leave.'

'But ...' Her hand went agitatedly to her breast. 'You will have a cup of tea first, Sir Donald? The kettle is on the hob and it will not take a minute to make. Or would you prefer a glass of sherry wine?'

The bottle of wine had been obtained that morning from Seddon's, on tick; as also had been a rich brown Madeira cake at which the girls had been casting longing eyes all afternoon. Sir Donald shook his head.

'No, ma'am. Thank you, but no. My cabbie is waiting.'

'But for a few minutes only ...' He was unmoved and she

recognized it. She said urgently: 'The other thing, Sir Donald.'
He looked at her, in bland inquiry. 'The help you said you
would give us in our present difficulties ...'

Sir Donald drew on a glove. 'As to that, I thought you
understood that the one is contingent on the other. If a
member of your family is so wilful as to refuse the major
benefit, it would seem to me merely an encouragement to
undutifulness and ingratitude to provide the minor.'

She looked desperately from him to me. 'I am sure when
Jenny has had time to reflect ...'

He inclined his head. 'That may be so. You may send word
to me at the Marine Hotel. But I leave for Carmaliot tomorrow
afternoon. She has till then—no longer.'

He bowed again to Mama, but left the room without giving
me another look.

I expected an onslaught of reproach and indignation from
Mama as the door closed behind him, but it did not come.
With a briskness unusual in her, she packed the girls off
upstairs to change out of their good clothes, bidding them
stay there till they were told otherwise; and despatched Harry
to Seddon's shop with the unopened wine and untouched cake
to ask Seddon to take them back. He accepted the commission
reluctantly, and I felt for him. He was a proud lad and Seddon,
though he would come round in the end, would make the
most of the humiliation, especially to someone who had
recently left his employ to better himself.

When we were alone she tackled me, though even then
more calmly than I had expected. Her pleading was urgent
but not overwrought. She laid stress on the desperateness of
our position and I, who had thought her frivolously indifferent
to it, could find nothing in that with which to disagree.

I was trying, with some difficulty, to collect my thoughts.
My reaction to Sir Donald's pronouncement had been auto-
matic: I could not believe he was truly saying it, and when I
did, found the idea intolerable. Nor could I believe anyone

23

could be so monstrous as to refuse help to other members of a family because one had declined to fall in with his whim and yield herself up to his possession. I tried, when Mama gave me an opportunity, to convey this feeling. She said, almost sadly:

'You *are* a child still. Do you not understand, after all the years with your father, that where women are concerned a man's whim is a command, to be obeyed without question or demur? And the richer, the more powerful the man, the truer that is.'

'I defied my father, when he wanted to strap me.'

'And would have been dismissed your home for it, to God knows what fate. For he meant it, you know, and I could not have helped you. It was an allowance on his part letting you stay the week.'

I said wearily: 'The allowance a cat gives a mouse. He enjoyed seeing me on the rack, as he thought, and you too.'

She tossed her head, unwilling to hear any criticism of him.

'That is past, and concerned only *your* future. This threatens all of us. What of the girls? What of Harry?'

'He will still help you, I am sure. He spoke as he did to frighten us. He will not keep to so cruel a purpose.'

'You do not *understand*, Jenny. He is a man of vast wealth, and a baronet. For him there is no cruelty in turning his back on anyone who thwarts his will. He has offered benefaction, but on his terms, and he will tolerate no amendment of them.'

'But it is so senseless! How could he want to take into his home someone who is reluctant to accept the invitation, benevolent though he may feel it to be?'

The wrangle went on. She declared I was being wilfully stupid in refusing to see what was obvious, and to some extent, though I would not admit it, she was right. I knew quite as well as she that inequality and injustice, rather than their nobler opposites, ruled the world. I knew that the poor had small chance of redress against the oppressions of the rich, and that women, except in a few fortunate cases, were the helpless chattels of men.

I knew these things, but something in me revolted against them with a passion beyond my control. Having defied a domestic tyrant, and seen fate reward that defiance with an improbable deliverance, I could not abide the thought of giving myself into another man's domination. The cage that was proposed might be gilded, but I could not tolerate the bars.

I did not attempt to express these feelings to Mama, knowing that in any case they provided a poor argument against her pleas. Was I, through an obsession with what I saw as freedom, to let the whole family sink under the weight of a penury which hung over us and soon must crush us? I tried not to think of that myself. I concentrated instead on reasoning that if Sir Donald could not be shamed, he might still be persuaded into changing his mind. He had clearly liked Maud, who was bright and pretty and would well justify an interest in her. Once he had recovered from his pique at my refusal, he would see the advantages of someone who in addition to being more attractive was younger, and so more pliable. The suggestion of adoption had been his, after all, so the project in itself probably still appealed to him.

Although Mama's case, I could not help but honestly think, was stronger, I was more forceful in argument. Also, I knew it had been her wish that Maud should be the one of us to be elevated to the grand life. This was not through any failure in affection—I think, as is true of many women, she was fonder of her last-born than of the others—but the reverse. She would miss her most, but was most ambitious for her advancement.

In the end, at any rate, she abandoned her pleadings and appeared to accept my proposition. It led her to a further resolve. She would go that evening to the Marine Hotel and seek out Sir Donald. She would deplore my folly, and sing Maud's praises. There might be just a chance of bringing him round.

More than just a chance, I assured her. And she must

spare nothing in her detraction from my character. A family, after all, was entitled to one black sheep, and the fleece of the rest would seem whiter by contrast. We were peaceable again, and I made us a pot of tea to mark the recovery of harmony.

That evening, after I had got the young ones off to bed, I set to work on my shirts. The house was quiet and peaceful. I had let the fire go out, to save what little coal we had left, but the night was not particularly cold so it was not too great a hardship. I had lit only one lamp, and Harry and I drew up our chairs on either side of it. This too served economy, but also provided a sense of closeness, a cosiness, that contented me. He was reading yet again his favourite book, *The Swiss Family Robinson*, his mind far away among blue Pacific seas and skies, engrossed in the wonders of a tropic isle. But in reality he was at my side, a comforting presence as I stitched away.

I felt surprisingly at ease. The excitement and agitations of the day had faded into an optimistic peace. It was perhaps not altogether reasonable, but I had convinced myself that the mission on which Mama was engaged would be successful. Sir Donald must see the advantages of taking a pretty and amenable child of six rather than an awkward and resentful young woman. That being agreed, he would make the provision he had promised for the others. I wanted nothing for myself—I could earn my living and did not mind how meagre it might be—but they needed help. And the couple of sovereigns a week which would save them from starvation would be nothing to a man of his means.

Meanwhile there was the wearying monotony of stitching, though with the saving grace of having Harry by me. Without looking up I could hear his breathing, the rustle of a page being turned. Time passed on undisturbing wings. All would be well, I thought, and was startled by the clacking of the latch as my mother opened the door from the street.

She looked tired and said: 'I could do with a cup of tea';

then looked at the cold grate and said: 'It doesn't matter.'

The night was chill suddenly. Harry asked:

'What did he say?'

'The same as before.'

I still would not accept or face it. I said:

'Give him time.'

'He goes back tomorrow.'

Her voice was listless. I said: 'I'll write to him', aware of the feebleness of it. Mama sat down in Father's armchair, heavily for one so small and thin.

'He was not unkind to me,' she said. 'He offered to send for tea or coffee, but I said no.' I was silent, and she went on: 'He talked about the children kindly, too. Especially Maud.'

'Then . . .'

'His mind is made up. He will not be thwarted.'

There was silence again, but it was no longer easy, or companionable. Mama shifted in the chair, and said:

'He talked of Harry. Of what a fine thing the Navy might be for him. He said he would have been able to arrange for him to get in, as a midshipman.'

As a midshipman—when he would have given an eye, like Nelson, to be taken as a cabin-boy. . . . I did not look at him—I knew what his face must show, however hard he tried to conceal it. It was unfair—unfair of Sir Donald to do what he had done, unfair of my mother to use such a weapon against me. And yet, thinking of the children and her situation, I could not say she was wrong.

Her eyes fixed on mine, more despairing than hopeful. She knew my nature.

I said, trying to sound unconcerned, even cheerful:

'In that case, there is only one thing to be done.'

3

If Sir Donald's arrival at Pratt Street had been less impressive than my anticipation had suggested, the manner of our leaving Portsmouth made up for it. He had, it proved, his own equipage at the hotel: a magnificent Berlin, painted glossy black with gold trim, with ship-crests on the panels, and with a pair of blue-liveried footmen to sit at the back, a top-hatted coachman brandishing a long whip on the box-seat, and four handsome black horses between the shafts.

It had been Mama's suggestion that everyone should come to see me off, but she seemed more relieved than disappointed when I said it would be too wearing for the little ones. I walked to the Marine Hotel with only Harry to carry my box. It was not a very big or heavy one, containing all my possessions that were worth transporting, but that not amounting to much. One of the footmen took it from him, contemptuously I thought, and stowed it away with Sir Donald's gold-clasped leather baggage. Then we waited for the great man, our benefactor, to complete his preparations for the journey. I did not have much to say for myself. Harry did most of the talking, trying his best to cheer me up.

Sir Donald arrived at last. He was in an amiable mood, greeting us genially, and assuring Harry that he would be in touch with the Admiralty concerning his future. Harry thanked him, and looked woebegone at me. I smiled at him, and added my thanks to Sir Donald, to which he nodded bland acknowledgement.

The morning was grey to match my feelings, and bitingly cold. Sir Donald was handed in to sit with his back to the coachman, and I was placed opposite. I was permitted to have the window open to wave goodbye to Harry, who ran out of the inn yard following the coach and stood in the road looking after us, his right arm flourished high above his head. When the road bent and took him from my sight and I sank back in my seat, Sir Donald closed the window. I had been provided with a rug and he tucked it round me, asking if I were warm enough. I nodded, too full of misery to speak.

I felt I hated this man almost as much as I had hated my father, though in a different way. My father's brutality had been closer and coarser; his was cold and more detached, but none the less real. To both I had been an object rather than a person.

I hated him, but knew I must not show it. The die being cast, the game had to be played out, at whatever cost. I was a hostage for Harry's future, for the very survival of Mama and the girls. Anger or sullenness might jeopardize the precarious bounty which they looked for from him. Since I was to be a sacrifice, I had better be a smiling one.

At this moment, though, try as I would, I could not bring myself to smile or talk. Fortunately, Sir Donald did not seem to mind. He would expect me to be unhappy at leaving my family; and in his conceit of himself would not look for resentment. I had been foolish but had been brought to see the error of my ways. That was enough for him.

The carriage rocked and swayed, a strange motion to one who had never travelled by such means before, but not unpleasant. After we had left the cobbled city streets behind and come out on to the turnpike, it was smoother, too. I had scarcely slept the night before, and what with weariness and the monotonous rhythm of our progress, sleep overcame me now. I dreamt: I do not know of what except that it was nothing cheerful.

I was awakened by a touch and cried out, but it was only

Sir Donald replacing the rug which had fallen while I slept. He asked if there was anything I wanted: a hamper which had been put in with us contained biscuits and oranges and a bottle of cordial. I shook my head, and managed to thank him in refusing.

He was disposed to talk. The turnpike at this point ran alongside a railway line and no more than twenty yards distant from it, and we saw a train come up from behind and pass us, with a glint of fire from the driver's cab and black smoke issuing from the chimney stack. It was an odd sight and interesting, I thought, but Sir Donald did not. He spoke of it with contempt as a hideous means of locomotion, unfit for a civilized people. As the train drew away ahead of us, the wind blowing in our direction briefly enveloped the carriage in its smoke, to his more extreme disgust. There should at least, he declared, be a law to prevent their tracks being laid within sight or hearing of roads on which coaches travelled. But what could one expect, in a world where day by day standards of decency and order were not merely being abandoned, but destroyed?

He went on in the same vein, and I nodded from time to time. He appeared to need no more than that: it was sufficient that he should talk, and I should listen.

We stayed the night at an inn. It was called The Forester, and its sign showed a man in green with a deer across his back. I had no idea of its situation, except that presumably it was somewhere between Portsmouth and Cornwall, and Sir Donald did not bother to tell me. It lay not far from the turnpike, with the woodlands crowding in: the following morning, from my bedroom window, I saw a real deer browsing close to the line of trees.

It was clear that Sir Donald was well known here. We were ushered into a private parlour, with a log fire blazing cheerfully in the hearth, and provided with refreshments while our luggage was taken up to our rooms. There was a hot toddy for Sir Donald, and black-currant cordial for me.

The landlord stood by while the drinks were served, and inquired of Sir Donald's preferences for dinner, humbly advancing some suggestions. For soup a consommé; followed by trout fresh that morning from the river. After that there was a pheasant that had been hanging twelve days exactly—in prime condition. Then perhaps, since Sir Donald was a delicate eater, a syllabub; with a Stilton that had been marinating in port since Christmas to finish. As for wine, he knew Sir Donald's taste in claret, and had taken the liberty of ordering a bottle of Lafite to be decanted, the moment the coach drove into the yard.

Sir Donald nodded judicious agreement, his only intervention being to require the cook to be careful of the bread sauce served with the pheasant: the last time it had not been as smooth as it should. The landlord declared he had berated the cook about it at the time and was sure that had not been forgotten; but he would assuredly warn him again.

I listened to all this with amazement. I thought of the humble supper of bread and dripping that would be served in Pratt Street this night. A delicate eater, indeed! I knew, of course, that the gentry ate their dinners in the evening and that such meals were lavish, but the reality shocked me.

But for all my disgust, and my mind's comparison between what we were to be offered and what my family would be eating, when the time came for a table to be brought into the parlour and laid with a white cloth and cutlery and glasses and linen napkins, I felt hungry. Sir Donald was attentive, urging me to eat, but I needed little pressing. Yet though I seemed to be consuming vast quantities, he did himself far better, taking second helpings both of fish and game. He urged me also to a glass of wine and I accepted, finding the taste a trifle sour but enjoyable in its way. Sir Donald finished the rest of the bottle, having previously drunk sherry wine with the soup and fish. I felt light-headed from my single glass, and did not understand how he could not be drunk.

I was waiting, in fact, for him to turn noisy, perhaps violent, as my father had done when in liquor. But he was calm and polite to me throughout, though more talkative as the evening advanced. At the end of the meal, after the table had been cleared and we had been brought tea, in my case, coffee and a brandy in his, he lit a cigar, after asking my permission, and said approvingly:

'You are a bright girl, Jane. I was struck by the correctness of your behaviour at table. I noticed the way you watched me, and took your cue in the use of knives and forks.'

I felt myself flushing, but said nothing. He went on:

'I saw this in you at our first encounter—the quickness, and observation. They are valuable assets. You will henceforth be living in a vastly different manner from that to which you have been accustomed, and it will be necessary for you to adapt yourself to gentler ways. There is much to learn. In speech, for instance. Your vowel sounds in particular require cultivation. But it is the readiness that counts, coupled with a sufficient intelligence. I judged that you had both, and am glad to be confirmed in my judgement.'

I burned with mortification as he spoke, but he gave no sign of noticing. Happily he did not continue long with me as his subject, but went on to speak of his family at Carmaliot—his wife and three sons—whose acquaintance I should make next day. Of two sons, Edgar and John, he spoke briefly, but on the topic of the third, Michael, waxed garrulous. Michael, it appeared, was his eldest son, and heir.

'You will understand,' he said, 'that the present Lady Bedivere was not my first wife.' I nodded, remembering Mama's talk. 'I was earlier married to a lady who was cousin to me, sister to your mother's mother. Alas, she died, giving birth to my first son. That means that, unlike his younger brothers, he has Bedivere blood on both sides. He is a true Roman.'

I had no notion what he meant by that, and was not disposed to ask. In any case he was happily engrossed in his subject. He went on hymning the praises of his son, and I gleaned an impression of someone who was a combination of courtly knight and warrior hero, a new St George. It was a panegyric which induced resentment: I was prepared to loathe him on sight or, for that matter, before. But I kept silent, and nodded and smiled, until at last I was obliged to stifle a yawn.

Sir Donald did notice that, and said:

'You are tired, my dear Jane. It has been a long day, and there is another ahead before we reach Carmaliot. It is time you sought your bed.'

He ordered another brandy as I bade him goodnight. A maid led the way upstairs with a lamp. There was a fire in my room, and she removed a warming pan from the bed. Crisp white linen sheets were turned back and my cotton night-dress, threadbare and patched, had been laid out on them. She would be speculating on it and me, I thought, but I was too tired to mind. I washed quickly, and was asleep almost as soon as I climbed into bed.

We made an early start and travelled all day, with only a short break for luncheon at an inn, but it was early evening before we arrived at our destination. We had long since left the turnpike, and the carriage had been trundling along a narrow bumpy road through desolate countryside. Moorland lay on either side, rising higher on the left than on the right but equally desolate. The day was fast darkening, and I thought night would find us travelling still when the road turned under a rocky brow and I could see that a village lay ahead. Sir Donald, who for some time had been silent, leaned forward and pointed out of the window.

'There is Carmaliot.'

The village huddled in a valley fold, its single street rising fairly steeply between converging slopes. Above and beyond the clutter of buildings, on the horizon, an immensely larger house was silhouetted against a sky whose fading but more perceptible brightness proclaimed the west.

A house, or possibly a castle. A round tower marked each flank, while at the centre a spire rose higher even than their turrets, a proud thrust of stone commanding attention, and awe. I had expected to be impressed, but the effect of this first sight was more striking than I could have guessed. It would have been an imposing edifice anywhere but in this setting, with the darker line of moor stretching away under the evening sky, it was magnificent. But the magnificence did not move me. I had expected to dislike it, too, and the seeing confirmed that. It was what the residence of someone like Sir Donald Bedivere should be: grand and arrogant, dominating the humble village at its feet. A loathsome place, I thought.

We lost sight of it as the road curved more sharply to go through the village. Cottages flashed by, some dark, some lamp-lit. An open door which spilled brighter light into the dusk looked like a tavern. As the incline grew sharper the horses laboured, and the coachman cracked his whip, urging them on. I had a glimpse of gate posts, a tiny lodge, and the lodge-keeper standing cap in hand, his wife and children in line beside him. There were shrubs and trees, twilit lawns. The carriage wheels crunched delicately on gravel. Then the carriage swung in a wide arc and I saw the house once more, looming up beside us, with lights behind high mullioned windows. The Berlin rocked to a halt by a flight of broad stone steps, on which half a dozen servants at least were drawn up to receive us. Sir Donald leaned forward and touched my arm.

'We are here, Jane. Welcome to Carmaliot.'

What followed was inevitably confusing, a blur of mixed impressions through which I moved part-fearful, part-resentful, wholly shy. The housekeeper, Mrs Muldoon, took me to my room, with a little maid marching behind us. Mrs Muldoon

34

was herself a small woman, but plump in black bombasine. She spoke in an Irish accent which I could not easily follow, but I nodded when she asked if everything was satisfactory, and refused the offer that the maid should stay and help me unpack.

The room was three times the area of the one I had shared with my three sisters in Pratt Street, and twice as high. It contained, apart from an oak bed wider than the iron one I had slept in with Maud, a wardrobe and chest-of-drawers of polished wood, two chairs, one of them facing a pretty writing table, a wash-stand with a pink marble top on which stood a flowered bowl and matching pitcher from which steam was rising; and everywhere warm woollen rugs that looked as though they had never yet been trodden. There were rugs on either side of the bed, rugs by the wash-stand and the writing table, a rug in front of the wardrobe and another, bigger and cherry-red, before the cheerfully crackling fire. A candle on a china stick stood on a small table beside the bed, but there were also lamps on the wash-stand and the chest-of-drawers. The room was bright and cosy and smelt of lavender and polish.

My box had been brought up, and I set about washing and changing into my best gown—the only one I possessed in actuality, apart from the one I had travelled in and a couple of garments too patched and frayed to be tolerable. When I had done I looked at myself in the mirrors—one in the wardrobe door, the other on the wash-stand. A poor shabby creature looked back.

I had been bidden to come downstairs when I was ready. I was as ready as I ever should be, but how could I face the prospect of going down—to face not only Sir Donald but Lady Bedivere, and his three grown-up sons? The thought of what I might read in their glances was too shameful. And yet if I stayed where I was they would send for me, and that would be worse. I looked at the girl's face above the drab woollen dress with one button different from the rest, and bade

35

her have courage: other ordeals lay ahead. And with that I went to the door, boldly opened it, and walked out on to the landing.

A scurrying maid bobbed to me at the foot of the stairs. I hesitated in the hall, lost and irresolute. Light showed through a partially opened door, and I heard a murmur of voices. What I should most have liked was to be a hundred miles from here, in the kitchen of the house in Pratt Street; failing that, to run back upstairs to the privacy of the room I had just quitted. But I could not have the first, and would not yield to the second. I walked across the hall and into the lighted room.

Lighted, indeed—I had thought my bedroom bright enough but this was dazzling, with lamps everywhere it seemed. And there was gold everywhere, too. The tables and sideboard were gilded, the yellow velvet chairs had golden buttons, the huge mirror over the fireplace had a broad band of gold at its foot and sides, a broader one painted with nymphs and shepherds above. Another mirror on the facing wall, its glass bulging outwards to show a scene tiny and distorted, was topped by a golden eagle with two gold balls hanging from its beak.

All this at the time I took in only vaguely, as a general impression of richness and brilliance. I was more immediately concerned with the confrontation I faced—with the people in the room. Their conversation broke off as they turned to look at me.

Sir Donald stood with his back to the big log fire, whose brass fender and irons gleamed more vividly than the surrounding gold leaf. He was flanked by two younger men, like him dressed in evening suits. They were tall and broad-shouldered like him, too, though less corpulent. One could trace resemblances, to Sir Donald and to each other, in their faces, but there were also marked differences. The one on his right gazed at me with an expression of grave and courteous interest, a look with his father's calm but lacking his severity.

36

He was quite handsome, his features regular and clean cut, and had Dundreary whiskers, the chin shaven and attractively strong. If I had not been so wary of everything at Carmaliot, I felt I might have taken to him.

His brother's face, concealed more by a brown bristling beard and bushy moustache, looked coarser, its lines drawn by a poorer artist. In addition he had a grin on his lips as he viewed me which I found unsettling. I was to learn that he was greatly given to grinning, but at the time it disconcerted me.

The fourth person, seated in one of the chairs, was Lady Bedivere. She was large and richly dressed and cheerful-looking: she too was smiling but in a more amiable, less disturbing fashion than her son. She was very big. Standing, she would have been within a couple of inches of her tall husband and sons, and her figure complemented her height. Her face was broad to the point of heaviness, her brows strong and black, mouth wide, chin doubled by a fold of flesh.

She wore a green silk dress, flounced and trimmed with violets, over a blue taffeta bodice and a brighter blue crinoline skirt. The dress, cut low over a swelling bosom, made me uncomfortably aware of my own—a dull brown day dress, buttoned up to the chin. A diamond brooch, shaped like a ship, was pinned to her dress. She carried a fan, small and pink, made of ostrich feathers.

Sir Donald led me to her. She put her hand out and grasped mine warmly.

'I am very happy to make your acquaintance, Jane.' Her look took in my appearance, but seemed more kindly than critical. 'It is bound to be unsettling for you, coming into a strange household, but we hope you will be very happy here.'

I was taken from her to the men. The elder, the grinning one, was Edgar: he was twenty-six, I found later. He also made a little speech of welcome but though it was phrased

37

correctly enough, I had the uncomfortable feeling that there was mockery in it. He took my hand and raised it to his lips, and I felt the bristle of his beard against my skin with repugnance. I was glad to turn away, but the feeling of being scrutinized, and with a contemptuous amusement, remained even when my back was to him.

John, the handsome one, was twenty-three, and as pleasant in his manner as in his looks. He was amiable, his eyes attentive without being too particular in their scrutiny. Edgar's voice, like Lady Bedivere's, had been somewhat loud, and in his case also coarse—in modulation rather than accent. John spoke more quietly. He said:

'You will be sadly missing your family, I am sure. Nothing can make up for that, but we shall do our best. Although the loss of one's home cannot be made good, we shall try to create a second one for you here.'

I thanked him, and meant it, as well as I could with my sensibilities frozen by the uprooting I had suffered. Sir Donald said:

'So you have met your new family, Jane, or all save one. There remains Michael. He is late down, but we make allowances for him.'

He spoke with an indulgent pride. John nodded agreement, but I noticed that Edgar turned his back on the company and made for the sideboard, where he replenished his glass with brandy and squirted soda into it.

Lady Bedivere called me back to her. She put questions to me, about my home. Her quizzing was direct, and might have been embarrassing but for the geniality of her manner. She boomed away good-humouredly and, being clearly un-concerned about my hesitancies, made me less conscious of them. I was talking of Harry to her, not at my ease but at least with greater fluency, when I was aware of someone coming in from the hall. I turned, obedient to Sir Donald's announcement.

'Here is Michael at last. Jane, permit me to introduce you to the eldest of your cousins.'

I stared as he bowed in greeting. It was true Sir Donald had said nothing of his appearance, but the glowing way in which he had spoken of him had fixed in my mind an image compounded of manly attributes and virtues. Meeting handsome John, and Edgar, who was a fraction taller and much more burly, I had envisaged the unknown Michael as combining their superior features, and surpassing them— someone bigger than Edgar, better looking than John, a flashing-eyed hero, with a wolfhound, maybe, at his heel.

What I saw was a small man, scarcely taller than myself, with a thin sickly face and a slight hunch to his narrow shoulders. His complexion was pallid, and as he offered me his hand he was taken with a fit of coughing. Our introduction had to wait some moments while his frail body was racked by it.

Had I been in a happier mood, I should have been obliged to suppress an urge to laughter. As it was, I gave him my hand with a feeling of amazement. The voice in which he addressed me was gentle and thin, and he had an impediment to his speech. Hesitant throughout, he gagged completely over the pronouncing of my name.

And this was Carmaliot's heir!

4

During the days that followed I inevitably grew more accustomed to things, and more at home in what I nevertheless regarded as a prison. But there was no denying that it was a comfortable one, nor that I was treated with consideration. The servants, whatever their private thoughts, seemed to accept me as a member of the family; as did the family themselves. Even Edgar, though I found his incessant grinning and guffawing irksome, could not be accused either of picking on or patronizing me.

Lady Bedivere, understandably since she was the only other female, was particularly active in her kindness. She kept a personal dressmaker, Mademoiselle as she was called, and set her to work at clothing me. It was a formidable undertaking, but Mademoiselle tackled it with enthusiasm. Orders were sent to Plymouth, and bolts of silk and taffeta, muslin and tarlatan, yards of lace and tulle and gauze, came back. After that there followed the measuring and pinning, the cutting and shaping and modelling. I found myself enjoying it against my inclination. This was partly through Mademoiselle communicating her own fervour—she was a small dark high-spirited Frenchwoman, and had perhaps been bored with the quietness of the English countryside, and the monotony of being confined to dressing Lady Bedivere's large frame.

It was also, of course, due to the sinful pleasure of vanity. However sternly I reminded myself that all this was charity, and charity which had been enforced on me against my will, the delight of seeing myself in the cheval-glass, transformed from a poor workaday girl to the semblance of a fine lady, was very great. I longed for a glimpse of Harry—would have taken the post back to Portsmouth like a shot if that had been possible—but found an unworthy consolation in the rustle of silk from my petticoats as I walked. I chided myself for such weakness for the greater part of a morning ... and then in the afternoon for the first time had the *cage-crinoline* affixed to my waist, and walked up and down the room, snatching glances at the mirrored vision in broad hoops of silk who accompanied me.

'You must walk more carefully, Miss Jane,' Mademoiselle admonished me. 'Little steps, equal steps. Like so!' And she demonstrated. 'Else it rides up, or wobbles. Then it is no longer graceful but most ugly. Like so.'

I did as she had told me and earned praise, which gratified me more than it should.

Not all my time was occupied with the labours and ardours of dress. A groom had been appointed to instruct me in the art of horse riding. I found it much more difficult, but this too was not entirely without satisfactions. Although apprehensive of losing my seat on the cob—an amiable creature but alarming to me who had had no experience of the species more intimate than timidly offering sugar to a dray-horse—the sense of elevation, of being at a higher level than the humdrum pedestrian world, had power to thrill for an instant before I clutched the reins tightly again in fear of falling.

There was also the exploration of the house and grounds. I was confused by the wealth of rooms and corridors and landings, by the front stairs and the back stairs, by the two conservatories (one an orangery) and the dairy, the laundry, the stables—all the additions and appurtenances. And I was awed by the chapel, which provided the central spire I had seen when I looked up at the house from the road below.

It had been built, I learned, by Sir Donald's father, the second baronet. The village of Carmaliot had no church, and

41

previously the family had attended Sunday worship at Morgit, a village five miles distant along the Boscastle road. Sir Percy, Edgar told me, had disliked the weekly journey, especially in bad weather, and had therefore torn down the rear of the house and built a chapel there.

'It cost more than ten thousand guineas,' he added, 'which was an expensive way of avoiding discomfort on a Sunday. But once he had started, it had to be grand, of course, with a spire to be seen for miles around, if there were ought save sheep on the moors to look at it.'

'If, as you say, the villagers attend, it makes it better for them, because I suppose they will have had to walk the five miles.'

'True enough, though I doubt if he had that in mind. Mark you, it's another way of keeping an eye on them, since they're bound to muster under Father's eye once a week.'

'And what do you do for a vicar?'

'The parson comes out from Morgit for the service. Better than us being obliged to go to him. He gets a fee for it, and his luncheon thrown in.'

He spoke of the clergyman with almost as much contempt as in his offhand reference to the villagers. I would have loathed his arrogance under any circumstances, but in the present ones, where he could only view me as jumped up from the lower classes he despised, it was particularly galling. But there was no redress for that: I made an excuse and left him.

Edgar was the only one who produced an active dislike in me. I retained a deep and inflexible resentment of Sir Donald as the instigator of all this—my abductor—but I saw little of him except at meals, where his behaviour to me was calm and amiable and unprovocative. I did my best to acquit the others of blame for what was after all the caprice of the master of the household, to whom they were bound to owe obedience; and was grateful to Lady Bedivere for her efforts on my behalf. The youngest brother, John, was kindly in a more positive way, taking trouble to talk to me in a fashion that was plainly designed to put me at my ease and make me forget the disruption I had been forced to endure. But he was attentive altogether, particularly to his heavy-browed mother whom he waited on with unfailing courtesy and affection. If I could have actually brought myself to like any of them, it would have been him. Michael I saw even less of than his father. His illness—for I learned that he had been suffering for more than a year from a weakness of the chest quite apart from his constitutional feebleness of physique—had taken a bad turn coincidental with my coming, and he spent much of the time confined to his room.

To me they were all alien, even the kindly John. I did my part as I conceived it necessary, answering inquiries politely and responding as best I could when engaged in conversation, but with a sense of obligation and constraint that excluded intimacy. I might have felt closer to the servants, but they themselves erected a barrier there. Having been used to the clamour of the girls, Mama's continual fluttering complaints, and the warm companionship of Harry, I was lonely, and lacked a means of assuaging the loneliness.

A human means, at any rate: there was Beast.

I should preface my account of him by mentioning that Carmaliot was prodigally supplied with dogs. To start with there were the foxhounds, who lived in kennels on the far side of the stables. The master of Carmaliot was also, by tradition, the master of the local hunt. Then there were the carriage hounds, half a dozen elegant creatures, white spotted with black. Edgar owned a pair of mastiffs which were usually kept chained up: to my relief because I was more than a little frightened by the sight of their huge bodies and ugly slavering faces and the sound of their deep angry baying. Lady Bedivere had a pug, which she cosseted and carried around and sometimes sat comically on the broad shelf of her bosom. And then Beast.

I came on him unexpectedly, the morning after my arrival.

43

Walking in the garden I turned the corner of a high box hedge and saw him lying in my path, dozing in the wintry sun. I was unsure for a moment whether it really was a dog I saw; his ugliness was so great as to give cause for doubt.

He was black and white in colour but with none of the decorative and harmonious blending of those opposites that the carriage dogs showed. His blacks and whites clashed in jagged streaks and distorted splotches. Nor did his coat have anything of their glossy smoothness; it was shaggy and un-kempt. His face was grotesque, with large hairy ears like flaps on either side of a white pointed muzzle across which a twisted stripe of black had the look of a scar.

Apart from his ugliness he was a big dog, and I viewed him with trepidation. (I had not met the mastiffs then, or I should have been more nervous still.) As he opened an eye and stared up at me, I had a mind to beat a retreat. But his timidity was greater than my own—scrambling awkwardly to his feet, he backed and then ran away. He was an even more comic sight in flight than he had been in repose. I could not recall seeing an animal so absurd.

Before we met a second time I had learnt something of his background and origin. The bitches were normally kept confined when they were in season, or mated with their own kind, but a couple of years earlier one of the carriage dogs had by accident been allowed to couple with one of Edgar's mastiffs. (I was told it was by accident; knowing, as I later did, Edgar's quirkish sense of humour, I could not be sure it had not been deliberate.) She had had a mongrel litter of four as a result.

Three of them were given to a groom to drown in the water-butt beside the stable door. The fourth was so much uglier even than his brothers and sisters that Edgar, fascinated with the spectacle, reprieved him from a similar fate. It was he, the mother bitch having the name of Beauty, who called him Beast.

While he was a bumbling puppy, Edgar remained amused

44

with him, but by the time he had grown to a dog this interest palled. I suspect he may have driven him off cruelly —he had a harsh way with animals and Beast's fear of human beings plainly had some cause. Subsequently he ignored him, as did everyone else. Beast skulked about the grounds, having nowhere else to go, picking up scraps as best he could. Cook disliked him, but would sometimes from pity throw him a bone.

I suppose it was understandable that I should feel a special sympathy for a creature who was, like myself, an outcast within the gate; and perhaps the more so because I was being treated better. The next encounter was when I surprised a stable boy throwing stones at him, and made him stop. I did it so angrily that the boy did not stay, but sped off in confusion.

Beast, of course, had not stayed either. I resolved to try my hand at winning his confidence, and with this in view obtained dainties from the cook which might tempt him, and set out on my quest. I discovered him in the sunken garden, from which he would certainly have been driven out had one of the gardeners happened on him, and countered his instinctive urge to flight with encouraging words—'Here, Beast! Good boy. Come here ...'—and the offer of meat.

The smell of the latter probably had a greater effect than the blandishments, but though he stopped running away he would not come to me. The paved paths that ran through the garden met at the centre where a small flagged space surrounded a sundial, and I laid the meat there and backed away myself. He watched for some moments, then hesitantly advanced, a wary eye cocked in my direction. I did not move and he came to the meat and wolfed it hungrily.

Taming him was easier than I had expected; behind the show of wildness he was almost as starved for affection as for food. The following morning he came right up to me, and the day after, shivering slightly, permitted me to stroke his rough coat and scratch behind his pendulous ears. Thereafter

45

our acquaintance prospered mightily. I had only to go out of the house and call, to have him bounding towards me in his curious lopsided gait.

And I for my part was very glad of his company. With Beast I had no need to watch and be wary, to dissemble my feelings. Putting my arms round his neck, cradling that misshapen head against me, did not remove my longing to have Harry to hug, but eased it a little. And I felt, however ridiculously, that in him I had a friend at Carmaliot, where otherwise I had found only condescending patrons.

Edgar, having seen us together, commented on it one afternoon when we were having tea, as was the household custom, in the library. In his drawling voice, with the usual edge of mockery, he said:

'I observe that the Beast has found himself a new Beauty to enslave him.'

I was handing round sandwiches and made no reply. He took two, of Gentleman's Relish of which he was greedily fond, and went on:

'We should never have kept that creature. By God, he must be the ugliest hound in England, if not the whole animal creation. And good for nothing. It would still be the best thing to put him down.'

I did not speak, but my eyes went involuntarily to his face. He was smiling, but he so often did. He saw my look and grinned more broadly.

'I'll have a word with Gilligan in the morning.' Gilligan was the head groom. 'He's grown somewhat big for the water-butt, but it's worth the expense of a cartridge.'

I shook my head quickly. 'No!'

'Are you a dog-lover then, Janey? Why, that's soon met, if so. I'll bring you back a puppy the next time I go to Barnstaple. A pug like Mama's, or a King Charles, maybe. Something a bit handsomer than that flea-ridden bag of bones, at any rate.'

'Please,' I said, 'I like him.'

46

'Do you, now? I've heard of such perverseness, like pretty women falling in love with crooked little men, but I've not met it before.'

I did not answer that. He handed his tea-cup to his mother for replenishing, and went on:

'And will you pay for your fancy?' I looked at him. 'What sort of tariff should one set on the life of a dog? A kiss, would you say? Well, Janey? Is the Beast worth that much to you?'

I was confused and embarrassed. It was only a jest, of course, a piece of cousinly teasing, but there was an ugliness to his humour which made me unsure. And our cousinship was distant, and unequal. He watched me, relishing my discomfort.

'Well, Janey?'

John came to the rescue, telling his brother to stop his nonsense: it was upsetting me. I should pay no attention to Edgar, he said, until I had the measure of his foolery. He added, since I still looked doubtful, that the dog would come to no harm, especially now that it seemed I favoured it.

Edgar did not deny the assertion, but railed at his brother as an idiot. He must not, he declared, assume that I was as lacking in wit as he was and as incapable of distinguishing between jest and earnest. He appealed to me for confirmation: I had known all along it was not meant seriously, had I not?

I did not want to plead guilty to a naivety which would increase his contempt. For that matter I was not sure that it had been a joke. And I liked John better, and was grateful for his intervention.

I would have said so, but I was not called on to reply. John retorted before I could and they first wrangled and then, after Edgar had aimed a playful blow, wrestled together. It was amiable, I thought, but they were not boys but tall powerful men. In the end, staggering round the room locked in this mock combat, they sent a chair crashing to the floor.

Only at that stage did Lady Bedivere, who had been

47

contentedly watching her pug lap milk from a saucer, appear to notice what was going on. She chided them : they were not to behave in such a fashion, especially with Michael ill upstairs. It was unseemly.

I did not quite understand the remark about Michael's illness. It was said to be no more than a cold on the chest, and in a mansion such as this it was hardly likely that the sound of an overturning chair would penetrate further than the hall outside. But I was relieved that the tussle was over : they abandoned it immediately on her command. Edgar was grinning still; John, I thought, showed signs of anger. Disliking the one, I approved of that in the other.

I thought of the Bedivere brothers next morning as I walked on the moors.

The weather since my coming into Cornwall had been altogether so much milder than the climate I had left behind in Hampshire as to make me feel I had been transported to a different, more tropical land. Frost had starred the window-panes on my last morning in Portsmouth, and in places ice had crackled underfoot as Harry and I trudged to the Marine Hotel, with our breaths pluming against a freezing greyness. At Carmaliot winter and its miseries seemed very far away : the air was soft and balmy.

And on this morning the sun was out, golden in a high blue sky with just a few small clouds in the west. I had no fitting with Mademoiselle and it was too early for my riding lesson. There was an urge to be in the open air, a longing to be free, if only for an hour, of the confinement of the house. I went into the garden, and found Beast waiting for me and ready to follow where I led.

The moor was Bedivere land, and the grounds of Carmaliot merged almost insensibly into it, the meadows beyond the stables becoming wilder and less securely hedged until hedges disappeared and one trod the invading heather. On the way I saw primroses, and daffodils in bud and some in flower though this was still mid February. An easy blossoming country. Life altogether was easy and unchallenging here.

For the Bedivere brothers, in particular: I wondered, not for the first time, about their lack of occupation.

In the case of Michael, it was more understandable. Apart from the indifference of his health, he was Sir Donald's heir and being groomed, presumably, for succession to the baronetcy and the government of the estate. But things were not so simple in the case of his younger brothers. They surely ought to have something better to do than idle their time away at Carmaliot.

Edgar, I had gathered, had served with the Army, as an officer in the Guards. But it seemed that he had abandoned that career a year or two ago, and was content to do nothing. John, until the previous summer, had been a student at Oxford. Having taken his degree he, too, had returned home rather than seek entry into a profession. Unlike Edgar, who seemed intent merely on frittering away his days, John studied still, excusing himself frequently from company and retiring to the seclusion of his room with that objective; but it still surprised me that he should be content to remain here, when his talents could be usefully employed in the world outside. He was unlike Edgar in that also, I thought. Edgar was by nature an idler and probably a wastrel: John struck me as more thoughtful and purposeful.

The explanation, I decided, must lie with Sir Donald. It was not a difficult conclusion to reach. My presence here, and the pressure that had been exercised to obtain the gratification of that whim of his, was sufficient evidence of his indifference to the desires of other human beings and his ruthlessness in thwarting them. He wanted not just his eldest son but the juniors also at his beck and call.

And how monstrous an imposition that was! In a sense he had been crueller to them than to me. For me there had been no future anyway, other than the possibility of marrying and serving a man the rest of my days—my best hope that of finding one less brutal than my father. But they were men, with more useful, more rewarding lives ahead of them. It was true their father supported them in comfort, luxury even, but they should have had careers. It did not matter much whether, as with Edgar, his despotism was directed towards indulging and encouraging a natural weakness, or whether, like John, his victim was being prevented from embarking on a productive course—the indulgence and the prevention alike were vicious. Moreover, where I could be dismissed as having no claim on his care—an unimportant girl, a poor relation—these were his sons.

A cock pheasant flapped up into the sky some ten yards from me. I was startled first, then struck by the beauty of its plumage, russet and green and purple against the blue. Beast, at my heels, had been surprised too, but recovered to launch himself, excitedly barking, into a chase. One could scarcely imagine anything more futile—the pheasant was a dozen feet off the ground before he got going—and I laughed at the absurdity of this shaggy black-and-white clown desperately trying to imagine himself winged like an eagle. The incident and my amusement took my mind off Sir Donald's vagaries, and I resolved not to return to the subject. I was away from the house, and the day was too fine to waste in detestation.

I had come a mile or more and over a slight ridge. Looking back all I could see of the house was the grey needle of the chapel spire. Ahead lay the rolling expanse of the moor, wide and empty, desolate of man or man's traces but none the worse for that. I felt a lift in my heart as I walked on. There had been no such pleasure ground as this at Portsmouth. I only wanted one thing: Harry, to enjoy it with me.

The second shock was as unexpected as the first, but much more frightening. The figure rose out of the ground in front of me, a shorter distance away than the bird had been. I stopped, my hand on my breast. It was a man: wild, dirty, menacing.

He had not actually risen out of the ground: I saw now

that he stood at the entrance to a shaft sunk into the side of a hillock. The entrance was partly concealed by a bush growing there and the shaft itself slanted at an angle from my path which was why I had not noticed it before. The man was dressed in trousers patched with leather and a blue cotton shirt, both old and shabby and torn. He did not have a beard, but the black stubble of whiskers on his face declared a two or three days' growth.

He was less tall and thinner than the younger Bedivere brothers, but his body had a powerful wiry look. His hands, I noticed, were not just dirty but bore the signs of hard work. He pointed an arm, on which hairs gleamed coppery red in the sunlight against corded muscle, towards Beast, still running and stupidly barking at the disappearing speck in the sky which was the pheasant.

'Is that thing in your charge?'

His voice was harsh but resonant. The question was rude and plainly hostile, but the accent was that of a gentleman. I felt a quick relief that my encounter had not been with some ruffian, but it was succeeded by resentment at his addressing me in such a manner. I said coldly:

'Yes, he is.'

'Then haven't you the sense to stop him flushing game, and out of season at that?'

'He did not flush anything. The pheasant flew up and he chased after it. That was all.'

Beast had heard our voices and abandoned his chase. He turned but did not attempt to come back to me, sinking instead onto his belly among the heather. Even at this distance I could tell he was frightened, and reflected that if the man had been intent on assaulting me I should have had small protection from my four-legged friend. I did not blame him, poor wretch: his life had not been one to nurture courage.

The man said: 'I recognize him now.' His voice was grimmer still. 'And if I had my gun with me, I'd settle his account.'

My anger was topped by contempt. 'For floundering harmlessly after a pheasant?'

He stared at me. His eyes were blue and hard.

'Harmlessly, d'you say?'

'He was never within yards of the bird.'

'And my sheep?'

It was my turn to stare. There was no sign of a sheep; no sign, now that the pheasant had vanished, of any living thing apart from the two of us and Beast. Was he mad, perhaps? But he went on:

'I have sheep on the moor, over by Lacdam. That dog of yours has been chasing them.'

I said: 'That's absurd. Look at him, cowering. He would be too frightened to chase his shadow. He even waited until he was sure the pheasant would not turn back and fight him before he went in pursuit.'

'My shepherd spotted him, only two nights ago. And we have ewes lambing.' He took a step in the direction of Beast, who got up off his belly but only to back cringingly away. 'If I had my gun ...'

'At night, you say? It could have been any dog.'

'It could, but it was that one.'

His stubborn unreasonableness infuriated me. I said:

'He only came out on the moor because I brought him. He does not venture far from the house on his own.'

'The house—Carmaliot?'

I assented with a small nod. The name Carmaliot must carry influence, and I was prepared to use it on Beast's behalf if not on my own. But the stranger seemed less impressed than I had hoped. He said roughly:

'I'd advise you not to bring him on the moor again. And keep him fast at night, if you set any value on his pelt.'

I made no reply to that. He started to turn away, but swung round again.

'Carmaliot, eh? You'll be the girl Bedivere's brought in.'

The blue eyes were curious, as well as hard. They unsettled me, and for all my own distaste for Sir Donald I did not care for this offhand reference. Whether it was statement or question, I chose not to answer it.

He looked at me for a long time, but I faced up to him. At last, with an abrupt 'Good day, ma'am', he turned again and went. I saw him striding across the heather as I called Beast to me.

5

I encountered John as I was crossing the hall to go upstairs. He greeted me and said:

'I saw you go out on the moor, and was tempted to ask you to wait and allow me to accompany you. The walk has plainly done you good. You have a splendid colour in your cheeks.'

His tone and look were admiring. I shook my head.

'If so, it is not from the fresh air, but anger.'

'Anger?'

I told him of the incident with the man in the blue shirt. When I had finished, John asked me to describe him more particularly. Then he said:

'Andy Pellinser. It could scarcely have been anyone else.'

'You know him?'

'Have done since we were boys.'

'And is he always so rude and uncouth?'

'Well, one would never have held him up as a model of behaviour. Or dress, for that matter. But I suspect he's deteriorated in recent years in both respects.'

'*Does* he farm sheep?'

'He has a few score head at Lacdam, but they're not up to much. His shepherd's an old man, and Andy himself spends too much time underground to see to things properly.'

'Underground?'

'That will be the shaft of an old tin mine he popped out of.

54

The moor is riddled with them—you must take care in your walking because some are vertical and overgrown. The Pellinsers made their wealth from mining but the ore ran out in Andy's father's time, and his father ruined himself driving shafts looking for more. There were stories of a rich lode which had been lost a century before. Andy has no money to hire men to dig now, but he himself hunts through the old shafts and galleries with a pick, trying to find it. The notion's mad, of course. The mine is worked out, but he will not admit it.'

'Might he really shoot Beast?'

Edgar came out of the billiard room as I was speaking. He drawled:

'Why, Janey, is someone else threatening your beloved hound?'

John answered for me: 'Andy Pellinser.' He went on to tell Edgar what had happened. Edgar said:

'I don't think even Pellinser is crazy enough to come on our land with his gun. Jamey would run him off fast enough if he did.'

Jamey was the gamekeeper. John said:

'I think I'll ride over and have a word with him, all the same.'

Edgar grinned at us. 'The Beast Protection Society at full gallop?'

John said: 'Never mind the dog. It's enough that he was rude to Jane.'

'A good point,' Edgar agreed. 'And it will pass an hour or two. But as your senior I claim the privilege.'

I would not have minded John, but the thought of Edgar championing me was entirely unwelcome. I shook my head.

'I would rather you let it be.'

'I have a better idea,' Edgar said, 'we could have a game of billiards to settle who goes.' He grinned again. 'And I'll give you twenty, to make the odds more equal. What do you say?'

'Please.' I looked at John. 'I would rather just forget it.'

55

'Would you?' Edgar asked. He shrugged. 'A lady's wish takes precedence over any other. Anyway, I still need someone to play with—I'm tired of knocking the balls about on my own. Tell you what, Johnny, we'll make it sixpence a point.'

Michael got up that morning, and joined us at luncheon. I heard him coughing as he approached the dining-room, and he looked more white than ever as he crossed through a shaft of sunlight to take his place at the table. Lady Bedivere was solicitous for his health, asking him if he were sure that he ought to have got up. He said gravely:

'Thank you Mama, but I feel m-much better.'

Sir Donald asked: 'Have you taken your Chlorodyne?'

'Doctor Roberts brought me some mixture of his own.'

'Then you should have taken them both,' Sir Donald declared. 'I have sent away for some pulmonic wafers, as well, but they are slow in coming.'

Michael nodded and thanked him. Sir Donald, with occasional contributions from Lady Bedivere, continued to dilate on the subject of Michael's health, while his heir picked his way through a modest meal, leaving a great deal on his plate. That, too, was noticed and commented on: he really must make an effort to take nourishment. Michael nodded docilely, and stammered a promise to do better.

I'm afraid I did not attend to all this with any sympathy. I was used to dealing with coughs and colds—Liza in particular was prone to such ailments—by means of goosegrease rubbed on the chest and a spoonful or two of linctus: those simple remedies and the passage of time were enough to work a cure. Visiting by doctors—Dr Roberts rode over on his black gelding practically every morning—and sending away for pulmonic wafers, whatever they might be, seemed to be taking a trifling disorder too seriously; especially when coupled with such over-attentiveness. And I was faintly disgusted by the meek way in which Michael accepted his

56

father's solicitous admonishments. I recalled the occasion the previous winter, when Harry had been quite worryingly ill with mumps, and I had had almost to use force to keep him to his bed. Michael's acquiescence in this fussing over a cold on the chest was simply another illustration of his feebleness: a feebleness which seemed to belong to his character as much as his physique. It renewed the disdain I had felt for him at first sight.

It was with no great relish therefore that I viewed the prospect of sitting with him after luncheon. Edgar and John had finally repaired, on Edgar's insistence, to play their game of billiards, Lady Bedivere had retired with her pug for the nap she took each afternoon, and Sir Donald forestalled my intention to go and write a letter to Harry by suggesting, in a fashion that amounted more to a command, that I should talk to Michael.

'He is starved of company,' he said. 'Try to amuse him, Jane.'

I had no idea how I was going to comply with that particular request. Apart from the distaste I felt, there was no common ground to explore and his dullness and quietness made it difficult to initiate anything. I asked after his health, the defect in which seemed to be the only thing of importance about him, and was civilly but briefly answered. After that I could think of nothing to say, and desperation began to set in as I racked my brain for a topic. We were sitting in the pink drawing-room, and to avoid gazing helplessly at him I went to make up the fire, though it did not really need it.

Michael said: 'You could have rung for the maid.'

'Yes. But I'm used to making up fires, and not used to maids and bells.'

'T-tell me about it.'

'What?'

'Your home, your family. The way you lived before you came to us.'

'It's not at all interesting.'

57

'Tell me.'

It would be something to say, but all the same I started reluctantly, not wanting to share my privacies, and least of all with this sickly creature. As he listened, though, and now and then prompted me, I found myself talking more readily. I told him about our life; about Harry and the girls and Mama. I spoke of my father's death and the poverty that had resulted from it. I mentioned Mama's letter and Sir Donald's reply. I said nothing of my first refusal of his offer and what had forced me to change my mind, but ended simply:

'So that is why I am here.'

He paused before saying: 'My f-father's a somewhat inflexible man. B-but his intentions are kindly, though you may find that difficult to appreciate at the moment.'

It was a comment on what I had not said, and I saw no cause to reply. Nor did I think it possible to do so without revealing my bitterness. He did not seem to mind, but went on:

'You are very fond of your b-brother.'

'Yes, very.'

I did not mind saying that; to do so brought him nearer. Michael said:

'And your father.' He paused. 'He must have been a hateful man.'

'I did not say so!'

I was indignant. I had been careful not to reveal my feelings in that quarter—my hatred would stay warmer for being hugged in secret—and had taken pains not to say anything critical of him.

'You did not need to.'

He was looking at me. His eyes were small and weak—a gold monocle was attached by a ribbon to his waistcoat and he used it frequently—but I noticed in his gaze a directness of which I had not before been aware. It was a mild look, but disconcertingly steady.

I was abashed a little, and also curious. I asked him:

58

'Why? What made you think it?'

He said calmly: 'It was in your voice. Not much—you have no cause to reproach yourself—but when you m-mentioned him there was something in your tone. A c-coldness. It was very slight. Perhaps it was your own character that made it noticeable.' He smiled, and despite its weakness his face had a kind of charm. 'You are a warm p-person, Jenny, and that makes it show.'

It was the first time I had been called Jenny since leaving home. I was not sure what I felt about that: it seemed a liberty and yet in a way I welcomed it. And I was disconcerted by the other things he had said; by his remark about my father and by the acuteness generally of his observation. I did not know what to say, and was spared the need to do so by his being overcome by a fit of coughing.

It racked his thin body harshly. He put a handkerchief to his mouth and a moment or two after that managed to mumble an excuse and left the room. As he went I was startled to see that the handkerchief was stained red with blood.

The day continued fine and that evening before supper Sir Donald asked me to take a turn with him outside. I had a silk shawl with me, one of my many new acquisitions, but he insisted that the maid be sent to bring down a woollen one.

'The night mists will be rising,' he said, 'and it is sensible to take precautions. A chill can strike, and settle on the chest. It is all too common.'

I guessed the reference was to Michael, who had once more retired to his room. He led the way, not to the rear as I had expected but to the front of the house, and I asked how Michael was now.

'He is well enough, thank you.' He spoke with easy confidence. 'It was simply that he got up too soon. Roberts is much too ready to indulge him in that respect. I shall speak to him about it when he comes tomorrow.'

I was puzzled by the mixture of lightness and earnestness

in his attitude to his son's health—by the contrast of anxious concern at the luncheon table and this present optimism. I thought of referring to the bloody handkerchief, but decided not to. I told myself it was no concern of mine.

A lawn, studded with yew and box trees cut into ornamental shapes, sloped down from the house with the two arms of the drive curving round it to the gates below. On either side of the drive stood dense shrubberies. The view was northerly, taking in the village, the lower land beyond and on good days a glimpse of the sea, ten miles away. Now, of course, it was lost in the murk of twilight.

Sir Donald walked me along the right-hand arc of the drive. The evening was cool, but not at all harsh. The air was still, our voices loud in a silence otherwise broken only by a late twittering bird in the shrubbery. I thought of the bustle of Portsmouth at this time of day—the flare and sizzle of naphtha, hawkers crying, the din spilling out from the open doors of the taverns, all the clamour of citified humanity. It seemed a long way away.

We had walked on the drive itself, with gravel softly crunching under our feet, but suddenly Sir Donald put a hand under my elbow and steered me on to the lawn. The grass was heavy with dew and I was glad I had stout boots on. We went across to a point roughly at the lawn's centre where stood one of the ornamental trees, a huge holly, ingeniously fashioned into the shape of a man on horseback.

'Do you know who that is, Jane?' I shook my head. 'It is meant to be King Arthur. Look there—see the scabbard, and the sword's hilt above it? Excalibur, the sword that was given him by the Lady of the Lake. You can see better by day how well the branches have been trained and trimmed. Old Hawkins, my head gardener, has been working more than a score of years on it.'

I was impressed but puzzled. I had a feeling that there had been a purpose other than mere recreation behind the suggestion of this stroll, and that it concerned the tree. I stared at the leafy shape, towering above us in the dusk, supported on its gnarled and knotted trunk.

Sir Donald said: 'This is Arthur's country, Jane: the last of the real old England, Roman England. And Arthur was the last Roman, defying the Saxon invader, reconquering the rest of the country and giving it Roman order again. He failed, in the end, through treachery, but first he had so bloodied the Saxon noses that ever after they walked warily in the south-west. And it is said that at some time Arthur will return, in one form or another, and this time triumph completely. Every true Cornishman believes it.'

He spoke with a vigour unlike his usual measured calm. I thought I had no need to do more than listen, but he turned to me abruptly and asked:

'Do you know where Arthur lived?'

'Was it not Camelot?'

'It was. And where was Camelot? Many places claim the honour. Winchester, for example, with its foolish Table, no more than a few hundred years old. The Saxons trying to claim our king!' He spoke with scorn. 'But Camelot could only be in Cornwall. Do you know what lies down there?'

He pointed far out into the northern twilight.

'The sea?' I ventured.

'The sea, yes. And Tintagel. Arthur's birthplace. No more than fifteen miles from here. You have heard of Lacdam, nearby?'

I remembered the wild figure on the moor, and his threat to Beast. I nodded my head, and Sir Donald went on:

'And do you have a little French?' I nodded again. 'Is it not possible that Lacdam once was Le Lac de la Dame? There is a lake there, and the ruins of a castle. So, close together, we have Tintagel where the King was born, and Lacdam where he was given his sword.' He spread out his arms. 'And here we have Carmaliot! This house was built on the ruins of a much older one. In our cellars there are signs of more ancient stonework still. So is it not likely that Carmaliot once was Camelot, the King's stronghold, set on the edge of the high moor and within sight of the sea?'

I did not know what to say, but he did not seem to require an answer.

'Arthur's land,' he said, 'and Arthur's stronghold—the heart of old England. And held by the Bediveres who have been Cornishmen for more than a thousand years. It is a fine heritage, one worth preserving. One for Michael Bedivere to pass on to his son, and his son's sons.'

I thought of poor Michael, spitting blood into his handkerchief. I no longer despised him as I had done, but it was a far cry from that sickly creature to the conquering warrior king, striking down England's enemies with his great gleaming sword. But everyone, I supposed, had their blindnesses, their false beliefs, and this seemed more harmless than most.

Sir Donald turned, and we walked back towards the house, whose windows now gleamed with light. More harmless, I thought bitterly, than a belief that a poor girl must be a puppet, to be disposed of as a rich man willed.

We walked in silence until we were close to the steps leading to the front door. Then he said:

'I am glad you have come to us, Jane—more glad than I can say. Your father's death—a tragedy, and I would not seek to deny or diminish that. But good can emerge out of evil. You have come to us. It is a great blessing.'

After dinner, John and I found ourselves alone in the drawing-room. He said:

'I could drink another cup of coffee. Thank you, Jane.'

I poured coffee for him and for myself. It was real coffee, not at all like the liquid extract which had passed for coffee at home. I had been uncertain at first, but now liked the taste. John stirred sugar into his cup, and said:

'The walk father took you on before dinner—I observed you went out into the front garden.' I nodded. 'Did he show you the Arthur tree?'

62

'Yes.'

'And told you how Carmaliot was once Camelot, I'll be bound.'

'Do you believe it?'

He shrugged lazily. 'I'm no expert on names and their origins. The parson told me once he thought it came from Carmel-yard, and marked the site of a monastery of the Carmelite friars. Mark you, he had a drop of brandy in him when he said it, and begged me later not to repeat the tale to Father, for fear it should upset him. He would not like to lose his Carmaliot fees. I suspect either of them might be right, or both of them wrong. I cannot see it matters.'

'It seems to matter a great deal to Sir Donald.'

'Yes. Did he also tell you about the original Bedivere, who fought at King Arthur's side, the last and most faithful of his knights?'

'Not exactly that. He said the family had been Cornish for over a thousand years.'

'Maybe so, but in a somewhat different form. We were Bedvers until great-grandfather bought himself a baronetcy and built Carmaliot. He thought the ennoblement deserved a better label. Bedivere sounded better. And such is the power of a name that his son, the second baronet, out of some fancy, maybe, about the Holy Grail, tore down half the house to build the chapel. And *his* son, our father, took up the notion of Arthur as the last king of Roman christendom, with the Bediveres holding his keep against the day of his return. Names have their power, I won't deny.'

We sat before a fire which, even though we were not likely to stay more than half an hour longer, had just been made up by one of the maids. The room was bright with lamps, warm from the glowing coals. I had eaten well and drunk a glass of wine. I glanced covertly at John and decided he was *much* more handsome than Edgar. And apart from his amiability, his cast of mind was attractive. The manner, light-hearted but tolerant, in which he spoke of Sir Donald's obsession appealed to me. I felt at ease with him. I said:

'John?'

'Yes.'

'Michael's illness—it is more than just a cold on the chest, is it not? He was coughing blood this afternoon.'

He looked at me seriously. There was a silence before he said:

'You cannot know, of course.'

'Know what?'

'That Michael is dying.' It was my turn to be shocked into silence. 'He has the consumption. He may last out a year, but scarcely longer.'

'But are you sure?' I could not believe it. 'There is nothing in the way your father and mother speak that suggests so dreadful a thing. And your father ... he was talking only this evening of the heritage—of what Michael would inherit ...'

'Father is not the first man to know something in one part of his mind and deny it with another. As you will have seen, he is devoted to Michael.' He spoke evenly, without a trace of bitterness such as might reasonably have come from a less favoured son. 'Perhaps by not looking at the truth he finds it less cruel to bear.'

'But when ... when it happens?'

'It will be a dark day—darker for the false light that blinds him now.'

I was quiet, thinking about it, but said at last:

'At least, he has two other sons.'

'Yes,' John agreed. 'He has two other sons, for what that's worth.'

6

The weather broke next day. A high wind got up, from the north-west, and after a time there were fierce drops of rain in it and at last a pelting downpour. All that day and the next, the wind howled around the house and it rained almost continuously. On the third day the air was quieter but the rain, less violent, dripped steadily from an ugly sky.

We were perforce confined, and endured the tedium in our various ways. Lady Bedivere grumbled at the weather, but since she rarely ventured out her activities (or lack of them) were not much altered. In fact, she benefited rather. Her only lively interest, apart from the pug, lay in the whist table, and with her two sons more readily available and myself as an obedient fourth, she could indulge it more. I noticed again how particularly fond John was of his mother, how thoughtful of her, and liked him for it.

Sir Donald had a habit of riding before breakfast which he refused to be deprived of; I saw him one morning returning drenched despite his oilskins and dripping water across the hall as he went up to his room where a hot bath had been filled for him. But his other custom of taking a constitutional walk late in the morning he did abandon. Instead I saw him stand looking out of the window, hands clasped behind his back, unmoving—making no audible complaint but registering, I guessed, a silent indignation against a universe which dared thwart him in this fashion.

Michael, reprieved from his sick-room, was a late riser and

an early retirer. In between he drifted about the house like a wraith almost, his mind seemingly fixed on things beyond the rain or, for that matter, the surroundings in which he moved. We spoke sometimes, but he did not again press me for confidences or disturb me with his trick of observation. I was glad of it. I was still confused, and troubled a little, by the conversation we had had; and what I had learned from John increased my reluctance towards intimacy. I was sorry if he were dying, but my youth and health turned me from him in an involuntary repulsion.

John was perhaps least affected of those whose reactions I could gauge. Although fond enough of outdoor pursuits he had interests of the mind which, for a few days at least, could amply fill their place. He would play whist at his mother's demand, or billiards or backgammon at his brother's, but his books contented him.

The one who most obviously found the confinement irksome was Edgar. His contemplations of the rain-bleared landscape were briefer than Sir Donald's, but very far from silent. After damning the weather frequently and loudly, he would turn restlessly away and require his brother to accompany him to the billiard room, or provoke him by raillery to the school-boyish wrestling I had witnessed previously. In one of their bouts a vase was toppled from its place on top of a cabinet and shattered on the floor. Sèvres, Lady Bedivere said, tutting at them mildly.

Edgar also went in more for teasing me, doing his best to provoke with comments on my appearance and ways of doing and saying things. I did not like it: the teasing itself was nothing, but I did not care for the looks that went with the chaffing. His eyes were bold, and made me feel uncomfortable. I avoided him as much as I could.

One good thing that happened during this time was the arrival of a letter from home, which I eagerly seized and bore off to my room, to read and re-read and then spend hours replying to. There was a long rambling dispatch from

66

Mama, from whose confusion it emerged that everything was going well, except that the girls had colds. There were brief clumsily written enclosures from the girls themselves (even Maud managing to letter her name beneath half a dozen crosses for kisses). And, most precious, there were two pages from Harry.

I wept a little over those. He wrote very cheerfully, saying he hoped I was well and was enjoying the fine life at Carmaliot. But his chief news was that Sir Donald had been as good as his word, and he had already heard from the Admiralty that they would soon call him for interview. It would be in London, and Sir Donald had sent him a couple of guineas for his fare and lodging there. To him, beyond any possible doubt, Sir Donald was a genial benefactor, and I most fortunate to have become his ward.

It was strange, I thought, how differently things could seem, seen through different eyes. And sad, though perhaps not strange, how unequal the affections could prove. Putting my handkerchief to my eyes so that I should not blot the page on which I was writing, I sorrowfully acknowledged that he was not missing me as I was missing him.

When I went downstairs again I heard Edgar's loud voice, and diverted my steps away from the sitting-room. I went instead to the chapel, which I had previously only visited for the Sunday service: Sir Donald's father had held a daily assembly of family and servants there, but he had not kept to such strict observance. The great oak door was ajar, and I quietly pushed it open and slipped inside.

It was built into the body of the house, but projected beyond it and was not connected: one had to go outside (though under the cover of a porch) and climb steps to the entrance. The nave was dark and shadowy, but half-way along high windows admitted light in blues and reds, yellows and greens. A gloom still, on such a day as this, but a somewhat brighter one. At the far end, behind the altar, a bigger window showed St Michael leading the army of Heaven against the hosts of

Evil, striking down Satan with a crimson sword.

I had intended to study the picture more closely, but as I started to take a step forward I realized that I was not the only person in the chapel. In the family pew at the front a figure was kneeling, and I saw that it was Michael. Watching him, hunched in prayer, I was reminded that there could be worse things than exile, or not being missed.

My slippers had made no sound on the stone floor, and he had not heard me. I turned, and tiptoed away.

At last the rain stopped and I awoke to a bright morning with the sun cruising through gulfs of blue between soft islands of white cloud. I found Edgar in the breakfast room, and in a far better mood. It would be wonderful to get out in the open again, he declared, and blow away the cobwebs of the past days. When I, for the sake of politeness, showed agreement, he immediately went on to propose that we go riding together after breakfast.

I demurred, but he insisted. He had had good reports of my progress as a horsewoman but wanted to see how I performed. He would not listen to any objections. The forcefulness of his manner irritated me and I was tempted to be as emphatic in refusal; but Lady Bedivere, who had joined us, declared it was a good notion—that I would benefit from the exercise and the fresh air. I remembered my position, and unwillingly acquiesced.

And there was no doubt that it was good to be outside, and in the saddle. I was far from being anything of a rider yet, but Edgar led the way at a gentle amble which taxed neither the cob nor my abilities. He appeared, too, to be making an effort to be pleasant. He complimented me instead of mocking, praising my handling of the reins with seeming sincerity.

The cleft in which the village huddled underneath the house was wooded on either side, and we took a bridle path along the western slope. The sun shone through the bare branches from which birds called merrily, and there was a

68

smell of freshness after rain. Our horses' hooves thudded softly on the carpet of last year's leaves. Once again I was struck by the mildness of this country's climate: but for the sharp fretwork of the trees, brown against blue, it could have seemed a summer's day. And already the land was budding for the spring.

Edgar chatted as we rode, sometimes side by side, sometimes forced into single file, along the hillside. He was complimenting me still. To start with, he said, he had thought me a child, but he had come to realize it was not so. I was a bright girl, with an older head on my shoulders than he had guessed. I listened, a touch surprised but glad to have a change from the usual teasing and buffoonery.

We came, after some twenty minutes, to a more open space. There were signs of the land here having once been cultivated —it was much more level, and the trees had been cleared. There was even a hut, but plainly a deserted one. No smoke rose from its broken chimney, the windows were blank holes, and the door stood open. I asked Edgar about it, and he told me it had been the cottage of the man who tilled the land but who had died some years ago. It had been abandoned since.

A wooden bench stood in front of the hut: villagers rested there, he said, when they went walking of a Sunday. He directed his horse that way and I followed. He dismounted, and helped me to dismount after him. Tethering the horses to the branch of a convenient tree, he walked me to the bench, a hand under my elbow, and with his sleeve brushed a space clean for me to sit down.

He did not sit beside me, but stood with one boot on the bench and pointed out the features of the view, including, in the distance, a line of silvery dazzle that was the sea. He asked if it were not a pretty prospect, and I agreed. He said:

'Aye, fair enough. But nothing like as fetching as the nearer view.'

I did not take his meaning until his bold stare down into my face made it plain. I did not feel flattered, but confused and resentful. To have him seeking to flirt with me was more of a trial than enduring his quips and boisterous humour. I ignored the remark, and sought to turn the subject by commenting on the saplings which were starting to spring up here and there: it would not be long before the woodland had regained its own.

Although I had looked away, I was aware that he was still closely regarding me. He said:

'That was something else I took a time appreciating— that you're a damned pretty girl, Janey. Because you are, you know. As pretty a wench as I've clapped eyes on in many a month.'

I did not know what to say, so said nothing. He was not perturbed. He asked:

'And you would not expect me to believe a handsome girl does not enjoy being told of it? A looking-glass serves well enough in its way, but the proclamation comes better from a man. And does it not earn a word or two of thanks?'

I said coldly: 'Thank you, cousin, for your commendation. But whatever your belief, I would rather choose another topic.'

Edgar paid no attention. 'And the reward, maybe, of a kiss?'

That was too much. I said: 'I think I should like to go on,' and started to rise to my feet. But as I did, he swooped towards me. His hands grasped both my upper arms, holding me while his face came down on mine. I averted my face but felt his lips on my cheek, his breath in the hollow of my neck.

I cried: 'Edgar, please ... You must not!'

His mouth sought for mine. One hand released an arm but only, shockingly, to attempt to caress my person. I was aware of his strength, and fearful as well as disgusted. Seeking anything which might end the embrace, I said:

'Let go of me ... Someone might come.'

I was relieved, though a little surprised, when his face at once drew back and the hatefully invading hand was removed. His other hand still held my left arm, but lightly. A grin started in his face.

70

'Well, now, that makes sense, my little Janey. It's a discretion I would expect of you. We shall have more privacy within.'

He moved towards the open door of the hut, attempting to draw me after him. I was shocked again by the full realization of his intentions, now undisguised. At the same time I understood that all this had been planned—that he had brought me here with a single end in view; as, almost certainly, he had brought other more compliant girls before. I resisted the pulling hand, and said:

'If you have no respect for your own honour as a gentleman, at least think of mine! What cause have you to think I would permit you liberties?'

He laughed. 'Cause enough, where a pretty girl is concerned!'

I said sharply: 'I see one thing—that you are no gentleman. Let me go.'

His fingers tightened on my arm. 'No gentleman, eh? The trouble is, you are starting to fancy yourself a lady. But wearing a riding habit and learning to sit a horse doesn't make a lady. Don't come the innocent maiden with me, my girl. And don't try to tell me you've not learned a saucy lesson or two in the Portsmouth alleyways. You should be glad I'm willing to overlook your squalid apprenticeship.'

My right hand was free. Without hesitation, I swung my arm and struck him hard across the face. The slap was loud and my fingers tingled from it.

Edgar stared at me again, not in admiration but black anger. His body tensed. I fancied he would assault me and, having had a taste of his strength, drew back. We were a long way from either the village or the house, and if I cried out I doubted that anyone would hear me. I had been wrong to strike him; by doing so I had only added fury to lust. I should have swallowed the insult, vile though it was.

But he did not attack me. Instead the hand that held my arm let go. He said, his voice low and savage:

71

'You were not wise to strike me, Janey. It is something you'll regret, I promise you.'

He untethered my horse and in a venomous silence helped me into the saddle. He mounted his own horse, and with an oath wrenched its head to turn it back on the way we had come. I set my horse to follow his, and we rode to the house without speaking.

John, that afternoon, asked me: 'What's amiss between you and Edgar?'

'Need anything be?'

'I know that black mood of his. And while you showed less, I observed that you avoided looking at him. Has he been plaguing you?'

I hesitated, but his look showed a concern and kindness so very different from his brother's callousness that I decided to confide in him. But I could not bring myself to tell the loathsome tale in full. I said only that Edgar had attempted to kiss me, and been angered when I refused.

He was indignant and sympathetic to the right degree. It was detestable that I, a cousin and a guest at Carmaliot, should be subjected to such an insult. He went on:

'Father would be immeasurably angry, if he knew.' Brown eyes looked considerately into mine. 'Do you propose making a complaint of it to him?'

I had no desire to approach Sir Donald about anything. I shook my head. 'No.'

'I approve your resolve. Leave it with me. I shall speak to Edgar. And I promise you it will not happen again.'

I realized it had not been an idle promise when Edgar came to me before dinner, and made a formal apology for his behaviour. His voice was cold, as was mine in accepting it, and we did not linger in conversation. But I was glad to have won that mark of respect at least; and grateful to John. It was something that, with one cousin detestable, his brother should be so agreeable; and should be able, although his junior, to exercise some control over him. There was Michael, too, I remembered, but he, poor fellow, did not really count.

My walks with Beast had been stopped by the weather, but I had not forgotten him. After the incident on the moor I had thought it best, out of prudence, to restrict his freedom somewhat, and I had got one of the boys to turn part of a stable into a kennel, securing him additionally by means of a collar, and a length of rope that gave him as wide a range of movement as possible. The boy had undertaken also to see that he was exercised, and fed and watered, and each day I had put on oilskins and gone out to the stables to make sure he was all right, and kept him company for half an hour.

I had planned to walk with him as soon as the weather cleared, but this had been prevented first by Edgar's insistence on that wretched ride, and in the afternoon by demands made on my company by Lady Bedivere. She claimed to be keen on embroidery, and had enrolled me as assistant in a huge flower panel. Her needle could scarcely be called a busy one, but this activity, like all others in which she engaged, was stretched out to the full.

So my visit to Beast that day was brief, too, and confined to the stable. He was glad to see me, and licked my face and thrashed the straw with his whip-like tail when I hugged him. Tomorrow, I promised, without fail we would take our walk, but not on the moor. There were fields down by the village where he could chase rabbits without fear of threats and anger.

In the morning I went out directly after breakfast. The stable door was open, and I called him as I went in, passing from the bright light of the yard to the dim shadows and the smells of horses and fodder. There was no answering bark, and I soon discovered why. The rope which had been attached to his collar was still tied to the post of the stall, but it hung loose and empty in the straw. The end was frayed from chewing.

The boy who had been set to look after him came up while

I was gazing at it. He was about twelve, gangling for his age but timid by nature and distressed close to the point of tears. I had been glad of his nervousness as something of a surety that he would not be unkind to the dog, as other boys might; and had been glad to see Beast responding more confidently to him as well as myself. But I thought now that another boy might have looked after him better.

The tale came from him disjointedly, hindered perhaps as much as encouraged by the sharpness of my questioning. Yes, he had seen him first thing. He had attended to his food and water. No, he hadn't noticed anything amiss. It was only just now that he had found him gone.

Beast must have been chewing the rope most of the night, and anyone with an atom of observation would have seen that. But there was no point in scolding the boy. Had he been seen outside, I demanded? The lad nodded. That was what had brought him here—Willy Darruck had told him he was loose. And just where was the dog, when Willy saw him?

'Out back in the fields, Miss.' He looked almost happy to be able to say something helpful. 'Heading towards the moor.'

I had a sick feeling of foreboding, which I did my best to subdue by activity. I told him to see that my horse was saddled right away, and he scurried off to do my bidding. It crossed my mind that it might be more sensible to go back to the house and secure John's aid, but he might not be easily found; and also there was something foolish in asking help to find a runaway mongrel.

Moreover the foreboding, I told myself while I waited impatiently for the horse to be got ready, was silly and irrational. Beast had not been gone more than half an hour. It was understandable that after days of confinement he should want to escape into the open; but there was no reason to think that he was likely to encounter Andrew Pellinser. Nor, for that matter, was it probable that Pellinser would harm him. The figure appearing out of the earth had frightened me, and the fear, lingering, had grown out of proportion.

Something else crossed my mind as I rode from meadowland into heather—that for so unskilled a horsewoman as I still was, there was more than a little folly in riding out on the moor alone. The cob was sure-footed but apart from mine-shafts, the moor was full of smaller concealed potholes and stones on which a horse might stumble. But there was no point in dwelling on that. I urged the horse on, scanning the rolling moor for sight of the dog. I called his name, but all that came back was the thin moan of a curlew.

Although he might have strayed in any direction, it was towards Lacdam that I set the horse's head. That was where Pellinser kept his sheep, where danger lay. I told myself not to be silly—that there was no danger, nothing but the figments of an over-active imagination. As I rode over the moor under a grey windy sky, I alternated between that mood and the other. My common sense assured me that my anxiety was unfounded, that by this time the dog might well be back in the stables and eating the bone I had brought him from the kitchen. But in another, deeper part of my mind, fear kept its hold, immune to hope and logic.

I rode up a long slope, and at the crest of the rise reined in. Lacdam lay in front of me. I had not seen it before but there was no mistaking the dark stretch of water, a ragged oval about a quarter of a mile across at its widest point. This side of it, heather and bracken gave way to scrubby grassland. There were houses by the lakeside, one quite large and rambling, the rest cottages. Solitary at the lake's end stood the ruins of what might well anciently have been a castle. There was a pocket handkerchief of an island not far from it, bearing a single tree.

I saw at first no sign of life except a bird wheeling high up, but I heard sounds: a confused bleating and excited high-pitched barking. They emerged from lower ground west of the ruin: a fleeting rabble of grey-white woolly bodies with an ugly black and white hound in yelping pursuit. I cried out, with all my strength:

75

'Beast!'

He did not hear me. He never heard anything again, except the shot which came as I called him a second time. He yelped on a different note, and dropped to lie sprawled on the grass. As I urged the horse downhill, I knew it was too late, and he was dead.

I slithered ungracefully from the saddle and knelt beside him. His side was torn and bloody from the shot and one eye stared blindly at the sky. There was blood on his muzzle as well. I cradled his head, still warm, in my arms, and sobbed helplessly for the loss of the one thing at Carmaliot I had found to love.

A figure overshadowed me. A voice hatefully familiar said:

'I'm sorry.' He did not sound it. 'There was nothing else for it.'

Slowly I let the dog's head rest on the grass, turned and rose to my feet. He stood before me in what looked like the same torn blue shirt, with the same black stubble of beard. He looked as grim and frightening as before, but I was too angry to be afraid. In a choked voice, I said:

'You killed him. He was playing, and you shot him without warning ...'

'Dogs don't play with sheep. They harry them. Even a town girl should know that.'

'He could only have been here a few minutes.'

'Long enough.'

He laughed as he said it. The laugh was harsh, ugly, and it snapped the last thread of my control. I threw myself at him, with no clear idea beyond hurting, killing him if I could.

For a moment he gave way, recoiling from the violence of my attack. But he recovered himself and gripped my wrists with steely fingers. We wrestled together, struggling and swaying. I got a hand free and clawed at his face, and heard him grunt with surprise and pain. Then he took hold of me and, stooping and lifting at the same time, brought me kicking across his shoulders.

76

I went on kicking as he carried me away, but if I hurt him he gave no sign. I shrieked abuse, which he bore in silence. It was only after he had dropped me ungently to the ground, quietening me with the impact, that he spoke again.

'The dog was stained with other blood than his own. That on his muzzle did not come from being shot.'

I stared up in mute hatred. There was a line of red down one lean cheek, where I had scored his flesh with my nails. Not deeply enough. He said:

'Look! Not at me. There.'

I was not prepared to obey him in anything, but he reached down and jerked my face round. Another body lay on the grass, a couple of feet away. It was the carcase of a sheep, its fleece smeared with scarlet, throat torn open. Pellinser said:

'And close to lambing. What do you say to that?'

'There was another dog. There must have been.'

'Listen.' He hauled me up as though I were a child of three. 'There was no other dog. You saw the blood on his muzzle. Do you want me to carry you back and show you the strands of wool wrapped round his teeth?'

I was not interested in the truth, or his justifications. All I knew was that here was another male, loathsome in his arrogant strength and brutality. My father was dead, but the world was full of them still.

He put his head closer to me. 'Well?'

I even caught the smell of spirits on his breath. It was my father, risen from death, cruel and invincible.

I whispered: 'I hate and despise you. I always will.'

7

Men on horseback met me as I rode miserably back across the moor: Sir Donald and John. Word had gone from the stables to the house of my hunt for the missing dog and, concerned for the hazards I might encounter, they had saddled at once and come in search. Sir Donald scolded me, though not roughly, for my recklessness. His head groom, I learned later, had been rated much more severely for failing to restrain me from setting out.

'To ride over the moor can be a risk for an experienced horsewoman, my dear Jane—over this moor in particular. And you are a novice still.'

I did not answer, and he went on:

'I admire your spirit.' It was said with unmistakeable approval, almost with pride. 'But you must not put yourself into danger. You are far too precious to us. You did not find the dog?'

I said dully: 'Yes, I found him.'

'Where is he, then?'

I told my story. I was drained of the emotions I had felt; of all save misery and disgust. They listened to me in silence. When I had finished, Sir Donald said:

'Pellinser was in the right.'

I did not answer. In my mind's eye I saw an ugly frightened cur, stoned and kicked from puppyhood, who had yet given me affection and comforted my loneliness. Yesterday he had licked my face when I promised him a walk. If this morning

I had gone out to the stables half an hour sooner ...

Magisterially Sir Donald went on:

'There's no crime a dog can commit worse than sheep-worrying.'

I said bitterly: 'I know.'

'And once they start, there's no curing them. However hard you try to keep them from the sport, they'll find a way to it. I've known a dog kill a score of sheep in a single night, and maim as many more. Pellinser was right to shoot him.'

He spoke with calm assurance, and what he said was incontrovertible. Pellinser had been right to kill poor Beast. But did that matter? It was enough surely that he was a man. Men needed no warrant for hurting and destroying. It was their nature and their privilege.

John spoke for the first time. 'It's a pity you should have been distressed by it.'

'True,' Sir Donald said. 'An unpleasant scene for you to witness.'

'I was wondering,' John said, 'if you would like him brought back to Carmaliot? We have a graveyard for dogs. We could have a stone put up if you would like that?'

He looked at me; and I wanted to cry but would not.

'I could ride over to Lacdam now, and see to it.'

'No, thank you.' I squeezed my eyelids tight for a moment. 'It doesn't matter.'

Lady Bedivere asked me if I would prefer not to come down for luncheon but have a tray sent up to my room. I was determined to make no demonstration, not even the demonstration of absence, and I refused the offer. I was grateful for the fact that no one said anything else; and that the conversation at the table was on the subject, perennially fascinating to Sir Donald, of Michael's health.

It appeared that cod-liver oil, which Dr Roberts had at one time strongly recommended, had been abandoned by Michael because it caused him nausea and indigestion. Now Sir Donald had seen an advertisement for Dr De Jongh's cod-liver oil which was made from the paler Newfoundland oils and was said to be more palatable. He had sent away for a trial bottle.

Michael listened politely, smiled and nodded, but said little. Later, though, when his father was talking of something else he had heard of—the Pulvermacher medical electric chain—he asked:

'I thought you were opposed to all the works of modern science, Father? Is not electricity something even worse than the railways?'

Sir Donald stared along the table at him.

'What you say is true, Michael. But I would have you travel by railway the length and breadth of the kingdom— yes, and do so myself—if such a thing would serve your health.'

He did not raise his voice, but a note of passion came into it which changed the tenor of their dialogue—reduced it in fact to a silence. I had not been entirely sure that what John had told me was true, either about the graveness of Michael's condition or that Sir Donald knew of it. The gloom that dropped like a smothering blanket was confirmation of both. It lasted, despite awkward attempts by Edgar and John to make conversation, for the remainder of luncheon. It was a poor consolation that under its influence no one noticed, or at any rate commented on, the plates I picked at and sent back.

In the afternoon I wandered about restlessly. I did not fancy the company of others, but found my own as cheerless. I tried to take comfort in thoughts of Harry, but Portsmouth seemed a world away. It was wonderful, I told myself, that he should be getting the thing he most wanted, and I knew he would have a splendid career in the Navy. Then I thought of the old days, of the little secrets and confidences and closenesses that had made up our companionship, and selfishly and hopelessly longed to have them back.

This was dreadful weakness, and I resolved to have no truck with it. The best way I had of helping Harry was to do my

duty at Carmaliot. Lady Bedivere had not, from consideration
I guessed, required me to attend on her at her embroidery, but I
decided I would do so voluntarily. I put aside aimlessness
and directed my steps firmly towards the little parlour in
which, when she was not having her nap, she sat during the
day.

I reached the door, but paused at the sound of voices. A
man's, coarse and confident and by now too well known:
Edgar's. I could not make out what was being said, but caught
words here and there. I heard 'dog' and 'Jane', and drew back.
Then I heard him laugh and felt my spine shiver. It was
nothing worse, I knew, than callousness, but somehow it
seemed more sinister. I heard Lady Bedivere's voice in reply—
chiding him, probably, but could not tell what she said.

I supposed I ought to have knocked and boldly entered,
but I felt I could not at that moment face either his mockery
or the concealment of it. I turned away, and as I did saw
Michael coming down the stairs into the hall. I thought of
pretending I had not seen him, of quickly going the opposite
way, but hesitated long enough for our glances to meet.

As he came across the hall towards me, I realized that I
must look something of a fool, standing irresolute outside
his mother's parlour. I thought he might refer to that, but
instead he asked simply:

'Would you walk with me, Jenny?' I hesitated again, and
he put out an arm. He smiled. 'It will d-do me good.'

He led us through to the orangery. It was warm, heated
by stoves set at intervals down the aisle, and we moved
through a green gloom, relieved here and there by the small
bright globes of growing fruit. There was an open space at
the centre, with chairs of wrought iron, painted white, and a
similar table: it was sometimes Sir Donald's fancy to take
tea here.

'Shall we sit down?' Michael said. 'Would you like me to
ring for cushions?'

I shook my head. 'Thank you, no.'

81

We sat together. There would have to be talk, I expected, but he would do the talking. I would smile, and say yes or no as needed, but I had nothing to say, to him or anybody. I was sorry for him if he were dying but there was nothing I could do to help.

He said quietly: 'Tell me about it.'

There was the directness in his look I had seen that earlier time. I said:

'About what?'

'About the d-dog.'

'You know what happened.'

'Just tell me.'

My own reluctance was even greater. I had thought I might talk about my home in a neutral way, but there could be nothing neutral said of what had occurred that morning. A telling must renew the bitterness and misery which I had since been trying to forget. I could not face it. And yet, as he went on silently looking at me, the small eyes in the thin face patient but insistent, I found myself talking.

When I had finished, I was crying. Michael found a handkerchief for me and I put it to my eyes. That was enough, I said to myself—I was not going to be foolish. For all my wretchedness I had not wept since I came here, even in the seclusion of my room, and I would not now in front of this poor creature. I sniffed and dried my eyes and set my chin high. Then, uncontrollably, a sob welled up, followed by another. The barrier was down: I wept and wept, my body shaking with it.

He put a hand on my arm and kept it there: no more than that. When at last I could speak, I said:

'I'm sorry. I'd better go.'

'No.'

I wanted to get up and leave, but could not move. There was a silence which seemed more like some real thing, a presence, than a lack of sound. He said at last:

'You must t-try not to ask so much of yourself.'

82

I looked at him, puzzling what he meant. I had feared he would talk of Beast, express a sympathy, and that it might start another storm of tears. He said:

'At home you took on many responsibilities, in the looking after of your b-brother and younger sisters particularly. It was necessary, and is no bad thing even for someone so young as you were—as you still are. But it can be c-carried too far.'

I shook my head. 'I don't understand.'

'You blame yourself for the dog's death. You feel you could—and should—have prevented it.'

I had not spoken of that any more than, the other time, I had mentioned my feelings for my father. He said:

'You hate yourself, more even than Pellinser. And you must not, Jenny. You are b-better than you think, but also less perfect than you want to be. And even if you could have the power over life you desire, it would do you little good. Harm, rather.'

I did not want his eye on me, especially on my inner self. And yet, although it disturbed me, I did not resent it as much as I should have expected. I shook my head again, without speaking.

'You are intolerant of your weaknesses, the more so p-probably because you are so strong a person. But there is weakness even in the strong, and it does no good to deny it. We must all take ourselves as we are.'

He started coughing then, and accepted the handkerchief I gave him back, sodden with my tears.

Next morning I walked down to the village. It was windy but sunny, with small clouds chasing overhead; a brisk and cheerful day. I passed by the fields in which I had planned to let Beast chase rabbits, and thought of him sadly but more calmly.

It was more properly a hamlet, I suppose, since it lacked a church, but apart from the inn it had a bakery, a blacksmith selling ironmongery from a small room in front of the forge, and a general shop whose stock ranged from comestibles to clothing and haberdashery—needles, thread and cloth for making shirts and dresses, plus a few of the latter ready-made and looking as though they had been there since the Great Exhibition, if not earlier.

The comestibles included sweets, ranged in display in one half of the window. I looked at them, thinking of the trouble I had had curbing the appetites of Mary and Liza and Maud for such goodies and wishing I still had it to do. I had been given a purse, and money to put in it. I remembered Liza's passion for liquorice bootlaces, and reflected that I could have bought the whole trayful and not missed the pennies. There were tins of toffees at the back. I went in and bought one to send off to them.

As I came out, a dog-cart was coming up the hill. I had been long enough in the country already to be attentive to any new thing, and I noticed that it was being driven by a girl in grey. The dog-cart stopped by the shop, and she got out nimbly. I wondered whether I should offer a greeting but decided it might be presumptuous, and started to walk on down the hill. But she called to me:

'Miss Cowper . . .'

Her voice was small and bright. I turned, and saw that her appearance matched it. She was dressed in grey—grey gown, grey gloves, grey bonnet—but gown and bonnet were trimmed with gay blue ribbons, and her face, though somewhat thin, was rosy, hair coppery, eyes hazel but with much warm brown in it.

'It is Miss Cowper, is it not?' I nodded. 'I was sure it must be. I'm Emily Pellinser. I've been so wanting to make your acquaintance. I should have left you a card, I know, and meant to do so. I hope you'll forgive my doing things improperly like this.'

She smiled, holding out a small hand. As I took it, making some sort of return to her greeting, I realized she was Andrew Pellinser's sister. I had been told he lived with her and his

84

mother. Her ease of manner abashed me, and so did that realization. I felt dreadfully gauche.

She said: 'I know you've met my brother, Andrew.'

I nodded but said nothing, awkwardness tying my tongue. She clasped my hand in both of hers.

'I want to tell you, above all else, how sorry I am for the manner of that meeting. And to speak for Andrew, too.'

I could not help a tightening of my lips. She said:

'I know how you must feel. It is scarcely forgiveable that he should have behaved as he did, actually daring to lay hands on you. But I will ask you to forgive him, all the same. He has been almost out of his mind with worry over those sheep. There is only old Miller to help him, and apart from his age he has been sick on and off all winter. Andrew has had to be with them most of the day, and up half the night as well.'

Her account of her brother's activities did not correspond with John's, of a man neglecting his business through pre-occupation with a fantasy about lost tin lodes; but one would expect her to be loyal. I remained confused. Although I was not prepared to alter my detestation of Andrew Pellinser, I found myself attracted to Emily.

When I did not speak, she said:

'He really is bitterly sorry.' I doubted that also. 'Please, Miss Cowper.'

'I would like to forget it—the whole thing.'

'But you will accept his apology, and pardon him? Or would you like him to offer it in person? I promise he will do so.'

I quickly shook my head. 'That isn't necessary.'

'Then will you confirm the amnesty by taking tea with us tomorrow?' She saw my look, and added: 'With my mother and me, that is. Andrew will not be there. Do say yes.' Her voice was warm and earnest. 'I can drive over and fetch you.'

'That wouldn't be necessary.'

'I know.' She laughed. 'With all those carriages and coach-men standing idle at Carmaliot!'

For a moment I suspected her of taking my remark as ostentation, and the comment as being designed to put me down. But her look dispelled the action. She went on:

'I enjoy driving our old dog-cart. I really would like to come for you. Please say I can.'

My instinctive reaction to the sister was as favourable as it had been antagonistic to the brother. I liked the way she had approached me, and was willing to see more of her. And it would be good to know someone outside the stifling circle of Carmaliot. I said:

'If you are sure you would like me to, I'll be happy to accept.'

'Good!' She squeezed my hand. 'I will call for you at three.'

Edgar was sullen that evening. It had been his intention, I gathered, to go out—to dine with a friend of his some miles away. There were to have been a number of his cronies there, and the evening's entertainments were to include cock-fighting. I could imagine that he would enjoy that. The project, however, had been vetoed by Sir Donald—a further example of his autocracy. He gave no reason beyond the fact that Michael was sufficiently improved to be able to stay up for dinner. Sir Donald required the rest of the family to be present as well.

I had grown accustomed to dressing for dinner, though the décolletage of the evening gowns Mademoiselle had made me occasionally embarrassed me still, especially when I observed Edgar's gaze rest on the swell of my bosom. It did so now and then tonight, though covertly in his father's presence.

The dinner was a special one. We dined well normally at Carmaliot—too well, I thought—but this particular meal, as I had gathered from a muttered snatch of conversation between two of the servants, had kept the kitchen hard at work for two days. The soup was a consommé of game, followed by truffled cutlets of salmon in a delicate sauce, and

86

that followed by guinea fowl, elaborately prepared and subtly flavoured. These dishes were all meant to be favourites of Michael, but he seemed to have an indifferent appetite for them.

A cool white wine with a long German name was served with the fish, and a red wine with the guinea fowl. It had a slightly harsh taste which made me guess it was claret. Edgar, sipping from his glass, perked up for the first time that evening.

'This is not bad.' He held the wine glass up against the light of the chandelier. 'Might I know which it is, Father?'

'You may, indeed. The Haut-Brion '21.'

Sir Donald spoke with his usual calm, but with an under-tone, I thought, of unusual good humour. Edgar gave a small whistle of surprise. He said:

'There can't be more than half a dozen left. Quite an occasion.'

Sir Donald smiled, but said nothing. It was not until our plates had been cleared and a second decanter brought by the butler, that he said:

'This is an occasion, as Edgar has suggested. I will tell you why.'

He wiped his lips with his napkin and nodded to the butler to recharge the glasses. I had scarcely touched mine, so there was little to add. There was silence as the butler proceeded slowly round the table. I wondered what it could be Sir Donald had to say, and judged from the expressions of the others that they were equally curious and equally unenlightened.

The butler retired at last, and Sir Donald said:

'Before I come to the main point, I should like to propose a toast.'

He lifted his glass, and I followed the others in doing the same. He said:

'To the health of our beautiful Jane.'

His eyes were on me, and the rest were not slow in finding the target. For a moment, embarrassed and confused, I kept

87

my own glass up; then realized what I was doing and put it down.

'In the short time we have had the pleasure—the joy, I might say—of knowing her,' Sir Donald said, 'she has become a valuable and valued member of our family circle. Apart from her beauty and the bloom of youth, we have learned to admire her wit and manners, and her willingness to join in and serve the family interests.'

John said: 'Hear, hear!' which Edgar less convincingly echoed. Lady Bedivere smiled benevolently. Michael said nothing. He was watching his father, a strange expression on his face.

Sir Donald went on: 'All this has gratified me, as justifying the decision I made, in the very moment of meeting her, to bring her to Carmaliot. I will now tell you that I had another purpose, apart from the consideration of the pleasure and profit her company might provide, in doing as I did.'

His gaze, which had been on me, went across the table to Michael.

'Michael is my son and heir. Jane, though new to our acquaintance, is by birth in cousinship with the Bediveres, as Michael's mother was. And it is my heartfelt and most earnest wish that these two should marry.'

8

When I awoke next day, I still shivered at the recollection.

The statement produced a silence far more crushing than the earlier one. Voices were mute, but eyes expressive. On the faces of both Edgar and John I saw shock, coupled with anger in Edgar's case, incredulity in his brother's. Of Michael I caught only a glimpse, because I could not look at him, but I saw a desperate hurt. Only Lady Bedivere matched Sir Donald in untroubled serenity. And yet I felt that what had been said had surprised her, too.

I did not for long study their expressions. As the significance came home to me, I dropped my eyes. Inured as I had become to Sir Donald's assumptions of command over the people surrounding him, to his cavalier dispositions, this took my breath away. I was too amazed at first to be angry. Only gradually, as I plumbed the depths of the affront, did my temper rise. I might have been obliged to accept a home and a way of life I did not desire, but that acquiescence was on a short term only. It did not follow that my whole life should be disposed of—that I should be handed over, my consent deemed unnecessary, to marital keeping of a sick, a dying man.

By now I was furious enough to tell him so. But as I started to lift my eyes I saw Michael's fixed on me. There was appeal in them, and his face was very white. I doubt if that would have kept me silent, but it gave me pause long enough to think of other, dearer features. If my anger provoked a similar emotion in Sir Donald, Harry's hopes of the Navy might be jeopardized. The words had formed already, but I bit them back.

It was Lady Bedivere who broke the silence. She said placidly:

'Why, Sir Donald, that sounds an excellent notion.'

The silence settled again. Sir Donald seemed indifferent to it. He had delivered himself of the formulation of his wish, and sought neither approbation nor comment. It was enough that he had spoken: he drank his claret with a faint smile of satisfaction.

Lady Bedivere, too, had said all she wanted. Edgar and John plainly did not know what to say, while I, though I had plenty in my mind, knew I must not speak it. Michael, though, said:

'Will you excuse me, Mama?' He always gave her that title, though not her son. He turned to his father. 'I am not feeling very well. I think I should like to retire.'

Sir Donald was at once solicitous. The sorbet had just been brought in, and he asked him if he would not try a little of it. The game, perhaps, had fevered his blood, and the ice would cool it. When Michael refused, he asked if he would like a hot toddy sent up to his room, and when that too was denied, urged him at least to be certain to take his medicine before he went to bed. Michael nodded, bowed to Lady Bedivere and me, and left the room.

The dinner continued as though nothing had been said. John was the first to make a contribution towards the re-establishment of normality, with a remark about the meet that was to be held the following week. Edgar, taking the cue, weighed in more ponderously with another. Sir Donald responded to them, and the ordinary familiar conversation of the dinner table ensued. No one offered any further reference to the astonishing announcement that had been made.

When, the following morning, I came down to breakfast

and discovered Edgar already present, he favoured me with his oafish grin.

'Good morning, coz. Or should I begin practising to call you sister?'

I stared at him in silent disgust. He gazed insolently back, but at that moment Sir Donald entered, and he looked away.

Sir Donald had looked in on Michael on his way down: it seemed he had passed a restless night and was staying in bed. He said to me, sliding eggs on to his plate and spearing several rashers of bacon:

'It might be a notion for you to go and see him, Jane.' He smiled in explanation. 'Your presence will maybe do him as much good as Dr Roberts' medicine—or perhaps more.'

The remark, with its implication that everything was proceeding according to his plan, enraged me again. But I had learned control. I said submissively: 'I will do as you wish, Sir Donald', and was rewarded—not by Sir Donald's complacent nod but by the look, combining uncertainty and hostility, flashed me by Edgar.

I thought of it, as I made my way upstairs. I had been so wrapped up in my own resentment that until now I had not considered the reaction other members of the family might have. Edgar, it seemed, disliked the thought almost as much as I did. Why should that be? Not, I was quite sure, out of jealousy arising from a fondness for me. He would have tumbled me had he been able, but only in the viciousness of lust. If he had any feeling for me, I knew it could only be the contempt he thought due to an upstart. In getting me as a wife, Michael would not be taking anything Edgar wanted.

But he hated the notion—I was sure of it. For what reason? When Michael died he would be Sir Donald's heir, and I could be tolerably certain that no compunctions over dead men's shoes would prevent him relishing that prospect. But that would still be the case: he could not imagine that marriage would work the miracle that Chlorodyne and Dr

Roberts' ministrations had failed to achieve. Unless ...

I stopped dead, my hand on the banister where it curved and levelled for the landing. Unless I were first got with child.

I felt the blood tingling in my face. It was another shock, a deeper and more shaming one. I had objected to Sir Donald's proposal primarily because, even more than bringing me here, it treated me as a puppet whose consent was not so much assumed as disregarded; secondarily because it was a still more vital violation of my rights. The thought of having to be companion and nurse to a dying man had been a trifle compared with those considerations. I should not have cared for it, but it could have been borne as a duty.

It had never crossed my mind that marriage in the true sense could be intended—that the violation was to include my body. I could not have believed it now, except that it was the only thing which explained Edgar's rancour. I took a grip on myself again. That, surely, was no more than a reflection of the lowness of Edgar's mind. Sir Donald could not have intended any such thing.

All the same I went to my own room before visiting Michael's, and splashed my face with water to cool it. Then I walked briskly down the corridor, knocked at his door, and was bidden to enter.

He was sitting up, with pillows propped behind him. He looked very white and the paleness emphasized the dark shadows beneath his eyes. He was coughing as I came in, and could not stop for some moments. When he did at last, he apologized in exhausted tones.

I said: 'Do not mind it. How are you, Michael? Is there anything I can get for you? Would you like me to plump up your pillows?'

I had thought I might speak to him of what had happened, and demand that he speak in turn to his father and tell him how impossible it was: Sir Donald would give him the consideration I could not expect. But when I saw how ill and weak he looked, I could not do it. He had enough to bear without my adding to it. Michael himself said, though:

'We must talk, Jane.' He pointed a thin hand at the chair beside the bed. 'Will you s-sit beside me?'

I said as I did so: 'If you're not feeling well ...'

'I'm all right. What was said last night—you know I knew nothing of it?'

I nodded. 'I guessed that.'

'I knew how you m-must feel. I should have liked to say something then. But it would have done no good, and might have done harm. I told you that Father is at heart a k-kindly man. But he is also an unbending one. And he b-believes he knows what is best for others better than they know themselves.'

He was showing a moral weakness, I thought, that repelled me more than the physical one. Despite my resolution, I did not keep the sharpness out of my voice, as I said:

'Kindliness means nothing if it does not respect one's right to decide for oneself. Especially on such a matter as this. If you are not prepared to tell him so, I must.'

I was hoping to shame him. I thought he might drop his eyes, but he looked steadily at me.

'Do not do that, Jenny. It is plain now that everything to do with your coming here is part of a scheme he has planned.'

'Do you think I don't know it?', I cried. 'And does that make it any better?'

'I do not think you would be wise to cross him openly.'

'But you can speak to him! You are his eldest son, the person he loves best. You know that is true. He will listen to you.' He shook his head slightly. 'He must! You are a man— you cannot be coerced so.'

'I d-do not think you grasp the depth of his feeling about it. Or his certainty of his own b-benevolence.'

'And am I to accept that benevolence which he wishes to thrust down my throat?' I spoke with angry scorn. 'Are you asking me to do his bidding, and marry you?'

He closed his eyes a moment. 'I am not asking that. Even

93

if marriage were a joy to which I could look forward, I could see no reward in t-taking a woman against her will. As it is ...'

I felt sorry for him, and calmer. In a quieter tone, I said: 'Then what are you asking?'

'As I say, everything he has done where you are concerned is part of a scheme, whose fixed aim he told us of last evening. Everything. I could reject it at once and out of hand. He might take some convincing, but I know it could be done. And if it were, I know for a c-certainty what would follow. The object being l-lost, he would send you back to Portsmouth.'

I said in astonishment: 'Do you think I should mind that?'

'I know very well you would not.' He broke off, coughing again, and resumed: 'But all else m-might be lost, as well. His assistance to your mother.' He paused. 'The sponsoring of your brother Harry.'

I said bitterly: 'And do you call him kindly?'

'When the sun is shining for him, yes. It is true of many people. Things are worse with him b-because there is one storm cloud he will not face.'

'And yet he must!'

The words came out before I had properly thought, and I would have called them back if I could. The storm cloud was Michael's own death. He looked at me, and I knew he knew it, too, and had already faced the cloud. He said:

'In time. And in time your brother will have got his appointment, and you and your m-mother be secure. The plan will have failed, but there will be none to blame for that. Jenny, t-trust me. And let him go on, taking comfort from his illusion. It is no more than that, I promise you.'

I was silent. He went on:

'Delay is more effective than opposition, with someone like Father at any rate. Leave that to me. You d-do not need to do anything, except keep silent.'

I could not argue with what he had said, and he too had

grasped the threat to Harry. If I could trust him, I should follow his advice.

I nodded slowly. He smiled:

'Good. That makes me happier. I'll admit a selfish consideration—I d-did not want to see you go away. I've grown used to your being here.'

His hand, white and bony, rested on the counterpane, and I held it in my stronger one. He said:

'You did not really think I would have been a party to such a thing?'

I shook my head. 'It would be too monstrous.' I saw his look, and added: 'As monstrous for you as for me.'

He did not answer, and did not keep his eyes on me but looked away, towards the window and the long view out to the distant sea. I knew something else in that moment. He would never speak of it, would hide it if he could, but he loved me in the way a man loves a woman—a man in health, with a future before him.

The thought was horrifying. I felt sorry for him, but could not bear it. I longed to be away—to be anywhere but in this room.

He looked at me again. His eyes were steady, knowing and accepting. He said gently:

'I feel a little tired. I think you'd b-better go now, Jenny.'

I had been looking forward to my second meeting with Emily, and the actuality did not disappoint me. She talked gaily as the horse clopped along the road out of the village, and I felt my spirits rising. It was good to be in her company; especially good to be away, if only for a few hours, from Carmaliot, from Sir Donald's obsessions and Edgar's ugly foolery and Michael's sickness.

The topics of her conversation also increased my sense of liberation. At Carmaliot there was occasional talk of external things, but they were mostly confined to sporting activities, and to the few acquaintances with whom a slight and supercilious social contact was maintained. It was taken for granted that no one within riding distance was really a fit familiar for the Bediveres.

Emily talked about the ordinary people of the neighbourhood—the villagers and the farmers and the farm labourers. She appeared to have a wide acquaintance with them, and twice she stopped the trap to greet someone and pass a few minutes in chat. She did not mention her brother again, for which I was not sorry, but spoke of their circumstances generally and, with a frankness I found engaging, of their poverty. They kept only two servants in the house, and she herself was obliged to do the cooking and, I guessed, a great deal else. It was a pleasant change from Lady Bedivere, and her readiness to ring for a maid to lift the sleeping pug back on to the cushion from which he had slipped.

The journey, though some seven miles by the road, passed pleasantly and quickly, bringing us to Lacdam and the Manor. On closer examination the house seemed larger—it was a rambling affair, lacking the solid structure of Carmaliot—but also more dilapidated. I commented on the chimneys above the central part, which were very tall with square tops and decorated with spirals. Elizabethan, she said, and added cheerfully that they were crumbling away: the next gale was likely to bring at least one of them down altogether.

Inside it was cleaner than I had expected: the two servants must be willing workers and well organized. But shabbiness, and a want of decoration, were much in evidence. In the hall, Emily said in warning:

'Do not be nervous of Mama. She is not so frightening as she seems.'

She spoke in an easy way which did not itself arouse any alarm, but when I was introduced to Mrs Pellinser I was taken aback all the same. She was a tall gaunt woman, dressed in an old-fashioned gown of black silk. Her eyes were deeply set, her nose long and thin, and there were deep lines round them and her thin-lipped mouth. When she spoke her voice was high but strong, and with a haughtiness of tone that disconcerted me even more than Sir Donald's arrogant assurance. She held out a heavily knuckled hand for me to take, and said:

'Miss Cowper. Emily has told me of you. You are staying at Carmaliot, I believe?' I nodded. 'And you yourself are a Bedver by blood.'

'A distant cousin only.'

I had ignored her use of the family's original name, but she did not let it go at that.

'The Bedvers,' she said, '—your cousins at Carmaliot—are very grand now. It was not always so.'

'Mama, please!'

Mrs Pellinser ignored her. 'Are you interested in the history of that branch of your family, Miss Cowper?'

I started to speak, but she did not wait to hear it.

'A hundred years ago, the Bedvers kept an inn at Plymouth; today Sir Donald Bedivere'—she spoke the name with ferocious contempt—'lives at Carmaliot and has footmen in livery, and a crest on his carriage. You know what crest—a ship. What a fine conceit that is, what a piece of effrontery! For they made the money which bought them the baronetcy out of ships, out of smuggling contraband. Inn-keepers and smugglers—they did not tell you of that, I'll warrant!'

'Do recollect yourself, Mama,' Emily said. 'Miss Cowper is our guest. This is not suitable conversation.'

Mrs Pellinser's face, old and lined but bold as an eagle, was set on mine. I said:

'Your guess is wrong ma'am. I have been told of the family's humble beginnings, by my cousin John. But if it had not been said, I cannot think it would have been a fault I see no great profit in dwelling on the happenings of a century ago. For that matter, keeping an inn seems to me an honest enough trade. And if crimes were committed then, I do not see that they have much to do with people living now.'

The fierce face stared into mine, and I was a little fearful of what my outspokenness might have provoked. But the grim features cracked into a smile.

'You're loyal, child, and that's no bad thing. Tell me, do you like your life at Carmaliot?'

I said warily: 'I have been treated with the greatest kindness by everybody there.'

'That is not an answer, but it will have to do. Your previous circumstances were, I understand, very different?'

Emily said: 'Mama!'

'Very different,' I said. 'The way of life of my family was never more than modest, and since my father's death we have been almost destitute.'

'Honest, too,' she said approvingly. 'And poverty's no shame, though that is something I did not know at your age. It would have saved me much bitterness, if I had.'

She spoke with a ruefulness which made me warm towards her; but her spleen was not to be quenched so easily. Heavy-browed, she said:

'But neither loyalty nor honesty will serve you where the Bedvers are concerned. I warn you, child, you will get no good of them, and maybe more harm than you conceive possible.'

During tea, served from a silver teapot bearing a crest so worn from use and polishing that I could tell no more than that it represented some kind of bird, Mrs Pellinser was as taciturn as she had previously been garrulous, and at an early stage she briefly excused herself and left. Looking after her, Emily said:

'She is unhappy, poor dear, for speaking as she did.'

'I am sorry if what I said upset her.'

'Oh, no. She liked it. It was plain she liked you, too, and that, when she came to consider it, made her regret her outburst all the more. It is I, of course, who should apologize to you, on both our behalfs. But I felt you would take it the right way and make allowances.'

Her bright eyes looked at me, and I felt again a sense of affinity.

'I was a little frightened of her,' I admitted. 'But sorry for her as well.' I recollected myself. 'I should not say that.'

Emily laughed. 'No matter, as long as she does not hear you! Mama is a very proud person. And whatever she may say about honest poverty, she still takes it hard. She was brought up accustomed to riches, and had no thought that her marriage would make any change in that respect. She has never reconciled herself to the reversal, and I doubt she ever will. It is for her much more than for himself, that Andrew spends so much time in the old workings, hunting for the lost lode of tin. He does not really believe it exists, but she does, and that is what matters.'

This, like her previous mention of his industry in looking after the sheep, did not fit in with my picture of her brother. Like the other it could be reasonably set down to the partiality of a sister. I did not want to talk of that, nor of him at all, and changed the subject, complimenting her on her dress. It was of red muslin with yellow mountings on either side of the skirt, simply cut but gaily pretty. She had made it herself, and I admired her skill.

We passed by a fairly natural process from dresses to balls: she had heard it rumoured there was to be one soon at Carmaliot and was curious about it. I told her as much as I knew, which was that one was proposed but a date had not yet been fixed. It was something for which I had felt more apprehension than anticipation, but it would be different, I felt, having a friend there—and realized that even on so brief an acquaintance I thought of her as such.

It was at this point that the drawing-room door, already ajar, was pushed open. We looked up to see Andrew Pellinser entering.

I was confused, and for a moment mistrustful of her: she had assured me of his absence. But I saw, as she rose quickly

99

to her feet, that she was as surprised as I. She said, her voice sharp:

'What are you doing here, Andrew? You said you would not be in this afternoon.'

He had shaved and, seeing him for the first time without a whiskery stubble, I was bound to admit that he was not ill favoured in looks. His face had the thinness and bore some resemblance to Emily's but was set in stronger masculine lines. I noticed that his hair, fairly long and curling slightly over his ears, was not black but brown, glinting redly in the light from the lamp Emily had had lit against the darkness of the afternoon. He had taken care with his appearance altogether, having put on a brown tweed suit, and wearing a blue cravat with it that matched the colour of his eyes.

He said: 'I know, Emily, but I wanted to see Miss Cowper.' There was harshness in the voice still, but I was more conscious of its depth. 'I wanted to beg her pardon in person for my unmannerliness.'

He came and stood in front of my chair. Even when still his body had the threat of action in it. He said:

'I am truly sorry about the dog, but I had no choice. You see that?'

I felt weak. 'There is no need to talk of it.'

'But there is!' He reached down and took my hand. I felt the roughness of his and was repelled, but not entirely. Emily spoke reprovingly to him, but he disregarded it. I looked up into blue eyes fixed on mine.

'I am sorry, desperately sorry, for my behaviour to you. And sorry for your unhappiness over the dog. Yet I had no choice but to do as I did.' The eyes would not let me look away. 'You know that, do you not?'

I did not answer. He demanded:

'Well?'

He was forcing me, as men always did, determined to have my consent whether I was prepared to give it or not. I should have liked to deny it him, if only for that. But he had come to me, however roughly, as a suppliant. My refusal would hurt him; and I knew also that what he said was true.

He waited, his face set; strong but capable of being wounded. And although in one part of my mind I called myself a fool, I did not want to hurt him.

'Yes,' I said. 'I know you had no choice.'

'And you forgive me for it—and for the rest?'

I nodded, and he looked so pleased, so much a triumphant man, that I should have liked to take back my forgiveness. But it was too late.

9

Although I tried not to think of Sir Donald's project for marrying me to Michael, it continued to disturb me. That Michael had declared himself my ally was some help, but not much. He had persuaded me at the time that an outright defiance was unwise and that I should leave matters in his hands, but my misgivings were merely allayed, and not removed. I did not feel able to trust either his strength or resolution. Even if I had been satisfied on that score, I think I should still have been unhappy. It was not in my nature to be content with another's ordering of something so important to me.

I did my best to dismiss these doubts during the day, only to find them attacking me the more strongly at night, when there were no distractions to defend me. In Portsmouth, especially during those final weeks when I had been up stitching into the small hours, sleep had come as a delayed and longed-for comforter, bringing oblivion. I had no such need at Carmaliot. I was wakeful and restless, reading by candlelight or merely staring out into the shadows of my bedroom.

The lack of sleep declared itself by day in occasional fits of yawning and, perhaps more positively than I guessed, in my looks. Sir Donald, one evening at dinner, took me to task on that account. He asked about my slumbers and when I denied any disturbance in them, firmly rejected the denial.

'I have made inquiries of your maid, who tells me that your bed is vastly disordered. Sleep, especially at your age, is a vital refreshment, my dear Jane. Your health can quickly be injured by a deprivation of it.'

He signalled to the butler, who came to refill his wine glass. Lifting it and staring approvingly at it, he said:

'This, I am convinced, is part of Michael's difficulty. I have spoken of it to Dr Roberts, who has prescribed a draught which will procure him a more substantial rest. You must take some, too, before you retire.'

The reference to inquiring of the maid, with its further indication of the proprietary rights which Sir Donald took for granted, had staggered me. As he went on I recovered, and was preparing to speak up when I saw Michael's face, silently pleading. I saw the others, too—John sympathetic, Lady Bedivere placidly munching, Edgar faintly jeering. There might well be an occasion when protest was called for—I felt sure there was bound to be eventually—but this was not it. I bowed my head and attended to my dish.

After dinner, while his three sons made up a whist table with Lady Bedivere, Sir Donald spoke to me. We sat together on the far side of the room from the card players, and were not likely to be overheard. Nonetheless, he kept his voice low.

'You must keep your health, Jane.'

'I will endeavour to, sir.'

'It is of such importance to us all.'

I was surprised by his earnestness. I said:

'My health has always been good.'

He nodded gravely. 'I do not doubt it. The bloom of health was one of the things that impressed me in you when I first discovered you. But even though your constitution may be strong, it is not something which should be taken for granted, or treated lightly.'

I nodded, resigning myself to the prospect of a lecture on health matters, and prepared to let his words echo unregarded. He went on:

'It is a blessing of which those who are lucky enough to have it are rarely conscious, and even more rarely grateful.'

His look went from me to the far side of the room, and the group of four seated round the card table. There was no way of being sure which of them he was staring at, but the expression, of fondness mixed with pain, told me well enough. Michael put down his cards to endure a fit of coughing, and I was sorry for him, for both of them. Sir Donald turned back to me.

'The human body is a temple, Jane. Each human body is. But some are destined to enjoy more precious offerings than others. Yours is one such.' His grey eyes under the thick silvery brows fixed on me hard. 'It will bear Carmaliot's heir.'

Even though I had, as I thought, accustomed myself to his purpose, I was once more taken aback. It had not occurred to me that he would broach it to me. I felt myself colouring. He said, his voice kindly:

'Your modesty becomes you. It is another confirmation of my judgement in the choice I made. I would not offend against that modesty under normal circumstances by such a reference. But the circumstances are not normal. I must tell you: Michael is more gravely ill than we have let it be known. Much more gravely ill.'

I did not know what to say. Although I had thought his pretence that Michael's sickness was no worse than a cold on the chest foolish, I did not want to listen to him telling me the ugly truth. I said:

'Please, Sir Donald ...'

'Hear me out.'

I had no choice. He was as implacable in this as he had been in making light of the condition. He spoke with no expression showing either in face or voice. Michael was dying. Nothing could prevent it, or hold it off for long. He looked at me, his face concentrated and serious.

'That is why your wedding is so important, and why it must not be much delayed. You understand?'

I stared at him, distressed and still quite lost for words. But he took my silence as maidenly modesty. Patting my hand, he said:

'We will not talk of it any more at present. I know you understand.'

I had hoped that the sleeping draught he had proposed might be forgotten, or failing this that it would be sent up to the privacy of my room. No such relief was granted: Michael and I were put on parade, like a couple of children, and the family watched us take our medicine. I suppose it was something that we were spared having it spooned into our mouths. The bottle was brought by Henry, the butler, and the dosage solemnly measured into wine glasses. Michael, glancing at me, shrugged ruefully, and I supposed that if he was required to bear the indignity I ought not to complain of it.

Dr Roberts' Black Drops, as Sir Donald called them, were not black but a dark green potion, sticky and somewhat sweet. Henry was waiting with glasses of water, and I was glad to rid myself of the taste, or most of it. A little stayed, cloying, on my tongue. Then, admonished to sleep well and arise refreshed, we were packed off to our beds.

In my room I undressed and washed and put on night-gown and cap. I felt no sleepier—rather, in an odd way, feverishly awake—and I wondered if Dr Roberts knew what he was about. I put out the main lamp, leaving the other burning beside my bed, climbed between the sheets, and picked up my copy of Mrs Gaskell's *North and South*.

That it engrossed me less this night was not through tiredness. My mind felt active, but at the same time less controlled. The author's words and images danced confusingly, interspersed with thoughts having no relation to the events or characters of the book. I thought of poor Beast—of Andrew's face fierce first in anger and then in suppliance—of Sir Donald and Michael ... And to my astonishment, I thought of my father.

It was not so much the fact of calling him to mind that was surprising, as the emotion that accompanied it. For as long as I could remember I had associated him with fear and anger, with an unquestioned loathing. But this time there was friendliness and warmth. It began to crumble as I rejected it, but even as it was fading something else came to me, from the misty region outside consciousness: a scene, vivid and sharp-edged.

'Where are the paddles, then, princess?' He was smiling hugely at me. 'You tell me where she's hidden her paddles!'

We were in the Portsmouth docks, on a sunny day with a light warm wind. He had taken me down there on a special trip, carrying me on his shoulders much of the way, and we stood on the quayside with all the noise of the port about us: the different squeals of iron and of rope, men's voices shouting the hiss of steam and flap of sail, seabirds squawking and wailing. The sounds and smells: the sharp salt scent of the sea, smells of tar and canvas and tobacco and, piercingly from a crate on the wharf, of oranges. His smell, too, close by me.

I stared at the ship at which he was pointing, and desperately wondered where the paddles were. The sides ran smooth and unbulging, so very different from the one berthed ahead of it with water still dripping from the slats of its big iron wheels. I felt uncertain and unhappy, and angry with myself for not being able to answer him. After all, I was three and a half years old.

Looking down at me, grinning, he saw my distress, and lifted me up again to perch on his shoulder. My hand, round his head, felt the rough reassuring whiskeriness. His right hand held me firmly in position: I was high and warm and safe.

'I'll not tease you, lass! She has no paddles, none at all. Then how does she travel, having no sails either? Because the steam turns a screw and the screw turns a propeller and that pushes her through the water. She's the *Archimedes*, the first of her kind but I'll wager not the last.'

He went on talking about ships, and I listened though not intently. It was enough to be here, enough to have him lift me and hold me. A man came along, someone who knew him, and asked if he were going to the tavern.

'Not today, Jack,' he said cheerfully. 'You can see I've got company.'

'She can wait outside, can't she?'

'Nay.' He laughed. 'You don't leave a princess waiting outside a boozer!' He gave me a squeeze. 'Do you, Jenny?'

I lay back in my bed at Carmaliot in the warm sheets, with the scent of lavender inside my pillow. I felt an aching sadness, for the way happiness can be forgotten so that it might never have existed, but more for the wretchedness into which it can turn. I asked the question why, but got no answer. I thought of him lying under the tarpaulin on the cart, with the cold rain puddling in his dead hand, and of the joy I had felt. I did not like myself for that.

Gradually the draught took effect. From being sharp with a fever's sharpness my mind clouded, until I forgot my misery in sleep.

I had dreams. I could not recall later what they had been, but I knew they were nightmarish. There was fear in them, a fear which was the more powerful for being undefined. Then at last the fear took shape, and not only shape but substance. Something was pressing down over my face, soft and warm and heavy on my mouth, stopping my breath.

I tried to free myself, and could not. I was hot and sweating, helpless against my attacker. If I could cry out ... but there was no hope of that. I attempted to brace myself, to force myself up against whatever was oppressing me. Relentlessly the weight bore me down.

All was soft and black and smothering. My lungs seemed ready to burst for want of air. I could not believe I was dying, but could not believe anything else, either. The muffling heaviness seemed to have been overlying me for so long that

I did not know how I could be living still. I wondered frantically if perhaps I no longer were—if this drawn-out agony was death, and punishment.

At that moment the burden shifted slightly. It was not by much and almost at once it seemed to press back, but it roused me to a despairing effort. I ceased trying to struggle up against it and put all my strength into a writhing sideways motion. Linen, swathing and tangled, still stopped my mouth; then, blessedly, I was free, drawing in air and letting it go in an exhausted cry.

Blood was pounding in my head. I breathed in again, deeply, the air more precious than food and drink could ever be. And I was on the point of crying out more loudly when I realized that the incubus was gone—that I lay on my bed, with nothing hampering or oppressing me.

Shakily I drew myself higher up in the bed. I called quietly, and got no answer. The room was black except where my window showed a starry sky. I listened, and heard nothing. Carefully, frightened still and ready to cry out at the faintest sound, I felt for the match-box on the table beside me, found and opened it, and with shaking fingers struck a light. It flared brightly, and I lit my candle from it. There was no one in the room, no sign of disorder except in my bed.

There disorder was all too evident. I lay among a twisted clutter of sheets and blankets, the top sheet wound about itself, a pillow thrust out of place and resting close to my hip, the patchwork quilt tumbled off and lying on the rug. The evidence of my threshing about was plain. What was not plain was the reason for it.

I tried, as my pulse eased from its frantic race, to recall the sensations of the previous moments. Not the suffocation— I did not want to think of that—but whatever else might have touched my senses. Had I heard footsteps going away, after I had succeeded in crying out? I thought I had, but now could not be sure. Looking out into the room again, I observed that my door was open, though not by much. I had closed it when I retired. A breeze (I slept with my window open) made my candle flicker and lifted a corner of the curtain. The door banged softly back. A gust could have opened it, too: the fastener was old and loose and I had not bolted it.

The bell rope hung at the side of the bed. I could pull it, and be rewarded, in five minutes or so, by the sight of a sleepy tousled maid. And what should I tell her, when she came? Was I to rouse the house—bring the Bediveres hurrying to see what was amiss? And what had been amiss, after all?

The door banged gently again, and I decided there was something I could do, and should. Slipping out of bed, I went quickly and pushed it fully to, then slid the bolt. It went home with a satisfying scrunch of metal, and I resolved never in future to omit that from my nightly routine. The next moment panic returned, with the thought that there might be someone lurking under the bed, and that in bolting the door I had imprisoned myself with him. I put my hand uncertainly on the handle, then summoned the courage to go back to the bed, drop to my knees on the rug, and look. There was nothing there. I straightened up more cheerfully, and found myself looking at the wardrobe door. It too could hide an intruder.

I lit the lamp, glad of the brighter light, and set about checking every place that might conceal someone. When I had finished I sat on the edge of my bed. There was no one in the room, nor had there been. It had all been part of a nightmare. I looked at the soft yellow light of the lamp, and remembered my fearful waking in the dark ... The lamp had been alight when I went to sleep.

Imagining the scene, I shivered. A hand quietly turning the knob of the door, a figure stealing in to stand beside my bed. Eyes watching me as I slept—pitiless murderous eyes. A mouth blowing out the light. The pillow lifted in the dark room, pressed down over my face ...

Whose figure? Edgar? I could not think of anyone but

him. He had been angry when Sir Donald spoke of his desire that I should marry Michael. My first realization of what the marriage might be aimed at had come from considering that. He expected to become the heir when Michael died, and the thought of a child stepping in between him and his ambition must be a bitter pill. Would he commit murder, rather than swallow it? It was something, too, that need not be detected. If I were found dead next morning, a sheet twisted across my face, why look for any other cause than self-suffocation, brought on in a nightmare, itself resulting from the sleeping draught?

I shivered again. My hair, soaking with perspiration, clung wetly to my face. If I went to Sir Donald with such an accusation, what would he say? That also I could imagine. His calm imperturbable voice: 'A nightmare indeed, Jane, for you to think of such a thing. Those novels that you read are not good for you. You must turn to more wholesome and improving literature.'

As though I were confronting him now, I marshalled the details: the open door, the lamp blown out, the footsteps ... Or had there been footsteps? Could I swear to that? The lamp, for that matter. I would not normally have gone to sleep with it lit. I thought I had done last night, because I had no recollection of putting it out. But things had not been usual last night, by reason of Dr Roberts' Black Drops. They had confused my mind and brought up that forgotten memory of my father. My state of mind was still an unsteady one. Sir Donald's voice echoed: 'A nightmare, Jane ...'

Could I deny it? I stared at the bolted door. Two days before I had found it off the latch. The maid, I had thought, not closing it properly, or the wind; and the wind more likely because Sir Donald was insistent that the servants should be scrupulous in all their duties. Would it have occurred to me to impute it to anything else, except in the aftermath of delirium?

I did not know what to think or believe. I looked at the

tumbled confusion of the bed. The Bediveres each and every one of them, would have known what to do about that: ring for the maid to make it afresh. I thought of Millie, sleeping peacefully in her attic room with a hard day's duties behind her and another before. Then I set to work, stripping the bed and remaking it.

By the time I had done and climbed back between orderly sheets, the nightmare seemed further off than ever. I settled down, tired and unsure, but this time deliberately I left the lamp burning. I was soon asleep.

I slept late, and felt blurred and heavy when I awoke. Looking at my fob-watch, a present from Lady Bedivere, I saw that it was nearly nine o'clock, a good hour past my usual time for waking. Millie was accustomed to call me a quarter before eight, and I wondered if her failure was yet another indication of Sir Donald's despotic rule over the details of my life—if he had given orders, because of the sleeping draught, that I was to be left to sleep.

Remembering the sleeping draught, though, I remembered the nightmare, and realized that with the door bolted Millie could not have come in to bring me my tea. She would have tried and tapped and, getting no answer, would have gone away.

Fearing that she might have spoken of this and that my lack of response coupled with the door being bolted might have caused alarm, I hurriedly washed and dressed. In fact my nervousness was unjustified. She was a willing pleasant girl but unimaginative, a little simple even, and would have thought nothing of it. The gentry had their strange ways, and as far as Millie was concerned I counted as such.

Edgar was coming from the breakfast room as I went towards it; he took that meal, even more than others, in a leisurely fashion. He stood before me, grinning.

'Well, coz, I don't need to ask you if Dr Roberts' Black Drops worked, do I? You must have slept like the dead.'

I looked at the dark heavy face with its oafish smile and tried, with a tremor of disgust and fear, to picture it hovering above me in the dark, straining with the effort of smothering me. I could not believe it.

No, it had been a hideous dream, no more. But all the same, I would bolt my door in future.

10

I did not see any more of Edgar that day, nor most of the rest, which was purely a relief. Acquitting him of an attempt to murder me did not make me think better of his person or manners. It seemed he had ridden over to Plymouth, on some business of his own. Sir Donald made slight, and slightly disapproving, reference to it at the luncheon table. 'Seeing his rackety friends, I suppose.' I wondered again about the presence of the younger sons at Carmaliot. Did he make them an allowance, conditional on their being there? And grant them such limited leave as Edgar, presumably, was now enjoying? I decided it was neither concern nor interest of mine, and concentrated on the pleasure of his absence.

Michael asked me how the sleeping draught had taken me, adding that he had himself slept heavily but had not really felt refreshed for doing so. I said only that I had had bad dreams, and he said, with unusual firmness, that I ought not to be subjected to such ministrations. He would speak to his father on the matter. I think he did: at any rate, there were no Black Drops on that night, or any other.

The hunt met at Carmaliot the day after Edgar's return. I watched them from a window at the front of the house as they assembled on the drive: the horsemen in their red jackets (which I knew I must call pink), ladies side-saddle in black with elegant hunting hats and crops, the horses scuffing the gravel, champing and snorting, the hunt servants; and everywhere, some whining but for the most part quiet, the hounds, snuffling aimlessly and amiably. Henry led out the footmen with the trays of stirrup cup. It was a bright blowy day again, and I should have liked to ride though not in that company. Yet I had to admit how colourful a scene it made.

A lady's habit more shabby than the others drew my eye, and I saw Emily, mounted on a chestnut mare. I had not realized she might be at the meet, though there was no reason for thinking she would not. I thought of going down to speak to her, but was shy of doing so in a crowd, and such a crowd as this. Next moment I saw Andrew, close by her on a grey gelding, which was an even more powerful reason for staying where I was. They talked together, their voices lost in the babble, and I saw them look towards the house. They were not looking at the window behind which I stood, but I still drew back.

Not long after that the pewter pots were handed back to the servants, Sir Donald standing in his stirrups called to the Huntsman who sounded his horn, and the hunt moved off. I watched them go away down the drive and out through the gates before I turned away. I was content to have the house, Lady Bedivere and the servants apart, to myself.

My satisfaction was increased half an hour later when the post arrived, and I found there was a letter from Harry. I opened it eagerly, thrilled by the sight of his handwriting, rounded and simple like my own but bolder. And the very first sentence filled me with joy. He had been for his interview at the Admiralty, and they had accepted him.

By now I had come to terms with the fact of our separation, and had ceased idle dreams of things being as they had been. Whatever became of me here at Carmaliot, there was no way of putting back the clock and returning to the old days at Portsmouth. I should see Harry again—of course, I should, many times: I could not bear the thought of anything else— but our lives could no longer intertwine in the way I had been used to, and had held so dear.

That being so, I wanted for Harry only what he himself

114

wanted, and this, beyond all else, was it. His own delight, though sketched in with restraint, was plain. He had been promised a place very soon, within weeks. This coming summer might see him cruising the Indian Ocean, or observing the wonders of the West Indies!

In my own last letter to him I had asked for more news of a girl I knew, a school friend, whom he had casually spoken of as about to be married. I re-read the whole of his letter, and found no answer to my query. It was understandable, I thought, that, concerned with his own great news, he should overlook this minor matter. Then I took in a sentence near the end. 'I suppose it is through your life being full of new exciting things that I've had but one letter this week—but I'm glad of it.'

It was not the case: I had not missed writing once. But that did not matter, and neither did the marriage of Annie Tanner. The important thing was the forthcoming installation of Midshipman Cowper. I took pen and plenty of paper, and voluminously wrote him my congratulations.

The huntsmen, except for Michael, were out all day. I had been a little astonished that he should attend—that Sir Donald should permit him to do so—and I was not surprised when he returned after a couple of hours, accompanied by a groom who, I realized, had been detailed to take care of him. He went wearily up to his room, and did not come down for luncheon. Lady Bedivere and I were the only ones at table. She chatted in her usual jovial fashion about various things, including the hunt. It was a pity I was not yet sufficiently skilled a horsewoman to take part in it; but by next season things would be different.

I said: 'I should not care to hunt even if I could ride well enough. I would find no pleasure in chasing a small frightened animal.'

Her laughter boomed down the table. 'Do not let Sir Donald hear you say so! Though his partiality for you is such that I

115

am confident it would survive it. But you will find you look at things differently in due course.'

'I do not think so. I can understand that other people may hold dissimilar views.' I thought of Emily. 'But I shall keep my own.'

She nodded to the footman and was brought another dish of apple-pie, thickly topped with cream.

'To be honest, I had no great fondness for the sport, in the days when I hunted. Not from pity for the fox—they are vermin, after all—but because so much of it was boring, and the rest uncomfortable. I was glad enough to retire, and spare the horses as well as myself. But it was something that was required of me *then*. As it will be of you, when you are mistress of Carmaliot.'

Her eyes studied me under their dark brows. It was a more speculative look than I had commonly seen in her, and I wondered if maybe she were shrewder and more observant than I had guessed. I determined to ignore the implication, and confine myself to the original point. I said simply:

'I do not think I shall hunt.'

She watched me a moment longer before, with a little shrug of her massive shoulders, she turned her attention to her pudding.

It was dusk when the others came back. There was the clump of heavy feet through the house, the roughness of male voices, the bustle of servants as hot water was taken up for their baths. Later, before dinner, they came to drink brandy and soda in the main drawing-room, though I had a notion they had already drunk enough from the hip flasks they carried with them as part of their equipment for combating the fearful fox.

I felt the intrusion of their masculinity, its roughness and arrogance, but other considerations were uppermost in my mind. As soon as there was an appropriate break in their talk, of how they had drawn that one in such a place, and run him from hither to yon, of scents and hounds and whippings-in, and the toss old so-and-so had taken at some stone wall, I spoke to Sir Donald, telling him I had had word from my brother.

He looked at me over the brandy glass, a slight smile on his lips.

'I am glad to hear of it, Jane.'

'He tells me he has been taken by the Navy. I wanted to say how grateful I am to you, for the assistance you have provided.'

'No need for that.'

His manner, though dignified still, was brisk and cheerful. The day's sport had exhilarated him, and his complexion had more colour in it. He put his hand on my arm, and said:

'I am glad to have been able to do something for the boy. And not for his sake only, but for the Navy's. He will be a credit to the service, I am confident of it. I had a letter from him, too—a very proper one. But I must confess I had heard the news beforehand, and more particularly. I know the ship he is to join, and that he does so in a fortnight's time.'

'As soon as that?'

I tried to be pleased for Harry's sake, but despite myself was dismayed. It was so final a step.

Sir Donald said: 'Yes, and the sooner the better for him, I'll wager. But I have a proposal I mean to put to him first. I intend asking him to spend a few days here at Carmaliot, before he goes to sea. Shall you like that, Jane?'

He was watching me indulgently. I said:

'I cannot tell you how much I would like it, sir.'

I spoke in a low voice, unsure whether he really meant it. It seemed too much to believe that I should see Harry again, and soon. I felt I knew how a prisoner, following long starvation, might fawn over his gaoler for the gift of a crust of bread.

Sir Donald nodded. 'Word will go to him tomorrow. And

before that there is something else that I hope will please you. This ball that was talked of. Lady Bedivere is sending out cards, and it is to be for Tuesday next. I'm told Mademoiselle is making you a gown to suit your beauty.' He smiled down at me. 'She will have a hard task.'

I said something. I know not what, by way of thanks. I had had no yearning for a ball, and even if I had the other news would have eclipsed it and extinguished it. But this too was a favour, and the benefactor looked for gratitude. Harry, I thought, here....

Sir Donald bent towards me. In a lower voice, he said:

'There is something which would please me in return. If during the course of the ball I could make a certain announcement ...'

The joy abruptly went. I looked at him. His face was kindly but rigorous. He said:

'It is something which would make me very happy. Think of it, Jane.'

My sleep was restless again that night, though there was consolation in the thought of the bolt firmly in place across my bedroom door. In the morning, the day being windy still but bright, I went for a walk. I headed for the moor. I had not been that way since Beast was shot, and resolved to conquer my reluctance. As I was going out, John hailed me and, when I stopped to let him come up, asked if I minded his accompanying me. I hesitated for a moment, not really wanting any company but my own. Had it been Edgar I should have made a brusque refusal. But John's attitude towards me had been so amiable that I could not justify rejecting this small request.

As we walked on he talked first about the hunt. He had either already gleaned my feelings on it, or else gathered them from my reaction now; for he spoke in quite a different fashion from his converse of the previous evening. There was, he admitted, an element of the barbarous—of the ridiculous for that matter—in a sport which pitted a pack of hounds and as many as two score huntsmen against one small animal with no power of fighting back. On the other hand the pleasure of the chase was real enough: a splendid exercise of body and exhilaration of spirit.

I found his open-mindedness sympathetic and we talked easily. He said suddenly:

'Emily Pellinser spoke of you, and warmly.'

'I am glad if she likes me. I like her very much.'

'But it was Andy who mentioned you first. It seems he had thought you would be at the meet.'

'That's absurd. Apart from anything else, I cannot ride well enough.'

John laughed. 'He has a high opinion of you, too! Very high, I would guess. I don't know what you said to him that day at Lacdam ...'

'Nothing pleasant, I promise you.'

'Whatever it was, it has had a powerful effect. I judge him to be quite smitten by you.'

'That's even more absurd.'

He looked at me quizzically, and I returned the look, smiling. He said:

'So the poor devil has no chance?'

I said firmly: 'It is not a subject worth the discussing.'

'You are quite right. I was joking. You are to marry Michael, are you not?'

I did not answer him, though I had a great urge to do so. I found him much the nicest of the people I had met at Carmaliot—nicer than anyone I had encountered since leaving home, apart from Emily. It would have been altogether easier than discussing it with Michael; because Michael and I were the puppets whose futures were being disposed of by Sir Donald, and Michael was in love with me which made things so much worse.

With John it might be possible to talk it over in a detached and rational way—to make sense of it and perhaps work out a solution. God knows I had need of an ally. But my silence was met with another from him, and the moment in which there could have been a chance of communication went. When he spoke again, it was to draw my attention to a crumbling grassy ruin—the remains, he said, of one of the old tin workings, perhaps hundreds of years old.

'Poor Pellinser's cross,' he added.

A bird perched on the ruin. It was quite large, with long pink legs and a long reddish bill, its back a greeny black but with a white belly and white throat and wing-tips. I remembered walking on a muddy beach with Harry and his telling me what it was. I said to John:

'An oyster-catcher?'

'Yes, though we call them sea-pies here.'

'But so far inland?'

'Blown by the wind. And unless it drops or changes, he will have a hard flight back when he has done resting. If he were sensible, he would forget what lies behind and go on with the wind to find another beach on the Channel coast. But birds have even less sense in their judgements than men and women.'

'He looks very pretty, sitting there.'

'Which is undeniably something.' He looked at me. 'But nowhere near as pretty as you, Jane, with the colour in your cheeks the walking has given you.'

We were quite out of sight of the house—of any living creature except the bird, any work of man but the grassy heap before us. Had Edgar been my companion, I should have been alarmed by the compliment, guessing that it would be followed by unwelcome attentions. I had no such apprehension of John.

This did not please me as much as I should have liked to think it did. I was glad, I told myself to feel so safe. I liked John, and thought him one of the most handsome men I had met, if not the most, but I did not want him to make love to me. At the same time it was not entirely agreeable that, even while he paid me compliments, I should sense this reserve in him. I did not want, I told myself, to be taken and kissed on the lonely moor, but it would not be unwelcome to believe that the thought was in his mind.

And why, if it were not? The probable explanation was all too plain; in fact he had referred to it not long before. I was reserved for Michael. His father had decreed it, and he would not—or dare not—challenge that edict. That put me much more out of sorts than the other had. I proposed going back and on the return journey John was obliged to carry the chief burden of conversation. I had to admit he did it very well.

If I could not talk of it with John, I must with Michael. There had been no chance the previous evening, so I sought him out that afternoon. I found him in the library, sitting before the fire and turning the pages of a copy of the *Illustrated London News*. He looked up, smiling, as I crossed the room towards him.

'How are you, Jenny? No b-bad dreams last night?' I shook my head. 'I'm glad.' He indicated the chair next to the one from which he had risen. 'But something troubles you. Tell me of it.'

I wasted no time in doing so. He listened and said:

'You d-did not answer him?'

'No. But he will speak of it again, before Tuesday.'

Michael nodded. 'Yes. He will.'

'And will not allow me to respond a second time with silence.'

There was a tap on the door, followed by someone entering. It was only one of the maids, coming in to make up the fire, but the interruption maddened me. In this great house with all its rooms one seemed to have no more privacy than in our terraced cottage in Pratt Street. That was not true, of course—my bedroom was bigger than the whole downstairs area there—but *there* I had not felt the need for it. The only irritant had been my father, and he had been out most of the time, at his work or drinking.

Michael glanced through the magazine again while the maid, infuriatingly slow, tipped coals on the fire and went on to brush the hearth. I sat and stared in front of me, willing her to be quicker. The moment the door had closed behind her, I said:

'You know he will demand an answer! There can be no doubt of that. His whole reason for giving a ball is so that he can announce to the county our engagement to be married.'

'Yes.'

'And I will not bear it!'

I saw the quick look of pain in his face, and was sorry for it and ashamed of myself for putting it there. But he said evenly:

'I know you cannot. But your brother is to come and stay with us soon after, is he not? I know you do not wish anything to happen that would prevent that, and defiance might. I told you before that d-delay is better, and that I would see to it.'

Even though ashamed, I was impatient. 'But what can you *do?*'

He smiled. 'That which I do best—be an invalid. On Tuesday I shall have an attack, and take to my bed. It will not be d-difficult to deceive them. I have studied my symptoms.'

I was uncertain. 'He may still wish to announce it, even if you are not there. Or he may postpone the ball until you are stronger.'

'As to the latter, it cannot be done. The invitations have gone out. For the former, I will speak to him. I do not think it will be difficult to persuade him to hold his hand. It would be natural, after all, for me to wish to b-be present for such a momentous occasion.'

I was unhappy still. My instinct was for defiance, whatever he said. But I knew he was right about the possible consequences. I nodded slowly.

122

'All right.'

'Without quite saying it, I can contrive to have him think things are falling as he wishes, but that a little more time is needed. And you must behave consistently with that. C-can you do so, Jenny?'

I drew breath deeply. 'I'll try.'

11

My earlier reluctant pleasure in being dressed by Mademoiselle had staled through custom, and I felt that I could take no interest in anything connected with a ball which I had not wanted and whose prospect inspired in me more apprehension than anything else. Nonetheless, as the days and fittings passed, I could not help but be impressed by Mademoiselle's skill, and just a little in love with the result. At my final fitting on the Tuesday morning, I gazed at myself in the cheval-glass with some of the surprise of viewing a stranger, and with a feeling of satisfaction, too, that I hoped I didn't show.

Mademoiselle had no such reserve, and no false modesty over her achievement.

'It is magnificent—without a doubt, magnificent! Miss Jane, turn yourself a little this way. No, not quite so much. There. Stay so.'

She stood behind me but, too small to see over my shoulder, was obliged to peer round my arm to look at my reflection in the glass. Her head bobbed like a bird's.

'Three things,' she said. 'The figure, the carriage, the youth. They are what is needed, and you have them all. The third does not do much without the other two, but when it is added to them ...'

I saw her hand, in the glass, lifted in admiration. And I saw myself again, the stranger, through her eyes.

The dress was of white tarlatan, flounced and trimmed with

rosebuds, over a lilac taffeta bodice and overshirt with bands of ruching edging the shirt and neckline. The berthe collar, showing an amount of bosom which a few weeks ago would have made me blush, was of white silk, as were the sleeves and the overshirt's edging. My hair had been done in curls falling down my neck on the left side, and she had fixed a spray of artificial lilac in it.

My arms were sheathed in long creamy white kid gloves, and I carried a pale blue lacy fan. (Mademoiselle's one criticism was that I had not yet learned to hold it properly, but she added that it was an exceedingly difficult accomplishment, and that I was improving.) Beneath the bell of the crinoline the toes of my slippers peeped out, white and gold. They had been ordered from London, and a delay in delivery had caused consternation. They had only arrived the previous day, to Mademoiselle's voluble relief.

'Sir Donald and Lady Bedivere will be very proud of you. It is pitiful that Mr Michael cannot be there too, to see you.'

Michael had been as good as his word and taken to his bed. I guessed he had also spoken to Sir Donald, whose manner on being told this news, was regretful but unruffled. He had said nothing more to me about announcements or engagements.

As Mademoiselle prepared to help me off with the gown, to be carefully laid on the bed and sheeted against the evening, I thanked her profusely for her efforts and all her help. It was the least I could do. She shrugged, lifting her hands in the French way.

'It is nothing, Miss Jane.' She gave me a quick look, smiling archly. 'And perhaps it is not long before I am making you an even finer dress, and picking the blossom from the orangery to attend it?'

Although she chattered almost continuously, it was the first such reference she had made. I realized, as I ought to have done before, that what was proposed could scarcely, in a place like Carmaliot, remain confined to members of the family: it must be the common gossip of the servants, both high and low. I felt a brief rush of anger, but suppressed it. It was not their fault, after all, and was bound to interest them.

I looked in the glass for the last time, before Mademoiselle lifted the dress over my head. It *was* lovely.

The main stairs at Carmaliot formed a twin flight on either side of the hall and, meeting at a half landing, ran doubled, only a central hand-rail marking their division, up the shorter climb to the first-floor. The doors of the ballroom, fastened back, were immediately facing, and Sir Donald and Lady Bedivere stood there to receive their guests. I stood, nervous and unhappy but trying not to show it, on Lady Bedivere's right. Behind us the sound of music from the orchestra—an oboist, a clarionetist, a flute-player, three fiddlers and a lady with a harp, specially imported from Plymouth—contended with the hum of voices and, as more and more people were greeted by us and passed through, was gradually submerged by it.

After the first few I did my duty mechanically, wondering if the smile fixed on my face could ever be removed. Sir Donald, introducing me, was correct but, especially with those he thought well of, much too concerned to show me off, and stress my cousinship. But perhaps I was being too sensitive, and as the line went by I accepted this mechanically like the rest.

They were a long blur of faces and hands, of smiles and meaningless remarks. Then the blur shifted into sharp recognition as someone stood before me; and the smile of convention left me at the sight of Andrew Pellinser. He bowed stiffly, his eyes fixed on mine. He said:

'You look very lovely tonight, Miss Cowper. I hope you will grant me some favours on your card.'

I had felt a disturbance—of resentment, but of something else as well, something that puzzled and troubled me. I told myself it was nothing: no more than the shock of seeing a known face after a procession of strangers. I had no time to pursue the thought, anyway, because Emily followed him. As we clasped hands, I asked her:

'Did you get my note?' She nodded. 'And can you stay?'

I had secured Lady Bedivere's permission to ask her to spend the night at Carmaliot rather than drive back to Lacdam, and sent over a note that afternoon. She had been out, so there had been no immediate reply. She said:

'I'll be very glad to do so, Jane. How pretty you look.'

Her own gown, of pale green silk trimmed with yellow was sweet, but far from new, and had been adapted to a crinoline with material that did not quite match. She herself, I thought, looked beautiful, and was someone I was unequivocally glad to see. I should have liked to hold her now, to talk to, but they were still crowding up the stairs. We squeezed hands and smiled, and I let her go.

The reception was over at last, and the orchestra struck up the opening waltz. Sir Donald led his lady on to the floor and they completed a circuit with more dignity than grace. A voice said: 'Well, coz', and I turned and saw Edgar grinning at my elbow.

'It seems I must do the duty of my poor sick brother.' He offered me his arm. 'Though I promise you I find it no duty but a pleasure.'

He led me on to the floor and set me to the waltz. To my surprise, he danced well. His ordinary movements were vigorous and clumsy, not merely in the scufflings and wrestlings he was continually provoking with John, but in the way he walked or sat or rode a horse. In the dance, though, he moved with unexpected rhythm and precision. He was a far better dancer than I, and his leading contrived to cover my defects as I followed.

The disadvantage, apart from my so heartily disliking him, was that he held me too close. This developed as the dance went on; at the beginning he had been reasonably decorous.

I tried to hold away from him but, smiling, he prevented me. As I had learned already, he was very strong.

I was glad when the dance ended, but my relief was short-lived. While we were still on the floor, he put out his hand and, before I knew what he was up to, took my card from me.

'It has always been a principle of mine to thrust home an advantage. Father decreed that I should give you the first whirl, but now I can do a little foraging on my own.' He studied the card. 'Every dance might seem to be taking things too far, or even every other dance. One in three would seem a reasonable allocation.' He grinned crookedly. 'For a second brother standing in for his senior.'

I protested: 'No ...'

I longed to snatch the card from his hand, but a hundred or more eyes were watching us and I did not want to create a scene. I stood helplessly while, without haste, he pencilled his name firmly at regular intervals down the list. He handed the card back to me.

'Our next engagement, I see, is for a set of Lancers. I should have preferred another waltz, but it will have to do. Au revoir, cousin.'

Whatever pleasure I might have got from the ball was ruined. Sir Donald partnered me in the second dance, and after that my card filled up rapidly, but to my eyes, and I felt to those of the young men who took the card to inscribe their names in accordance with my preference, the boldly written succession of EB stood blatantly pre-emptive. Andrew Pellinser, granted two dances, commented on it.

'Edgar Bedivere has staked a heavy claim on you this evening.'

I said brightly: 'A cousinly consideration, for fear I should lack partners.'

'He is too considerate by far. And more blind, I should say, than cousinly. But if it were a kindness, one can see already that it was unneeded. Allow me to scratch out a few of them, and write my own name in.'

I shook my head. 'I do not like an altered card.'

He stared at me. 'I am sure you practise consistency, and admire you for it. But it can be carried too far. You do not need to make your excuses to Bedivere. I will readily do that for you.'

I was angry again, and the more angry because I must not show it. His first glance at the card and the tone in which he commented on it had made clear his hostility to Edgar, which I guessed was something that long antedated this occasion. I could imagine how he might go about speaking to his rival, and the response he was likely to get. For all the dubiety of my feelings towards Andrew I would have much preferred him as a partner. (After all, I reminded myself, he was Emily's brother.) But not at the cost of a scene, a brawl possibly, of which I would plainly be the cause. Smiling, I said:

'You are kind, Mr Pellinser, but I prefer to leave things as they are.'

I fancied I had spoken firmly, but he paid little heed. Still holding the card, he said:

'It is an unfair monopoly, and I do not think I ought to tolerate it. If I ...'

I cut in on him, cold now. 'I am astonished that you should persist, when you know my mind. Do not make me regret granting those dances which I have to you.'

He looked at me, tight-lipped, bowed, and left; and Edgar replaced him.

'Almost time for us to take the floor again, coz. Andy Pellinser looked miffed, I would say. You have not upset him, I hope? A worthy fellow, for a sheep-farmer.'

I ignored both sneer and question. I did my best not to speak to him but he chattered for both of us, and was skilful in putting things to which I must respond, or else look sullen to the other dancers in the set. I saw Andrew staring at us with no friendly look, but pointedly ignored him. It was more than enough having Edgar to contend with.

The supper dance was one of the many Edgar had secured. He continued his assiduous show of attention, and brought me a plate laden with delicacies.

'Cornish lobster, Janey, and Cornish salmon. The most toothsome items one is likely to find anywhere.' He grinned with loathsome affection. 'Apart from your dainty self, that is.'

Later, while he was away seeking ice-cream, Sir Donald spoke to me, asking me if I were enjoying myself. I made the expected reply, and he said:

'I perceive that Edgar is looking after you.'

'Yes, sir.'

I spoke submissively, with little expression. He paused before saying:

'I am glad that you and he hit it off so well. I'd thought at first maybe you did not.'

I had no answer for that, and did not attempt one. His own expression had something other than calmness and superiority in it, which I read finally as slight puzzlement. He said:

'It is a great pity that Michael was taken poorly. The entire evening would perhaps have been too much for him, but I feel sure he could have managed till supper.'

His voice, as he spoke, took on its more natural note of confidence. He went on:

'But he will be better soon. And there will be other balls at which you will dance together.'

I had my second dance with Andrew not long after. At the beginning he was better behaved, talking easily and paying me pleasant compliments. I warmed to him and myself spoke more naturally. The interchange was light but congenial; something like my walk on the moor with John had been and yet with the difference that I was more sharply aware of him, and of his admiration for me—an admiration not only of the mind. Then, close by, Edgar's laugh rang out and, with compulsive dislike, I turned my head to look at him.

'I cannot stand that bray of his,' Andrew said. 'Or anything else about him.'

The animosity in his voice showed that he had misread the prompting for my look, and that our brief interval of friendly intercourse was over. I was not prepared to discuss the Bediveres and my attitude towards them, and resented his desire to coerce me into echoing his hostility. If I were to hate Edgar, it would be on my own terms and no one else's. I gave him a chilly response, which presumably confirmed him in whatever guess he had made. When the dance ended, he bowed to me in silence.

It was over at last, the strains of the last waltz dying on the exhausted air, the flurry of compliments and goodbyes, the cries of coachmen and snorting and whinnying of horses, the fading scrunch of carriage wheels on the gravel outside. Emily and I went upstairs. She had been given a room near by, but we had cups of chocolate sent into my room and drank them together.

The weather, which had been poor over the weekend, a series of storms and uneasy intervening calms, had fortunately settled fair the morning of the ball. A half moon, bisected by the top of my window frame, hung in a starry sky. Though I thought I had grown accustomed to this climate, the air's mildness still surprised me. The breeze brought with it scents of growing things and I thought, though possibly I was deceiving myself, the tang of the distant sea.

Emily had loved the ball. The Carmaliot balls, she said, were famously the best in the county, and this one the finest ever. She had danced several times with a charming Major from the Hussars, who were stationed near Launceston, and he had asked leave to call on her. Though his chief value, engaging as he was, had been in quickening the interest of a certain young man she liked more, but who was desperately slow.

She turned her attention to me. '*You* seemed to be doing

very well, with your cousin Edgar. More than one person remarked on it.'

Her comment, though innocent, was too much. The reference to Edgar triggered off the feelings I had been obliged to keep pent up during the evening. I said very positively how much I had come to dislike him, and told of the way my card had been pre-empted. If I had wanted anything for detestation, that would have provided it.

'I am surprised,' Emily said. 'You control your expression well. You showed nothing of it.'

'I'm glad, if so. It does not prevent my loathing him.'

'He, I am sure, is enamoured of you.'

I thought of telling her of the episode of our ride together, but although I liked her I was shy of that. I said only:

'I do not think so, but it would make no difference if he were.'

She said speculatively: 'One hears no good news of Michael's health. And he is the second son.'

I said, bitterly and involuntarily: 'Scarcely a weighty consideration, when I am intended for the first.'

Emily stared at me. 'For the first? You do not mean Michael?'

I hesitated, but this, unlike Edgar's advances, was something that I wanted to talk about. I did not imagine there was any way in which she could help me, but confiding would be a relief. She listened while I told her of Sir Donald's project, showing a lively interest and yet not appearing as shocked as I might have expected. In the end, she said:

'You mean to refuse?'

'What else? But I am bound to go warily.'

'And Michael?' I looked at her. 'What does he think of it?'

I would not mention my conviction of his love: it would be too like a betrayal. I said:

'Michael is for delaying things, and not risking Sir Donald's anger. That is why he took to his bed today, to prevent there being an announcement.'

132

She was quiet for a moment or two, then said:

'You have no doubts?'

'Doubts? Of what?'

'Of refusing Michael.'

I laughed. 'It was not Michael who asked me! His father decreed it.'

She said thoughtfully: 'That may be. But from what I hear Michael is not much given to defying his father; and in a matter such as this I think it even less likely. You are a belle, he a man poorly favoured and in bad health. I do not think you would find it hard to get Michael to make a declaration on his own account.'

'I doubt it, but even if it were true ... how could I contemplate it?' I hesitated again, but went on: 'The plain fact is, it is not thought Michael can live long.'

She nodded. 'I've heard as much.'

'So my function is intended to be that of a brood mare: a means of producing an heir from the heir to whom Sir Donald is devoted, and whom he knows he must lose.'

'I perceive that. But there would be compensations, would there not? Even if you became a widow rather than Lady Bedivere, you would be secure of a fortune, with your son, if you had one, the next baronet. And as a widow—young, pretty, rich ... you would have good prospects.'

'And for that I am to give myself to a dying man?'

She shrugged. 'Girls have done worse, and got less from it.'

I stared at her. She was smiling slightly. I said:

'You are joking.'

'Oh, no.'

'Are you telling me that you would enter into such a contract?'

She laughed. 'I see no chance of it!'

'Or do you think that because my family is humble, it is impertinent of me to lay any claim to pride?'

I was already half resentful of that possible imputation, and when she stared blankly at me my resentment grew. Even

133

though I liked her, I would accept no condescension. But she gasped, laughing again.

'Jane, Jane, sometimes I despair!' She put out her arms and hugged me. 'It is nothing like that, I promise you. It is that we are such different people. I have pride enough, I think, but nothing like yours. Since you ask me, I will tell you honestly that if I had such a chance I do not know what my answer would be. But I do know I would not flatly reject it. I should think of it very carefully, weigh things up, and I fear I should not be at all romantic in my final judgement. My galloping Major was quite delightful for a few dances and I should not at all mind a flirtation with him at greater length. But even if *he* were serious, I should not be without having much more promising information about his circumstances than I think it likely I would get. Whereas Willie Caradoc will come into an estate worth having. Nowhere near Bedivere levels, but handsome enough.'

She held my arms and we looked at each other. I was surprised at her views, but loved her candid manner of expressing them. She smiled.

'But it is what you want that matters. Nothing else.'

Andrew had driven the dog-cart back the previous night, and I had the carriage take us both to Lacdam next day. The small rift of misunderstanding had closed, leaving our friendship more firmly cemented, and we chatted merrily on the way over. Emily would have liked me to stay to luncheon, but I had told them at Carmaliot I should be back. Besides, I had mixed feelings about seeing Andrew. I felt I did not dislike him now—I could not, liking Emily as I did—but was uneasy at the thought of encountering him.

The wind had returned, blowing from the west, driving a race of blackening cloud across the sky. I sat back in the carriage on the return journey to Carmaliot, thinking of Emily, and of Andrew. The road curved under a bluff on our left, supporting three or four storm-tattered trees. I thought at first the sound was thunder, or else the coachman's whip cracking. But it was too sharp for the first, too distant for the other. It came again, and this time I heard the whistle of a bullet. It must be someone shooting on the moor.

But I had heard the bullet. I was indignant with whatever careless idiot could be practising his sport so close to the highway. It was a height of folly.

The crack and the whistle came again, but with an addition : a sharp splintering of glass. I stared, more amazed than frightened, at the neat hole drilled in the glass of the carriage window, matched by another opposite. But fear was not long following. I heard the coachman call out something indistinguishable, but I was already crouching undignified on the floor as he whipped the horses on to the gallop.

12

No sooner were we safely back at Carmaliot, and the story told, than a party set out, led by Edgar, John being away for the day, to hunt for the sniper. Sir Donald and Lady Bedivere expressed their concern, and their relief that I had come through the peril unharmed. And Sir Donald had no doubt as to the identity, at least in a general sense, of my assailant.

'A tinner,' he said, 'for a certainty.'

That was, I knew, the name for tin-miners. I said:

'But are not all the mines in these parts closed?'

'Not only here, but far and wide throughout the county. Now that they have found tin in the land of the Malays there's too little profit in working the Cornish mines. The men are thrown out of work and roam the countryside, living as best they can. Some of them have turned highwaymen.'

'Highwaymen ...?'

'You had little enough about you, but they were not to know that. And who is to know what might not have happened if they had succeeded in halting the coach? They are desperate men. Robert did well to put his whip to the horses. To stop might have been the means of bringing on disaster.'

I had imagined up to that point that the shots had been meant for me in person, and had linked the incident with that other in the night. But there was no reason, I realized, to believe the two were connected, nor in fact that either was aimed at me. Edgar, whom I had suspected of being my night assailant, had been at Carmaliot when the shots were fired on the moor, and had ridden out to hunt for the man responsible. No, the second was as clearly due to the casual barbarity of desperate men as the first had been a nightmare. I felt ashamed for arrogating such importance to myself.

'But we must take no chances from now on,' Sir Donald declared. 'You will have an armed footman with you when you go abroad.'

I shook my head. 'It is not necessary, sir. Such a thing is unlikely to happen twice.'

'It should not have happened once!' His voice was charged with fervency. 'You are precious to us, my dear Jane, with a preciousness that is not ordinary.'

He paused, but with the clear intention of continuing. He put his thumbs behind the lapels of his smoking jacket, and looked at me. There was something else he wanted to say, and in the wake of his last remark one subject leapt to mind. I felt a quick alarm.

Sir Donald repeated: 'Very precious, indeed. Jane, I have news for you. I hope you will think it good news.'

Could he, I wondered wildly, be about to name our wedding day? It seemed unlikely, but no more than his previous public declaration of his wishes in the matter. And since for him such a thing would be good news, he would see no reason why I should not think it so.

Michael was in the drawing-room with us. He had said little of what had happened, but I had seen concern in his face. I looked at him now, and drew a small smile of reassurance. But his expression was strained.

'Yes,' Sir Donald said, 'I am hopeful you will like what I have to tell you. The post came while you were away. There was a letter in it, in reply to one of mine. I sent your brother my request that he should come here as soon as possible, having learned his enlistment in the Navy is to be sooner

137

than was thought. He writes to say he will be arriving by tomorrow's post.'

He looked at me with grave benevolence. 'Well, Jane, does that suit you?'

In my happiness I forgot all hazards and problems—shots on the moor, talk of weddings, Edgar's tormentings. I could think of only one thing, one person. I said warmly:

'I cannot tell you how much, sir!'

We were only to have three days together, a short time indeed, and I determined to waste none of it. I was waiting down in the village a good half hour before the post could possibly arrive, and saw him right away, seated up beside the driver, as the coach turned the corner and groaned up the hill. As he leapt down I ran to him and embraced him eagerly; then drew back fearing that, no boy now but a bold midshipman in the Queen's service, he might not care for such a demonstration of sisterly affection. But he grinned, and hugged me back, and added a smacking kiss, regardless of the attention of bystanders.

The carriage had brought me down to the village, and was waiting to take us both back, but I proposed walking. I wanted to have time to talk to him in private before the walls of Carmaliot swallowed us up. So we let his box be taken up, and set off arm in arm. (It was a new box, I saw, and a handsome one, obtained no doubt from Sir Donald's bounty.) The day was warm and bright, and spring flowers bloomed by the wayside, early arrivals in this temperate clime. I saw cowslip and deadnettle and yellow rocket.

But my eyes were not engaged by them. Covertly I stole glances at Harry as he walked beside me, telling me the news from home. He was wearing a new suit, with long trousers, and looked very smart. He looked older, too, but his cheeks were as pink and his brown hair as unruly as ever, his nose snubby, familiar, beloved. I squeezed his arm, when he had stopped talking, and said:

'You've not changed, Harry.'

'Have I not?'

He grinned at me but looked a shade put out. I realized that change was something he looked for in himself—who had been an errand-boy and now had a great future ahead of him—and added quickly:

'Except that you're handsomer and—and taller, I think—and astonishingly elegantly dressed.'

He roared with his old laughter, which had comforted me so often in the past.

'Well, that's enough to be going on with!' He turned his gaze on me critically. 'And you've changed, too, Jenny.'

'Have I?'

'I would not say you're any taller, but you look better. It seems the Cornish air agrees with you. As to elegance ...' He looked admiringly at my blue velvet coat, trimmed with ermine and lined with pale blue silk. 'I've never seen the like! But there's your voice, as well.'

'My voice?'

'Voice,' he repeated, emphasizing the vowel sound. 'You're learning to speak like a lady.'

His remark confused me. It was certainly not something I had consciously set out to do, and I was embarrassed and also a little angry that Carmaliot and its inhabitants should be capable of working such a change in me.

Fortunately we were not obliged to continue with the subject. We came to the gates, with the gate-keeper doffing his hat to us as we passed through. Above us, beyond the sloping lawn with its sculpted trees, stood Carmaliot—the great granite sweep of the front, the towers at either end, the lance of the chapel glowing in sunlight. Looking at it, Harry gave a low respectful whistle.

I had not thought much in advance of Harry's meeting with the rest of the Bediveres. My position simply was that they had better like him, or the worse for them. I might be willing on my own account to accept the dictates of Sir Donald and Lady Bedivere, the odious jibes of Edgar, but I would tolerate no insult to Harry. The thought came to me more sharply as I led him downstairs, having seen him lodged in the room next to mine which Emily had used, and introduced him to the family.

To some extent, though I was unwilling to admit this, I was anxious on his account. I had watched and learned the way things were done and said, but Harry had a more simple and open nature. He might well, through ignorance, make an impression they could regard as bad. If that happened, and I saw so much as the beginnings of a grin on Edgar's bearded lips, I was ready to fly at him.

But I need not have worried: Harry's very simplicity, the good manners which were part of his nature rather than studied and observed, served him well. He marched up to Lady Bedivere, treated her to a solemn but graceful little bow, and thanked her in a clear firm voice for her kindness in receiving him at Carmaliot. From her he went to Sir Donald, and thence in turn to the sons, requiring no direction or prompting from me.

In fact he got on well with all of them, not merely then but during his stay. I noticed he seemed a little more quiet with Michael and more boisterous with Edgar, but in a natural way. And they responded amiably; even Edgar, whom I closely watched. Lady Bedivere that evening remarked how pleasant a young man he was. I had reason, she said, to be proud of my brother; and I most heartily agreed.

The size and extent of the house did not seem to bother him as it had done me, and he very quickly made himself at home. He drank the glass of claret which was offered him at dinner with a confidence that won Sir Donald's approval.

'You will need to have a strong head on your shoulders if you are to serve as an officer in the Navy.'

And he took enthusiastically and with considerable aptitude to horse-riding, though his legs were soon sore from gripping the animal's flanks. Edgar led him off at one point to instruct him in billiards, and returned proclaiming him a natural player, only wanting practice to be capable of holding a cue with any man in the kingdom.

Although he would have been happy enough to stay at Carmaliot, with plenty to occupy him, I took him away on his second day, to show him off to Emily. When the carriage was brought round in the early afternoon, John accompanied us out. I noticed that a footman sat beside the driver, a rifle cradled in his arms. I had forgotten Sir Donald's remark— almost forgotten the incident which had provoked it in the excitement of having Harry with me—and I exclaimed. Surely it wasn't necessary?

'Father's orders,' John explained. 'It is to be a regular thing in future. We never laid that fellow by the heels, and even if our chase made him decide these parts were too warm for him, there are plenty of other vagabonds abroad this winter. A farmhouse was broken into over towards Bodmin only two days since, and the farmer's wife terrified.'

Harry, as the carriage rolled down the hill to the village, asked what John's reference had meant. I told him, making light of it and contriving to suggest that no bullet had come anywhere near. (The windows of the coach had been promptly mended in Plymouth the next day.) He took it as lightly, and amused himself surveying the moor for gunmen. It was all, I realized, a part of an exciting holiday as far as he was concerned, and was pleased on that account. Whatever my resentments against Sir Donald, I was grateful to him for providing this for Harry; and for me.

Mrs Pellinser, as I suppose was only to be expected, provided an exception to the chorus of amiability which had greeted him in Cornwall.

She wore the same black silk gown in which I had first met her, with the same jet beads as her only ornament, and stared down, several inches the taller though he was well built for his age, with the same sharp, almost hostile scrutiny.

'So you are Master Cowper.'

He nodded politely. 'Yes, ma'am.'

'And you fancy yourself as a naval officer?'

'I hope some day to gain that rank, ma'am, and to prove worthy of it.'

'At least,' she said bitterly, 'it is your intention to serve the Queen on the sea, and not line your pockets by the subversion of her ordinances, as your fine relations the Bedvers did.'

Harry looked at her, showing a little surprise but no discomposure. He said politely:

'I know nothing of that, ma'am. Sir Donald has been very good to me, that's all I know.'

She stared, her mouth tight and long thin nose menacing. I thought she might be about to censure him, and was ready to leap to the defence. But when at last she spoke, she said:

'You have chosen well. I knew a sailor once, who had your bearing.' She shook her head. 'It was a long time ago.'

With Andrew Harry got on even better than he had with Edgar and John. He was taken to look at the sheep, and to see the ruins of the main mine working, which was less than a mile from the house. They came back late for tea, talking and laughing together, and for the first time I saw Andrew as boyish, too: neither angry nor brooding nor awkward, but open and cheerful. They ate like a pair of schoolboys, ravenous from being out of doors, downing great quantities of crumpets oozing with butter.

Before we went back I found myself alone with Andrew, Emily having taken Harry, at Mrs Pellinser's request, to the parlour to which she had retired earlier. We sat together companionably for a few moments, but our casual talk faltered and came to an end. The silence that followed was not so easy. His expression was awkward again. I felt he wanted to say something but did not know how to go about it. And I was not sure if I could help him, or if I wanted to. He said at last, abruptly:

'Jane—I may call you Jane?'

'Of course.'

He shook his head. 'There's no "of course" to it. I have behaved so badly with you up to now. At our early meetings, and then on the night of the ball ...'

I said quickly: 'Please do not think of it.'

'No, let me say on. When you came here before, I begged your forgiveness and you granted it. My behaviour at Carmaliot can only have confirmed your view of me as hopelessly boorish. And to turn begging forgiveness into a habit is less likely to mend things than to make them worse.'

He had a look on his face that was a comical blending of indignation and remorse. I had an impulse to laugh, which I repressed. I said:

'I promise you there is no need for it, Mr Pellinser.' I caught his look, and amended: 'Andrew. It's an unprofitable subject, and we should leave it.'

'No, we will not!' He spoke with a renewal of vigour. 'Because while I cannot hope to excuse myself, I am determined in some part to explain it. The fact is, I am inexperienced in dealing with ladies and sadly inadequate. Emily has scolded me for it before. But I have not been much to dances and such things—I should not have gone to that one except for you—and I have not learned the graces that I ought. I would have said to myself it was because I had too much to do, but I doubt the truth of that. I think it is more that a man learns these things under the tender care of his mother, and mine has been less inclined to such embellishments than some.'

He paused, but I said nothing. He then went on:

'She deserves no blame. She is a good woman, who has suffered greatly.'

'I am sure of it.'

His look was grateful. 'I owe her much, but not an awareness of the gentle ways with which a man should approach a woman. I did not think it mattered, but I see now that was only because women themselves did not matter to me—apart

143

from my mother and Emily, who were used to me and did not mind the crudeness of my manners.'

He spoke in an earnest and yet self-critical fashion that I liked. Acutely conscious of my own defects, I warmed to someone who grappled so hard and honestly with his. But I could see no reason why he should do so in my presence. It might be that our encounters—my reactions to his incivilities and his response to those reactions—had brought on this self-examination, but I did not feel that justified so lengthy an explanation. As though reading my thought, he said abruptly :

'I am trying your patience, am I not? But that is from timidness in part.'

He rose to his feet and paced about the room, while I did my best to make sense of the remark. Then, more sharply still, he turned and stood before me.

'Jane, listen to me.'

The harshness, which I had grown used to and even in a way come to like, was more distinct in his voice. He stared at me, the blue eyes intent.

'Women did not matter to me—then. Things are vastly different now. They changed—changed utterly—when I met you.'

I started to protest : 'Please . . .' He would not be halted.

'That first time . . . I knew that something had happened, but I did not know what. I came up out of the mine, as I had done hundreds of times before, and saw you there. Not the emptiness of the moor, which I knew so well, but you. It was so unexpected . . . and you were so beautiful . . . that I was at a loss. I spoke rudely, and when you answered me as I deserved admired you for it, but could not help myself going on.

'Afterwards I thought about you. That's a poor way of putting it. You were in my mind, the way no one has ever been. But I still did not properly know what my feelings were —only that more than anything I could imagine, I wanted to see you again. And when I did . . . I found my ewe dead,

144

the dog standing over her with a bloody muzzle. I was so blind with rage I do not know how I aimed the gun. I went after him, and found you with him, and anger and everything else were so mixed up that I don't know what I said.'

He had brought back the day, and the memory of Beast, my single comfort in those wretched first days at Carmaliot. I shook my head, trying to drive it away.

I whispered: 'It doesn't matter now. Forget it all.'

'How can I? Afterwards I remembered—not the words that had been spoken but you. I remembered holding you in my arms. And knew I loved you.'

I had been trying, though scarcely able to believe it was happening, to prepare myself for the declaration. But the effort did me no good at all; I just looked helplessly at him.

'I had angered you so much—caused you such distress—that I thought I had no chance. And when at the ball you danced so often with Edgar Bedivere and he paid court to you, I thought you favoured him, that he was perhaps already accepted as your lover. I should not have spoken as I did, but I cannot tell you how miserable I felt. Nor the difference it made to me when Emily told me that he meant nothing to you.'

I was silent still. He said:

'You will not blame Emily for telling me? She is fond of you, and has a sister's concern for me. She scolded me for my manners at the ball, and on account of my general mood of late, and in the end I confided in her. That was when she spoke of your indifference to Edgar. She encouraged me to hope. And has taken your brother off to give me this opportunity—to tell you I love you, and ask you to be my wife.'

She had given me, I thought with indignation, no warning; not even a hint of what might be in store for me. But even as I resented it, I reflected that she had been serving what she conceived to be her brother's best interests—and would I have done any less for Harry? Moreover, in a family hard pressed for the means of keeping a weather-tight roof over their heads, she was seeking to help him get a wife who could bring him nothing, who was herself a pauper. That showed a partiality for me as well, and I thought fondly of her again. I should not mind having Emily for a sister.

Andrew stooped and took my hand. I did not resist as he lifted it to his lips. He said:

'I spoke to you first because you have no close relation here. I will attend on Sir Donald, if you wish—or approach your mother. Only say that you will marry me.'

He had gained in confidence during my failure to respond. That last sentence was less a plea than a statement. I felt the old shivers down my spine, the old hostility to male presumption. To find the notion of a closer relation with Emily attractive was not the same as welcoming that tyranny back. Moreover I felt, along with resentment, a sudden panic at the thought of him attending on Sir Donald, and what might come of it. Enmeshed in Carmaliot affairs, I had no desire for someone else to blunder in and make matters worse.

And it was absurd. I did not love him—did not love any male creature but Harry. And could not. I took back my hand.

'It is no good.'

'No good?'

I was doing it badly: there were conventions to observe. I said:

'Thank you, Andrew. It is a great compliment. But I cannot.'

'Cannot? Have I no hope?'

I shook my head. 'No. I am sorry.'

His look was wretched, and I felt truly sorry for him. I got to my feet, and said gently:

'I think we should go and find the others.'

The hours passed so quickly; in no time Harry was due to leave. I managed to secure for us the privilege again of walking down to the village to join the post, and when he had said his thanks and goodbyes to the Bediveres, we set off. The weather had mostly been fine during his stay, and was fair now, the sky almost equally divided between blue and drifting white and the air warm enough for summer. Harry commented on this and went on to talk of other felicities provided by Cornwall and Carmaliot.

'I am glad to see you in so pleasant a way, Jane,' he said. 'Very glad. And glad that I have been able to witness it. Your letters were cheerful enough, but one must have doubts unless one sees things at close hand. You are quite capable of concealing things you think may worry people.'

I was glad myself that he should go away untroubled. I said:

'Now you know how well off I am.'

'And they all are plainly happy to have you with them. Sir Donald seems to look to it as something without a term.'

He had not, to my relief, spoken further of his particular plans in Harry's presence. We reached the gates, and Harry stopped to look back for a final view of the green sweep up to the grey and pink granite of the house. He gripped my arm.

'It's good to know you are being looked after while I shall be away at sea. And that there is to be provision for Mama and the girls. It only needs be for a few years, and then we can make a capital little home together, you and I.'

I laughed. 'A few years? Do you plan to become an admiral, and retire, so soon as that?'

He grinned. 'Perhaps not quite so soon! But I shall have begun to make my way by then, and it will be good to have a snug nest in England to return to, and Jenny keeping my slippers warm for me.'

He had changed so much already in the short time we had been apart—we both had. And even if we changed no more to each other, he would change in his views of happiness and of his heart's needs. He would look for someone else to guard the nest while he was away—to rear his children as well as keeping his slippers warm. That was certain, and as it should be. I felt the sadness of an even greater parting than the one that lay ahead, but would not show it. For a few minutes longer we could play at dreams together.

So I entered into the game, and we walked down the hill to the village, talking of where we would fix our home. Cornwall, he said cheerfully, was as good a place as any, as far as he could see. But we need be in no hurry to come to a decision on that. And it did not much matter, as long as we were together.

We came in sight of the village inn, and two children playing outside. They belonged to the inn-keeper: a boy of three or four, a girl some years older. She was scolding her little brother over something he had done, but lovingly. It might have been Harry and I, ten years past.

He said: 'Things have fallen out very well, Jenny. For you and me both. It is not just that Sir Donald's interest has got me my place in the Navy. He likes me, and will continue to help. And he has influence with the Admiralty. Even today, that counts for a great deal. I shall do my best to justify his favour, but it will be his further favours that assist me to do so. It is easy to be overlooked for promotion if one has no friends in high places. And I mean to do well.'

He spoke with great determination. My heart was chilled, and I had nothing to say. We reached our destination as a clatter of hooves and wheels could be heard lower down.

'Hello,' he said cheerfully. 'The post is early today.'

13

With Harry gone, the bill for my happiness of the past few days came in. I had known it would—I had never looked to get anything without payment—but the sum of it devastated me nonetheless. If I was spared the particular misery of uncertainty and strangeness which had attended my arrival at Carmaliot, there were other considerations which made this second loss of my brother more difficult to bear. I walked alone on the moor, and thought of them.

To begin with, the moment of decision in Sir Donald's project for my marriage loomed nearer. That had been made plain in the evening following Harry's departure. Sir Donald had not spoken of it directly, but the hints had been inescapable. He was mightily pleased with my brother's visit, not only because he was a bright and promising lad, but also in that it had given me such pleasure. (I had had my treat.) It was a pity that his stay had to be so short, but now we must look forward, and find other happinesses. (He wanted his in return.) Above all he thanked God for the blessing of my presence. (The precious vessel, to carry Carmaliot's heir. . . .)

It was something which, indulging my joy in Harry's company, I had succeeded pretty well in putting to one side; not quite forgetting but, when the thought came up, consigning it to a future on which I was not anyway prepared to look. That future now was here and, realizing this, I confronted another disillusionment as well. Michael was my ally, but of what value? He had urged me to leave matters to him, and for want of anything better I had been prepared to do so. But I had been foolish to think there was any way in which he could save me.

Sir Donald's determination—the determination of a man not only strong and powerful but fixed in the pursuit of an unalterable obsession—had not changed. Michael was feeble, sick, accustomed by long usage to filial obedience. He was his father's superior only in rationality, and what had reason to do with authority? The pressure was being resumed, and would continue the more strongly for any retreat into apparent illness that Michael might use to check it. Reminders of the approaching loss of his heir could only spur Sir Donald on to circumvent it. In the end, Michael would give way; from weakness if from nothing else.

So I was on my own—and worse. Harry had been my hostage to fortune. Once he was in the Navy, Sir Donald could not very well get him out again. There were Mama and the little ones, of course, but I had not thought so much of them. I would find work and support them somehow. They might have to do without some of the comforts Sir Donald had put their way, but that could not be helped. We should manage to get by.

But now, unexpectedly and crushingly, I had something else to face. As I walked across the moor, with the sky a ragged grey, threatening rain, and a curlew mournfully quee-queeing in the distance, I thought of Harry's words during our last conversation. 'He likes me, and will continue to help. And he has influence with the Admiralty ... it will be his further favours that assist me ...' I knew what favours he could expect if I were to thwart his benefactor.

I tried to tell myself that this too did not matter. Once he was in the Navy, Harry could make his way unaided, like many another young man. It was a great thing for him to have the chance—six weeks ago he would not even have dared to dream of it. Neither, I well knew, would he ask for help granted at such cost to me; nor accept it if he knew the circumstances. I had been anxious that he should not worry about me, and it was clear I had succeeded, with the assistance of the amiable reception which he himself had been given, in persuading him that here at Carmaliot I was in no way disadvantaged; but quite the reverse.

I stopped and looked about me. I had come far enough to be out of sight of the house. The moor stretched away, grey and flat under a flat grey sky. A drop of rain stung my cheek. There was silence except for the rustle of wind in the heather; even the curlew had ceased his wailing. I thought of Andrew's sudden appearance, that other time on the moor, and the shock it had given me. That could not happen again. I would not want it to. But suddenly I felt very much alone.

There was nothing to stop my writing to Harry and telling him how things lay. I knew what sort of reply I should get if I did: warm, indignant over the pressure to which I was being subjected, firm in its counsel to resist. He might even, I thought with alarm, abandon his post with the *Belphoebe*, and come to rescue me.

I started walking slowly back, towards Carmaliot. The alarm was needless. I would not write that letter.

I thought of Emily. I was missing her, too, though less acutely. I had been minded, in fact, to send a note, asking her to come over or proposing alternatively that I visit her at Lacdam. But I felt shy about the episode with Andrew, which we had had no chance to discuss. All the same I wished she were with me now.

And yet, if she were, could I doubt what advice she would give? She had stated her opinion clearly on the night of the ball. Since then, having discovered her brother's feelings for me, she had been willing to promote his case; and doubtless still would if she thought there were a chance of it succeeding. But if I were determined not to have him, she would think me a fool not to take Michael. I was being offered position and wealth, and the toleration of a feeble dying husband did not weigh very heavily in the scales against such blessings.

Who could say she was wrong? And even if one discounted the material benefits, was it not pride and selfishness that were the chief reasons for my reluctance? As a person I had come to like Michael. He was weak, in character as well as in constitution, but was that not better than the vaunted strengths of men which I so well knew, and loathed? He loved me—I was sure of it. Was it too much to ask that I should subdue my pride and the distaste I felt for his body, and give myself to him?

The moor was wide and empty, and loneliness lay heavy on me. I remembered Beast and wished he were with me now, comical and ugly and making no demands. But the memory itself reminded me how fallible my inclinations could prove. The only thing at Carmaliot I had loved had been revealed as a slaughterer of the innocent.

More spots of rain came down and the sky was darker. The house was in sight, and I hurried towards it.

There was another hunt next day, but they met away from Carmaliot. Sir Donald and his sons rode out early, accompanied by the hunt servants and the hounds. I watched them go, and thought how unfit Michael looked for such an enterprise. He tried to keep from coughing, though without much success; and I noticed at one point that he held on to the post at the foot of the stairs, supporting himself while he struggled to draw breath.

Once more I was amazed by the division in Sir Donald's attitude towards him: on the one hand cosseting and sending him to bed with some new medical cure-all, on the other watching with indifference while this wretched invalid mounted his horse. A groom assisted him, and the morning was raw for Cornwall, the wind, unusually, from the northeast.

But it was not indifference, of course: that calm survey he gave his eldest son concealed pride. This, Carmaliot's heir setting out for the hunt, was the flower the cossetings were meant to nourish. Just as Michael himself was a flower whose cutting down could be made good by seed planted in a fertile soil. I shivered, and turned away.

It had been an early start and with Lady Bedivere not yet risen from her bed, I was left to my own devices. I had started a letter to Harry the previous day but been too dispirited to finish it. I could complete it and it would go by the day's post. I felt cheerless still, but even though he had been so greatly looking forward to his ship he might be glad of a letter.

I had left it in my room, and I could have settled down there with it: the fire had been made up and crackled warmly in the hearth. But I decided to take it down to the library which was my favourite room in the house. I preferred the long rows of leather bindings to the rich elegance of other rooms, especially when I could be certain of having it to myself. I found a big comfortable chair near the fire and took myself and my writing case into its embrace.

But before I had written more than half a dozen lines, the clop of hooves disturbed me. They were coming up the drive, and I went to the window which overlooked it. I saw hunting pink, and was certain it must be Michael. I felt concern: he must be feeling very ill to have retired so early. Then I recognized the horseman: it was Edgar.

Automatically I drew back so that he should not see me at the window. He dismounted by the steps at the front door, and I heard him shouting for a servant to take his horse. I went back to my chair and the letter, feeling a slight irritation at his return and about as much curiosity over the reason for it. I told myself that perhaps he had forgotten something and would be going after the others again once he had got it. I hoped so, not wanting his company at luncheon. His demeanour towards me had been much better of late, but I preferred his absence to his presence.

At least, I decided, I was safe from him at the moment: he

would not expect me to be in the library. I dipped my pen in the ink and was starting a new sentence when the door was thrust open. Edgar entered, his face crooked in a grin.

'I spied with my little eye something beginning with J,' he declared, 'even though she quickly scuttled back into the room. How are you, Janey? Busy with your correspondence? Not to a lover, I trust?'

The comparative amiability that had recently marked our intercourse was preferable to what had gone before. My chief hope was that he should go about his business with as little delay as need be, but it was far from certain that hostility would achieve that. I ignored the remark he had made, but said in an even, not unfriendly voice:

'What brings you back, Edgar?'

'Damned horse went lame. Excuse me, coz.'

He ambled across the room and flung himself into the chair next to mine. The smell of horse, and sweat, was in my nostrils. I said:

'You'll take another out?'

He nodded. 'Presently, but I'm in no hurry. Old Cople-stone serves a foul cup—I'd as soon drink my own brandy. And to tell the truth, I find it as pleasant to sit and talk to a pretty girl as to follow the hounds on a morning such as this. The old fool doesn't tend to his earths properly, either.'

I said warily: 'I'm writing a letter, as you see.'

He grinned. 'That can wait, too. You've all day to write your letters. The fact is, Janey, I've been wanting to have a talk with you.'

I was silent. I smelt his sweat again. It was unlikely they would have done much more than amble on their way over to the meet, but he was hot from exercise, his face flushed. Had he galloped back? On a lame horse? Or was that simply the excuse he had made?

'On an important subject.' He was grinning, but the eyes studied me keenly. 'Very important indeed.'

I stood up, clutching my writing case.

154

'Perhaps another time. I . . .'

He stood up quickly, as I did. He loomed above me, close enough for me to touch. Or be touched by. I shrank back a little, and he said:

'Sit down, Janey.' His voice was hard. I hesitated. 'I've told you you'll have time for your letters later. I won't keep you long.'

I did not like his closeness, and was unsure of what he might do if I attempted to get past him and make for the door. I sat down again. He said, approvingly:

'That's a good girl.' He did not resume his own seat, but stood with his back to the blazing fire. 'I have a great liking for you, Janey.'

I thought of the incident on the ride, and could not help saying:

'If so it is something you have not always displayed to the best advantage.'

He slapped his crop against the leather of his boots.

'I'll not deny it. I took you for something else than what you were. I know better now. A liking, as I say, and admiration too.'

I regretted having said anything since any remark might provide him with a springboard for another, and all I wanted was to end the interview. So I looked at him in silence.

'You're a fine girl,' he said. He stared at me, pursing his lips. 'Much too fine to be thrown away on someone like Michael.'

I still did not answer, and he went on:

'That's a mad notion of my father's. Would you not say so? He looks for you to be with child before the poor devil snuffs it. But the chances are, it's too late already.' He laughed coarsely. 'I doubt he still has the vigour to sire one, even on so fetching a wench as you are.'

I turned my head away. He said genially:

'I forget myself, do I not? I promise I'll do better. I like a woman who insists on what's due to her modesty. You'll have no complaint of me in that respect as a husband.'

I looked at him quickly, my resolve of muteness shattered by his words.

'Are you mad?'

'Never been more sane.' His tone was cheerful. 'It's the best possible thing for both of us. I can see us getting on famously together. You've got spirit, but I like that too.'

I thought of Andrew's declaration. The contrast between the emotion he had shown, moving even though I could not possibly return it, and this casual proposition labelled the latter the enormity it was. I said:

'Do I hear you right? You said husband. This is meant as a proposal of marriage?'

'Exactly so.'

'A trifle bare.'

He laughed. 'It wants a few gallantries preceding it? But they're not my style, and you're too sensible a girl to be taken in by them, anyway.'

'And your father, Sir Donald?'

'What of him?'

'Have you spoken to him of your intention? What do you think he would say to it?'

'Well, now, we've come to a point worth discussing.'

He stretched himself, expanding his large chest under the red jacket; then resumed his seat. Crossing one leg over the other and prodding the toe of his boot with the crop, he said:

'He won't like it. He wants the line to go through Michael —you can see, he's mad for it. But if he can't have that, he'll settle for the next best. He doesn't show much but I can read his looks, and I tell you that since you've been here you've come to mean almost as much to him as Michael does. Damn it, I think as much! And I'm his son. He has small regard for it now, but he may think differently when Michael's gone.'

His voice, as he said that, had a tinge of bitterness. I realized he had suffered, too, and perhaps the suffering had made him what he was. But it did not make me like him. I said:

'It may be you underestimate the strength of his desire to have ... to have me and Michael marry. And therefore the consequences of thwarting it.'

'I watched him when I was playing up to you at the ball. He did not much like it, but he showed no anger.'

'Because he cannot believe anything could truly come between his wish and its achievement. If such a thing really happened, his anger would be terrible.'

'It might be,' he conceded. 'We might find ourselves banished from Carmaliot, the pair of us. I think we could rub along, if so. I suspect Mama would help us, on the quiet. And what happens after that? He will not find another bride for Michael. He would not have the heart to try. You came as a gift from the gods, and it is the kind of gift you do not get twice There's not enough time left, anyway. He'll be dead before the year's out.'

He spoke with a brutal indifference which made me loathe him more than ever. Staring into the fire, he went on:

'I'll wager he'd come round. Though even if he did not, it makes no difference. The baronetcy comes to the eldest son, and the estate is entailed on him. He won't be able to deny me my rights.'

I had wondered, disliking him as I did, why I had permitted this conversation to go on—why, after the shock of hearing him refer to the possibility of our marriage, I had not reverted to my earlier silence. I understood now that, without knowing what I was about, I had been dredging for just the monstrous truth which he had reflectively and indifferently brought into the light. Perhaps I had been a fool not to see it before. At least it came to me with no sense of surprise, only revulsion.

'That's why you wish to marry me,' I said. 'Of course. Before I came, you were waiting for Michael to die. Your father's project threatened the loss of all you had been looking

157

for. But if you could marry me instead ...'

He looked up, grinning and unperturbed. 'As I said, a capital thing for us both. You get a man, instead of a wasting bag of bones who'll cough consumption into you as like as not. You'll be Lady Bedivere in due time, instead of the Widow Bedivere. And we both come into the estate. What could be better?'

He paused, and when I said nothing, added:

'If you're afraid I might treat you badly, you needn't be. It's a bargain between us, and I'll keep my side of it. I'll do right by you. Damn it, Janey, I like you as much as any gal I've seen. And I shan't need to look for a dowry if I have my rights.'

I said: 'Peddle your bargain elsewhere. It does not interest me.'

'Be reasonable.' I looked at him with silent contempt. 'I'm not rushing you into anything. There's time to give it thought. Though to my mind the sooner we hammer things into Father's head the better.'

I got up from my chair again, unable to bear being seated near him. I said:

'It is not just that I would not marry you for money, however vast the fortune. If the saving of my life depended on it, I still would not.'

His face darkened: I think my tone stung him more than the words. He said angrily:

'So you think the dying man a better bet? Maybe you look to getting your hands on all of it, and sooner.'

I did not reply to that. He rose also, and stood before me. He was very close. I was aware of his strength as well as his anger, of the broad shoulders and heavily muscled arms. My glance went, for reassurance, to the bell-rope hanging beside the chimney-piece. I was safe with servants within call.

He laughed suddenly, harshly. 'Do not bank on it, coz! You may find your calculations mistaken.'

He turned away at that, and stumped out of the room.

I heard Edgar ride out, on his way to rejoin the hunt. Later in the morning another horseman returned. I saw Michael for a few moments before, white-faced and exhausted, he dragged himself off to his room.

I felt things hemming me in: things and people. I had an impulse to say to Michael more than the few casual words I gave him—to woo him even into wooing me. I did not think it would be difficult. After the vile contract Edgar had proposed, the thought of marrying Michael was, by comparison, tolerable. I imagined myself in his arms with a small shiver of repugnance, but reaffirmed: yes, tolerable.

As he walked to the stairs, I almost called him back. What restrained me was the awareness of finality, not so much where he was concerned as in myself. Michael would always let me change my mind—he was too gentle to hold me to a promise—but once I had set my foot on such a path, I knew I could not turn back.

It was not an aspect of my nature that I admired or valued. In fact it was a stiff-necked quality which had served me ill in the past. I remembered a neighbour, when Harry and I were little, who had taken us to the Christmas pantomime along with her own daughter. She had done so two years running, but in the third winter I had fallen out with the girl and she had made some jibe to the effect that I would be whistling a different tune by Boxing Day. I told her I should never accept her mother's invitation to the pantomime again.

That had been mid-November. Within a week the quarrel had been made up. She was astonished when, a month later, she came with the usual offer and I refused. I accepted on Harry's behalf, but would not go myself. She had so forgotten what had happened that she asked me why, and I, rather than bring it all to mind, declared I was grown too old for pantomimes.

She argued with me, and then begged me to come, to be company for her. I could not. I remembered the declaration I had made—that I would not go with them again—and even if I had been foolish would not forswear my folly. We quarrelled a second time, and on that occasion I sought her out to make it up. But I still refused the pantomime.

Of course, had the invitation to Harry been withdrawn unless I went, I should have gone. But they did not think of that and I stayed at home, and wept through the long afternoon of Boxing Day over what I was missing.

No, I was not proud of it, but I could not help it. If I gave my word to Michael and Sir Donald, I would keep it, whatever befell. And it was knowing that which made me let him go.

14

Michael had a bad turn and was several days in bed. He ran a fever and coughed blood, and Dr Roberts rode over twice a day. Once he brought leeches—I saw the ugly things in a glass jar as he carried it into the house—which he set to his body. I would have thought he had lost enough blood, but I supposed that a doctor should know more of that than someone like myself, ignorant of the ways of physicking an invalid.

In that time, though there was anxiety in the house and Sir Donald paced more, and more silently, things did not go so badly for me. The pressure appeared to have slackened a little as far as my future was concerned—I realized Michael's relapse had much to do with that—and my present suffered less harassment.

Edgar kept out of my way, spending most of the day out of doors with two of the grooms who were his special cronies. I heard the three of them laughing together once when I was having a horse saddled to go riding, and left the stable so that I should not encounter them. But to my surprise his manner towards me on occasions when we were obliged to meet—for family meals or playing whist or suchlike—was unchanged. Or rather, I observed with some wonder, it was still more amiable. I remembered the black anger he had shown, but I made the responses that politeness and the presence of the other members of the family demanded. I could play a game as well as he, but I watched him warily all the same.

Apart from that, though, I could please myself what I did. My riding had continued to improve, and I ventured over one day as far as Lacdam. I had sent no word in advance, but Emily greeted me warmly. Her mother was the same black bitter hawk, and made the usual denunciation of the Bediveres, their wealth and its newness, but I had a feeling she too was glad to see me. Andrew, as I had hoped would be the case, was away from the house—either seeing to the sheep or delving in his mines.

It was a gorgeous day, the finest yet, more June than April, with the westerly breeze pleasantly fanning the warm air, the sky a perfect blue. Too good to stay indoors, Emily said, and proposed a picnic tea. Mrs Pellinser would not join us, but the maids took tea things out and we found a grassy spot beside a rampart of turf and crumbling stone, on the shore of the lake. The waters were calm, and clear and blue as the sky.

I wondered if, once we were alone together, she would speak of Andrew and the declaration for which, as he had told me, she had prepared the way. I was ready to say I did not wish to talk of it or him. Yet once she had made it clear that she had no intention of introducing the topic I wished, with female contrariness, that she would. I even in the end spoke of Andrew myself, asking if he were well.

She said serenely: 'Very well, at least in body. Troubled in mind, maybe, but that's his own fault—if you believe we can control our natures. He takes things a deal too seriously.'

She showed something less than sisterly sympathy, I thought. As though aware of that, she went on:

'I am sorry for him, but what can one do? Heartache cannot be shared, and you cannot tend it like a cold or a fever. In fact nursing it may very likely make it worse. And it cures itself in due course. I take my stand with Rosalind:

"men have died from time to time, and worms have eaten them, but not for love".'

She looked at me quizzically, and continued:

'How are *your* affairs of the heart? Have you made your mind up yet, about taking Michael?'

Although I suspected that my own temperament matched Andrew's more nearly than hers, the coolness of her common sense was refreshing. I said:

'Would you believe I've had another proposal?'

The lift of her brows showed she knew I was not speaking of Andrew.

'May I ask, from whom?'

I told her about Edgar. She smiled at the end.

'You are greatly in demand, it seems. I envy you that, at least. For all his protestations my galloping Major has neither written nor called, and neither has Willie Caradoc since that night. I fear my coquetry may have had an opposite effect to the one I wished. You refused him?'

'Yes.'

'He is a better figure of a man than poor Michael, providing one takes the view that a healthy husband is more worth having than one who may give you weeds within the year. And one could not quarrel with his argument: Sir Donald would come round, and if he did not, it would make no difference in the long run. But I applaud your refusal, all the same.'

'To propose it to me so coldly ...'

She smiled again. 'I can see that would offend your romantic nature.'

'I have not a romantic nature! It would be a compact sealed in Michael's blood.'

'Strongly put, but I take your meaning. It is something I should have found distasteful, too. But that is not my only reason for agreeing with your saying no. There is Edgar himself.'

'There is, indeed. Even under the happiest circumstances,

163

I could not have contemplated accepting such a clown.'

Emily laughed. 'Romantic, and forthright! A formidable combination. He is a clown, I agree, but not just that. He is more dangerous than he looks—more cunning. There was a farmer over by Lifton a year ago who tried to take him in over a horse, and got taken in very heavily himself. No, even if the bargain had been worth making, you could never have trusted him, and would have found yourself linked with a man wily as well as treacherous. Which is a still more formidable combination. As far as I can judge, many husbands prove treacherous, but fortunately most of them are less clever than their wives.'

'You may be right. But let's not talk of Edgar, on so fine a day.'

'He spoils it, I agree. Look, that silly spirit-stove has got the kettle boiling at last. If you bring over the pot, I will make the tea.'

As she did so, I looked at the rampart beside us. The stone which formed its framework was worn and broken, but bore the marks of human shaping. I mentioned it, and Emily said:

'Yes. The ruins of the castle further along the lake are twelfth century, but these are said to be the remains of an earlier structure. Roman, maybe.'

'Or the castle in which the Lady of the Lake lived—the one who gave Arthur Excalibur.'

'You've heard that story, then?'

'Sir Donald told me. And about Carmaliot being Camelot.'

'The countryside is full of such tales, but it surprises me any sensible person takes them seriously. The lake is said to be bottomless, too. When we were children, Andrew and I took out a boat and plumbed it, with a weight on the end of a rope. The furthest depth we found was not much more than seven feet!'

'Which of you proposed the measuring?'

She shrugged. 'I don't remember.'

'I will guess it was you. You are too practical altogether.'

'One needs to be in Cornwall, in self-defence. If not, one might find oneself believing all sorts of things: witchcraft, and owls and ravens being evil spirits, and hares being ghosts of the dead. The tinners used to frighten themselves with tales of knackers.'

'Knackers?'

'They were supposed to be gnomes who lived underground. They looked like little old wrinkled men, but they were also said to be able to change their shapes, and to vanish into smoke. Consistency is not the chief quality of country tales. They were held to be very evil and malicious, too, and since the mine workings were their favoured haunts, tinners were reluctant to go below unaccompanied.'

I thought of underground rocky galleries, pitch black except for the light of the miner's lamp, and shivered.

'I can imagine that.'

Emily poured us tea. She said:

'Anyway, the Lady of the Lake did not have a castle— she lived under the lake.'

The shiver had passed. The day was warm and bright, and Emily was putting milk in my tea. The lake stretched blue and calm beside us. I felt lazily content. I said:

'How could she—live under the lake, I mean?'

Emily passed me my cup.

'I have a notion you are the kind of romantic who expects romance to be governed by reason. How very unreasonable of you.'

We encountered Andrew as we walked back to the house; he was coming away. He saw us, looked irresolute, then came to greet us.

He went on: 'I had to come back to the house ... I thought you'd be away ... I saw you over by the lake ...'

He was apologizing for his presence in case I might be embarrassed by it, stressing that he had done his best to keep clear during my visit. But his eyes on my face were hungry.

I wondered, as we parted and went different ways, if he had been entirely honest. I had a feeling he might have watched us from a distance, and contrived this brief meeting. But I did not resent it if he had; in fact was touched. I no longer hated him, or wanted him to be hurt.

In the evening, John solicited Harry's address from me. He said he wanted to send him a few guineas to help him over his early days: he believed the Navy was not overly generous to the midshipmen it recruited.

I thanked him and gave him the address, but said I hoped the kindness was not necessary: I knew Sir Donald had made provision for him. John said:

'I don't think an extra couple of guineas ever went amiss with a young man. But I wanted to write to him as well. He will be lonely, away from home for the first time.'

I liked that thought, and his consideration. We talked pleasantly; at first of Harry, with John commending his good qualities and me appreciating his commendations, later of more general things. He mentioned Michael, and I realized after a time that his conversation had a purpose: he was probing delicately after my intentions.

It did not nettle me that he should do so, because I felt that his interest, unlike that of others I could think of, was, if not positively friendly, at least free from selfish considerations. To Edgar as the second son the question of heirship was a crucial one; but John, the third, had no personal stake in it. He would be no better off whether Michael or Edgar, or for that matter Michael's son succeeded.

I debated speaking to him of Edgar's proposal, but drew back. It had not resulted in any continuing unpleasantness—Edgar had greeted me with every appearance of cousinly affection only an hour or so earlier—and was best forgotten as far as the circle of the Bedivere family was concerned. John had already taken his brother to task once on my behalf. He

166

might feel constrained to do so again, and that might well cause trouble.

I was better inclined to deal frankly over my feelings about Michael. I continued to feel more at ease with John than with anyone else at Carmaliot. He still showed me no signs of gallantry, and my intuition was that this was not from policy but represented a lack of something another man might have felt; but I was no longer piqued by it. My life was not devoid of male interest after all: quite the reverse. After the pragmatic but also physical attentions of Edgar, the intensity of Andrew, the silent and more ethereal desire of Michael, it was a relief to be in the company of a man prepared to treat me less as a woman than a friend.

From that standpoint, then, I might well have been ready to indulge his curiosity. But to do so would mean formulating and clarifying ideas and sensations which were far from certain in my own mind. More than that, whatever I said would constitute a kind of declaration, to which my stubbornness could bind me subsequently.

So I parried his implied inquiries, though gently. He for his part did not seem to mind: the questions themselves had been not at all direct, and he did not press them against my evasions. We parted for the night entirely amiably. I thought, as I walked along the lamp-lit landing to my bedroom, that I should not be at all averse to having John as an extra brother. But did that mean I was prepared to take Michael, as a husband?

My instincts gave me the answer, and unequivocally. And yet the thought was in my mind, recurring more and more frequently. In the end would instinct weaken, borne down by the weight of reason and practicality? I had an idea it could be so.

It would be different if Michael were not so sick and feeble. Perhaps it was a weakness in me to be repelled by that, but I could not help it. Except, of course, that the argument was futile. If Michael had been vigorous and healthy, Sir Donald would never have thought of securing a second-generation heir. He would never have brought me to Carmaliot.

The message was brought to me next afternoon while Lady Bedivere was having her nap and I was at work on embroidery in the parlour. One of the maids, Marion, brought it. I did not like her: she was thin-faced with pouting lips and big sly-looking eyes. She bobbed and said Sir Donald wished to see me, in the chapel.

'In the chapel? Are you quite sure?'

'That's what was said, ma'am.'

I had thought Sir Donald was out riding. Nor could I see any reason why he should propose the chapel as a meeting place. But the girl could not have made it up; and things unlikely in someone else might seem reasonable to a man as bound up in obsession as he was. Might he even have some notion that the atmosphere of the chapel could be a help in gaining the end he sought?

It took on a weird probability as I put my embroidery away and prepared to do as I had been requested. A setting of holy solemnity for the promotion of an enterprise which to him was both solemn and holy. I had a recollection, out of history lessons with the younger Miss Tranny, of the story of William of Normandy getting Harold to swear allegiance over the box of saints' relics. Sir Donald was unlikely to attempt anything of that sort, but he might well feel the chapel was the place in which to force me to decision—to obtain the precise consent which so far he had been content to assume.

This reasoning, as I made my way through the house, convinced me; and apprehension grew with the conviction. The unusualness increased the interview's significance, and seemed to lessen the chance of my continuing in evasiveness. I should not be able to escape saying something—and what was I to say? I could not entirely check a trembling in my limbs as I pushed open the heavy door to the chapel.

I saw no one. The chapel seemed quite empty: just the

rows of wooden chairs which the villagers and servants used and further up the family pews, equally untenanted. It was a grey day outside, and the side windows were subdued and gloomy in their colours.

I called softly: 'Sir Donald ...'

No answer came. In front of me St Michael, in the big window, brandished a dull red sword against the Enemy, himself garbed in lack-lustre green. He might be behind the altar, intent on something—praying, perhaps, for the grandson he desperately longed for. I walked down the aisle, my shoes tip-tapping on the stone. I said more loudly:

'I am here, Sir Donald.'

The figure came out from behind the altar as I reached it. But it was not Sir Donald. It was Edgar.

My first sensation was of relief that I was to be spared the decision I had thought faced me. After that came anger that he should have had the impudence to summon me by a false message. And curiosity, then, as to why he had thought it worth while. I was about to give expression to the anger, when he said:

'My apologies, Janey, for the fib about Father.' He grinned, quite amiably. 'You must not blame the girl: she conveyed what I had told her.'

She had conveyed it, I recalled, as though the message were direct from Sir Donald; but it was not a point worth arguing. I said:

'Perhaps you would be kind enough, before I take my leave, to say why you told such a lie, and involved a servant in it?'

He wagged his head, admiringly. 'You are coming on, Janey—learning to speak as to the manner born. It will not be long before you're a match for a duchess.'

Not wanting to bandy words, I turned to go, but stopped when he said:

'Be patient, and I will tell you all. In simple, I wanted to talk with you again, and in a place where we were not likely to be disturbed. And I felt that if I proposed such a rendezvous, the proposition would get short shrift.'

'You are right in that. We have nothing to discuss.'

'Exactly. I refer to your attitude, not to the need for discussion. And the chapel struck me as an excellent meeting ground: somewhere we are unlikely to be disturbed and unlikely to disturb anyone else. Have you ever been in the main part of the house during Sunday service? An organ bellowing, a hundred lusty voices giving tongue—and not a sound comes through. It is most solidly built.'

I repeated: 'We have nothing to discuss,' and again prepared to go. But he said:

'We have something.' He drew a folded sheet of writing paper from his pocket. 'A letter.'

'What letter?'

He held it between thumb and forefinger. 'I do not recall the precise words. The message, though, is clear. It offers an assignation, in the writer's room at night. It is most affectionately penned. And it is addressed to me. Can you think who might have signed it?'

'I neither know nor care! And I do not see what it has to do with me.'

'Do you not? Well, let me tell you—or should I say, remind you? It is signed, with love ... Jane.'

'So you have a doxy who bears my name. Thousands do.'

'True.' He unfolded the paper slowly. 'But this one has your handwriting.'

He waved the paper in the air so that I could see the writing plainly. I felt a shock of amazement and horror. The writing *was* mine, or a close resemblance to it. I reached out my hand to take it from him, but he pulled his own hand back. He re-folded the letter, and put it in his pocket.

'You deserve an explanation. As to the letter, first. I know some fellows in Plymouth outside, one might say, the best society. But they have talents. One of them can counterfeit a man's hand well enough to pass a banker's or attorney's scrutiny. He owes me a favour or two, and in any case I can afford to pay for his services. He can counterfeit a man's hand, as I say; or a woman's. All he needs is a fair specimen to work from. That was not too difficult to obtain. You place your letters with everyone else's on the table in the hall; and you write frequently to your brother. I watched you deposit the envelope one morning, from the stairs. I thought young Harry would not miss one out of so many.'

I remembered the inquiry to which I had got no answer, and felt cold. Emily had warned me of his cunning, but surely she could not have anticipated such deep-laid villainy as this?

'So,' he said, 'I have this letter, signed with your name, in your fair hand. I should not like to use it; and there is no reason why such a use, so shaming to you, should be made. I have you at a disadvantage, coz, but I shall deal fairly with you. I ask your hand in marriage—offer mine in friendship.'

I stared at him incredulously. Marriage? Friendship? He stretched his hand out.

'What do you say, Janey?'

'That I despise you. No more.'

He shook his head but did not seem perturbed.

'Allow yourself time for reflection before you make rash answers. It is in my power to provide Father with convincing evidence of your unchastity. I can assure you he would not want an unchaste wife for Michael.' He laughed, coarsely. 'It would never do for him to be uncertain which of his sons it was had got you with child!'

I stared at him in cold defiance. 'I am not with child by either, nor likely to be. Tell what lies you choose—purchase as many forgeries as you like—I do not care!'

'Can I not persuade you to take a more practical view?'

'Never!'

He paused. He was grinning still, and I thought there had never been anything I loathed more than that grimace—not even my father's face twisted in drunkenness. He said:

'And if I were to carry out my threat, it might not do,

might it? As you say, you are not with child. In fact, it might well be you have your maidenhood still—I'd be inclined to believe you have. And that is something that can be tested.'

I flushed before the insolence of his look but kept my chin up. I did not deign to reply.

'Which brings me to another reason for choosing a rendez-vous such as this, a place where no one is likely to come and from which the noise even of a bellowing congregation cannot be heard. I'm prepared to accept you came here a maiden. But rest assured you will not leave it in the same condition.'

I was sure he was bluffing but nonetheless horrified that he should speak of such a thing, in such a place. I said:

'I cannot believe that even someone as debased as you would attempt an act that desecrated a holy chapel.'

The smile left his face but what remained was more frightening: an ugly look of resolution.

'Do they not say the better the day, the better the deed? It goes for places, too. I am going to have you, Janey, here in this holy chapel. And afterwards I'll make it good by marrying you here. You can wear white, as a virgin bride should. But we'll know better.'

'As to marrying you—never! As to the other foulness ... I know you are stronger than I, and probably no one would hear my cries, either. But I promise you something: you will need to kill me before you get me.'

'I do not think so. Not kill. But I've already discovered you for a wild cat, and I can imagine you would struggle hard. You would bear the marks of my mastering you, and if you ran crying with them to my father my story might not be easy to sustain.' He shook his head regretfully. 'A pity, that.'

It had been a bluff, hideous but no more, and I had out-faced him. I said:

'I am going now. Do not try to stop me.'

I thought he might reach for me as I turned away, but he did not. Disconcertingly, the grin was back on his lips. I turned about and, for the first time since coming into the chapel looked at the door by which I had entered. I stopped, shocked at what I saw. The door which I had left open had quietly been closed. And standing there, hidden by it when I came in but in plain view now, were the two grooms who were his cronies.

I turned back. He said:

'Well, Janey?'

I whispered: 'You had them there, all along? Let them listen to all that was said?'

'I am doing my best to be reasonable,' he said. 'I still have some consideration for your modesty, providing you are concerned enough for it to accept the inevitable. I have only to say the word and they will station themselves discreetly outside, while we conduct the business that needs doing. Do not make things difficult for yourself.'

For answer, I flung myself at him. But quick as I was, he was ready and caught my arms in his hands. As I kicked with ineffectual shoes against his leather-encased legs, he called to the men at the door. Twisting in his grasp, I saw them coming down the aisle. I begged them:

'Help me! Please help me ... You cannot do such a thing.'

They were both tall men, one broad, one thin. The thin one's face showed a vile anticipation, the broad one's an indifference that was in its way more chilling. I screamed as they reached me, and heard the scream echo futilely from the chapel walls. Then a hand was clapped across my mouth, gagging me. Another hand took over the prisoning of my wrists from Edgar.

Between them they picked me up and carried me as easily as one might carry a kitten towards the family pews. Edgar, unencumbered, instructed them:

'Be careful of her. I do not want a single bruise, the least tear or dishevelment in her dress. She must have no wound, except the wound of love.'

Of love ... I felt sick and faint. I tried my strength again against the gripping hands, and could do nothing. I was at man's mercy as I had never been before, and knew no mercy would be shown. A wave of faintness came again, and I was tempted to give way to it: to blot out awareness of the outrage I had no power to resist. And yet, whatever the pain and shame, I would not surrender. I looked at Edgar's face. I would have spit in it had the hard cruel hand across my mouth not prevented that. I could only blaze hatred from my eyes.

Behind him transient sunlight turned the saint's sword to glowing scarlet. I felt the hardness of the pew against my neck and legs. And then, unhurrying, irresistible, his hand on my body.

At that, I closed my eyes. I would have prayed, except that God, too, was a man.

Then behind me a voice cried out:

'What are you doing?'

15

It was Michael's voice. I tried again to cry out but the hand was iron-hard against my mouth. I heard Edgar curse softly. He said in a low voice:

'You damned fool, Willie ... I told you to slip that bolt.'

Michael spoke again. 'What is happening there?'

Edgar said: 'A game, Michael. It does not concern you.'

I heard Michael come forward a step or two from the door. He asked incredulously:

'You have not brought a girl in *here*?'

'Stay.' The tone was warning. 'This is not an affair for you to meddle in, Michael.'

'But your men are holding her. L-let her go.'

'It is a game, as I told you. Robust, maybe, by your standards, but she likes it that way. Some wenches do, though you would not know it.'

My head was below the level of the pew and he could not see me. I tried to heave up, and failed. There was a silence following Edgar's speech: brief, but it seemed an age. Michael would back out, I was sure. Edgar and his grooms playing with one of the village girls or a maid ... it would sicken him probably, especially in its desecration of the chapel, but what could he do about it? After all he himself was an invalid, scarcely half a man.

But the footsteps came forward along the aisle. Edgar told him again to get back, but he paid no heed. They were level with the pew. I managed to twist my head an inch or two. My eyes looked into his amazed ones.

'Jenny!' He spoke to the men who had hold of me. 'F-free her.'

'Do not.'

Edgar's voice was strong and hard against his thin stammering one. The hands held tight. Edgar said:

'You're a fool, brother. I don't know what brought you here but it was unfortunate for someone. For us, plainly, if you go away to tell the tale.'

Michael was looking at the man behind me on my right, the bigger of the two. He said:

'Gawston, you m-must set her free at once.'

'Hold her, Willie. You did badly enough, leaving the door unbolted. If this reaches my father he'll hammer you. You'll not get away with less than transportation, and likely a flogging beforehand. Do as I say, and you'll be all right.'

'How c-can he be?'

Edgar turned back to Michael. 'I said: unfortunate for someone. If not for us, for you. I was willing to wait while your lungs rotted away, but you have altered things by blundering in here. A troublesome situation, but easily remedied. I can crack that puny neck of yours as easily as topping an egg. And if I throw you down those steps outside, what is it but a sorry accident? You missed your footing, full of holy thoughts.'

'Jane ...'

Edgar laughed. 'You think the presence of a witness may protect you? And so it might, if the witness were on hand. But she will not be. A dead man cannot sire, so she will be dispensable. Perhaps they will think she has run back to her Portsmouth slum—or maybe that she found you lying dead, and took fright! It does not matter what they think, as long as no tongue still wags that could accuse me, and I have two faithful ones to swear I was ten miles from Carmaliot all afternoon.'

176

Michael did not speak. I had expected little, but still felt betrayed. He was so feeble compared with Edgar: he would not fight for his life, or mine—not even speak up. I felt despair, as well. I was at the mercy of man's weakness as well as strength.

'I will give you a chance, brother,' Edgar said. 'Stand aside, while I complete this business, and I will let you die in your bed. Because I do not think you will carry a tale of how you watched the bride meant for your use taken by a better man. And if you do not fancy watching, you can close your eyes. You can be best man at our wedding—is that not generous?'

He spoke with assurance and contempt. I could see Michael's face, thin and white, and Edgar's, ruddy, robust, grinning. Michael tried to speak, but a coughing fit came on him. Edgar laughed.

'I must see we have pulmonic wafers at the bridal feast! Sit down and rest. The affair will not take long.'

Michael moved towards us. He was going to plead, I thought, and it would do no good. Whatever he begged for— his life, my virtue, both—was already lost. Mercy had no more meaning than justice: male strength ruled all, and Edgar's strength, compared with his, was a furnace fire compared with a guttering match.

He did not speak to Edgar. To Gawston, he said:

'I have told you: set her free.'

Edgar said: 'Shall I crack your neck now, Michael, to quiet you?'

Michael ignored him. He said again: 'Set her free.' There was no trace of impediment in his speech now, but something else, a quality I had never heard before. 'Do as I say, Gawston.'

Edgar said: 'You take my orders, Willie, not his. And your liberty depends on it. Hold her.'

Although not looking at him, Michael stood no more than a foot or two from his brother. Edgar could have reached out to seize him, or smashed him down with his fist. But he did

177

neither, and there had been a difference in his voice, too. The assurance was less strong.

'I am talking to you, Gawston.'

Michael's voice was low, but commanding—a master's to his man. I felt the grip on me slacken. Edgar said:

'Pay no heed.'

It lay between them—everything lay between them. But Edgar's voice, though deeper toned, now somehow had a shrillness in it. And Michael said, without fear, with authority:

'Let her go.'

Their hold on me relaxed. My mouth was free of the gagging hand. The shorter of them clumsily helped me rise to my feet.

Michael asked: 'You are not hurt, in any way?'

I shook my head. 'No.'

He looked at the two men, and Edgar. 'It is you they laid hands on. I leave them to your judgement, Jenny.'

'I only want them gone. No more.'

'Then they will go. You are generous, b-but I knew that. And it is probably best. Anything else would cause distress, and do no good.'

He turned to Edgar. 'Go, and take them with you. Make up any story you choose. But understand one thing: you will not return to Carmaliot. You leave this place forever.'

I thought even now Edgar might argue, but he said nothing. He went, his bullies at his heels, and we were left alone in the chapel. Michael suddenly looked weak, as though vigour had drained out of him. I begged him to sit down, and he wearily obeyed. He looked up at me.

'Are you truly all right. You s-suffered no injury?'

'None. But only because you saved me.'

'It was fortunate.' He shook his head. 'I come here sometimes.' He hesitated. 'To p-pray.'

'I know. I saw you once, but did not wish to disturb you.'

'You should have spoken to me.' He managed a tired smile. 'You would never disturb my prayers.'

I did not see Edgar again. I gathered from the talk at dinner that there had been an excuse of sudden pressing business in London: Lady Bedivere spoke of it with fond exasperation—for young men, these days, everything was always pressing....

Sir Donald made no comment at all, which surprised me rather. The following Sunday, coming out of the chapel with Michael after Mattins, I referred to that. He said:

'I suspect he is too pleased to be rid of him to question his reason for going. Shall we take a turn in the garden, Jenny?'

It was a grey day but mild, with a residue of the night's rain hanging pearl-like from the greening hedges. I said:

'I should like to. Do you really think he wished to be rid of him? I thought it was your father who kept him and John here, in wasteful idleness, to show his power over them.'

He smiled. 'You are confident in your judgements of people, and often right. But not always. Edgar stayed of his own volition. There was one thing Carmaliot gave him which no other place could.'

'What was that?'

'The chance to count my coughs.'

He was seized with coughing as he said it. I took his arm and pressed it gently. I still did not care to touch him, but told myself the feeling was less strong. I said:

'And John? Why does he stay?'

'Simply from idleness—he has more taste for it than Edgar, for all his talk of studying. And to please Lady Bedivere.'

'I should not have thought her so doting a mother.'

'Should you not? Well, there you miss again. Though I agree she shows little of it. But she shows little of anything.'

'Then how will she take it when she finds Edgar does not soon come back?'

He said slowly: 'I do not know.' He paused. 'There is something else that concerns me more.'

'What, Michael?'

'Letting him go, as we did. It seemed the best thing then.'

'It was.'

'I am not so sure. You heard what he c-called me—a dying man.'

'He said it hoping to cow you.'

'No. Look at me, Jenny.'

We had reached the sunken garden, where I had wooed poor Beast with scraps of meat. I stopped, and we turned towards each other. He blinked his weak eyes.

'It is true. You know it, too. There's no way of t-telling how long I have, but it will be months rather than years. And when it happens ...'

'You are wrong. And I will not talk of it.'

'We must. Because then Edgar can come back to Carmaliot. There will be n-nothing to stop him. He will be my father's heir. I worry for you.'

'He will not harm me again.'

'He m-might.'

'No.'

I hesitated. I had said nothing of the reason for Edgar's attempt on my person, leaving him to assume that lust accounted for it. This was only in part from delicacy; more from unwillingness to touch on the subject which he himself had now raised. But since he had raised it, since he was concerned for me, there was no sense in drawing back. I told him of Edgar's offer of marriage, and of what had been said in the chapel. He listened, and said:

'I always knew him for a brute, but not such a brute as that. I think it would be best to speak to Father.'

'No. I am safe now—do you not see? If ...' I summoned courage to look him in the face. 'If you should die, he has no need of me. He will have what he wants.'

He shook his head. 'He still might do you injury. He must hate you bitterly.'

I walked away from him along the path. My mind was in a turmoil, and yet my thoughts were clear. He followed me and I turned to face him again, the sundial at my back.

'There is a way to make me safe.'

'T-tell me.'

'We can do what your father wants.'

He stared in silence, then once more shook his head.

'No, Jenny.'

'Why not?'

'Does it need saying? I am no fit husband for any woman, let alone ...'

He did not finish, but his eyes supplied what was missing. Let alone for one I love. I said:

'The woman is the judge of that, not you. And I tell you that you are.' He was silent. 'Do not make it harder for me than need be.' I smiled. 'It is not easy for a girl to propose marriage—that is usually the man's part.'

'I am selfish enough—as selfish as any man. But that is a sacrifice I could not accept.'

'No sacrifice.'

His mouth was trembling. 'No, Jenny. I c-cannot take it from you.'

I put my hands out and took hold of his.

'Listen. Will you believe me when I say I tell you something truly?'

He smiled a little. 'I would never doubt your honesty.'

'Then believe me when I tell you this would not be a sacrifice. It is what I choose, and want.'

'If I could think so ...'

'Believe it.'

I drew him close, and kissed him on the mouth.

I had not lied to him. Although the actual occasion had happened unexpectedly, the thought and the intention had

181

been growing in me for days; from the moment he delivered me from Edgar. I had been helpless as never before in my life that I could recall—helpless and condemned to suffer a humiliation and disgrace such as my worst nightmares had never painted. Nor was it a hurt which would pass and be forgotten. Even had I fled Carmaliot, the memory of it would have gone with me. The memory, and maybe more. I had woken in the night since, shivering, imagining what it must be like to carry and bear a child so loathsomely conceived. It was a fate I knew other women had learned to accept, but I did not think I could have survived it.

It seemed to me that I owed Michael not merely a deliverance from violation, but life itself. Nothing I could do would settle the debt, but nothing should be shirked in paying off what I could. It was in my power to offer him some joy, and I took joy in that thought.

I would be a true and faithful wife to him. I would serve what remained of his life, and give battle to Death who hovered at his back. Nor would I despair of winning the battle, however great the odds. Now he was resigned to dying, but I would change that. He would have, if I could instil it in him, something better than any potion Dr Roberts or the medical advertisements could prescribe: the will to live. And I would do it.

I thought of these things as we stood before Sir Donald and gave him our news, and received his blessing. He could scarcely pronounce it, he was so stunned with joy. He took both our hands, and I saw tears in his eyes.

They did not move me. I no longer felt resentment for the way he had taken charge of my life; for any part of the things that had happened since that afternoon in Pratt Street. But I felt no affection, either—felt nothing for him. It was Michael who was my concern, Michael I would cherish. He coughed again. The day had turned more raw since morning—we had waited till evening to speak to his father—and he had been coughing a good deal. A drier climate might be better for his chest, I thought, than this damp air. If so, I would take him from Carmaliot, and no one should stand in my way.

I had not lied to him. I had said it was what I chose and wanted. Neither of us had spoken of love.

Lady Bedivere and John declared their satisfaction more easily than Sir Donald had been able to do. Lady Bedivere said:

'It was a great pleasure to welcome you here, dear Jane, but this is so much greater. I did not dream when you came to join us that we should one day know the joy of having you as a member of the family in so full a sense. I am sorry Edgar is not present to hear the news. I will write directly and tell him, and tell him to have done with his London business and come back to give you his congratulations.'

Had she had no idea, I wondered, of her son's envy of his half-brother; nor of the bitterness her letter would convey? The warmth of her speech made it seem unlikely that she had. And certainly she could not have conceived of the monstrousness of which he was capable. The shrewdest eye was blind to defects in the loved one. But that was no bad thing. Blind spots might be preferable to an all-critical view.

John said: 'I shall like having you for a sister, Jane.'

I smiled. 'And I you, for a brother.'

I told Emily when she came to visit the following afternoon. Lady Bedivere was at her nap, Sir Donald and the others were absent, and we took tea together in the parlour while rain sent drops running down the windows. She looked at me for a moment in surprise; then laughed.

'So you saw sense, after all! I must congratulate you for that, as I congratulate Michael on his good fortune. I confess I am amazed. I thought you were too stubborn to see where your interest lay.'

But although she tried to disguise it, there was a falseness

183

in her tone. She might have advised me in that way, and most likely honestly, but she was disappointed in me all the same. She had expected better of me.

It was that which prevented me telling her how it had come about. Although I did not relish the thought of describing what had happened in the chapel, I was prepared to do so; but would not now. If she chose to think ill of me I would rather let her than say anything which might seem a justification.

We talked together as normally as we could, but a shadow lay between us. I knew she was glad when it was time for her to leave. The rain, though it had eased, had not yet stopped, and I suggested she should delay her going since the dog-cart did not give a full protection from the elements. But when she smilingly refused, I did not press her.

I thought of her later as I walked down the drive towards the gates. The rain had gone, the dusk was calm, the sky glowing in the west, and I felt the need for fresh air after being cooped up all day in the house. And the need for a solitariness no room could provide.

I was unhappy about Emily. She had spoken of my stubbornness, and I cursed that alliance of it with pride which had kept me from being frank with her. I was to have a husband and would care for him, but I did not want to lose a friend. My need was greater now rather than less.

But it was silly, a quirk of melancholy, to think I should lose her because of that. Misunderstandings were a natural hazard of friendship, and she was much too sensible to let it grow into an estrangement. Even I, I told myself with rare charity, was too sensible, and that being so, my own stiff-necked nature having been responsible for our being at cross-purposes, I must take the initiative in putting things right. I resolved that before I went to bed I would write her a note. Not about anything in particular, but simply friendly. She would understand.

That having been resolved, I felt better. I was abreast of the Arthur tree, and on an impulse decided to look more closely at it: in the half-light it looked even more real, a green rider on a green horse. I turned from the gravel drive and walked across the lawn which, water-logged from the rain, squelched gently under my boots. I stood under the tree and stared up at it, remembering that other time and Sir Donald telling me of the Roman King.

He had fought for old good things against fearful odds. And against those odds he had held the bloody onslaught of the Saxons, driven them back, regained the land of his fore-fathers. But what was left him in the end, with Guinevere lost, Lancelot estranged, Mordred proved treacherous? A sense of duty done? The story said he had not died, but been taken to Avalon to heal his grievous wound. I could not believe that part. There was no Avalon and had never been. Only death; and the knowledge, because he was a wise man and courageous, that it had all been for nothing. The Round Table was dissolved, the land once more defenceless to the savage greed of the Saxon.

A gloomy thought for a calm grey evening, with the rain gone and the sky promising a better day tomorrow. It was very still, but a rhythm beat faintly in the distance. I heard the sound grow louder—the rattle of a horse's hooves, ridden at the gallop. I looked towards the gates, and saw the figure appear, galloping still up the drive in the direction of the house.

I was curious about the rider's urgency, and his identity: I could think of no one likely to be calling at this hour and with such impetuousness. Then I recognized the grey gelding as Andrew's, and was visited with panic. Had something happened to Emily? Instinctively I called out.

He checked his horse, turned it about and rode across the lawn towards me. His face, as he came near enough to see, was set and strained. He flung from the horse, and stood in front of me. I said:

'Is Emily ...?'

He did not let me finish. 'Tell me she has it wrong.'

His voice was hoarse. I felt cold, and weak.

'What?'

'That you are not to marry Bedivere. It cannot be true!'

I stared at him. His demand was rude; he had no right to put that question to me, and in such a tone. It merited censure, and I should mete it out. But I felt a reluctance, and for the first time since my match had been arranged, a sense of shame.

'Tell me,' he said again. 'You must.'

His voice, his look, would suffer no refusal. I said, hearing my own voice strangely in my ears:

'It is true. Michael and I are to marry.'

'You cannot!' I did not reply. 'It is unthinkable.'

'No.' I looked away from him. 'It is not unthinkable. We are to marry.'

'I will not accept it.' I saw his hand clench tightly into a fist. 'God knows I am not worthy of you, but he much less. You cannot love him, any more than spring could love winter. So why? Why?'

It was no business of his, and I should dismiss him. He had no right to tell me whom I should love, or could. But the shame lingered and, the more unaccountably after my behaviour with Emily, a need to justify myself. I said, tonelessly:

'The Bediveres have been kind to me—Michael more than any.'

'Kind!'

It was no good. There was nothing I could say to put things right. I tried to tell myself again that none of it was his concern. I shook my head.

'Go, Andrew. Please go.'

His horse cropped the meagre pasture of the lawn. He half-turned towards it, and I thought he would mount and ride away. But unexpectedly he turned back. His arms reached out and grasped me, drawing me in. I should have turned my head away, but before I could his lips seized hold of mine.

There was the smell of maleness, the roughness of his coat against my hand as I struggled to free myself, the awareness of strength so much greater than my own. I pulled away, but still was held. I felt anger, but mixed with other things. And helplessness, but a different helplessness from that I had known in the chapel.

His lips were warm and strong. I twisted my head and managed to get free. I knew then what the difference was; in this weakness there was the seed of self-betrayal. I wanted him to hold, even to master me—wanted those lips again.

It was that, the realization of my treachery to myself, that gave me the power to resist. His grasp slackened, and we stood apart. Breath shuddered in my breast. With the chill of despair, I said:

'Go at once. And do not dare behave like that again.'

Then I watched him as he rode off into the dusk.

16

Apart from the irritance of Edgar's presence, life had been easy at Carmaliot all along: only my resentments had contrived to turn it sour. But the whole place seemed imbued with a new and greater cheer. It was best exemplified in Sir Donald, whose gravity was now continuously lit with good humour. In his references to our coming marriage, one could read the depths of uncertainty which had underlain his apparent confidence. He had pursued a dream, with relentless vigour but knowing in his heart that it was a dream; and the dream had become reality. Astonishment marched with exhilaration, and heightened it.

It was a different case with Michael. He had hidden his desire and still feared to contemplate it openly. But in the looks he gave me, especially when he thought I was not watching him, there was an even greater joy—uncertain, but less so with each passing day.

Lady Bedivere and John had nothing personal to rejoice over, but they both appeared to take pleasure in the delight of others. And the servants, too, seemed to share in the atmosphere of celebration, or so I felt. All was set fair for the future. Michael looked better, I told myself, and was coughing less. Death like the Saxons had been driven back from Carmaliot.

I realized that not all of the change was in others: that a good part lay in myself. The resentments I had felt before had gone—I had dismissed them, along with so much else, when I made my decision over Michael. Previously I had seen my life at Carmaliot as something to be endured, and for no longer than need be. In resolving to marry Michael I accepted the prospect of its continuance indefinitely. To harbour rancours which belonged to the past would mean qualifying that resolution and acceptance; and I would not do that.

The die had been cast, this time by me, and I was determined not to waver in pursuit of the course I had set myself. I reflected on this as I sat before my dressing-table, and drew the brush through my hair. I looked at my mirrored image and the brown eyes looked back. No, I would not look either to left or right—I must not.

And thinking that, I thought of Andrew. It was a reflection I had schooled my mind against, but briefly I indulged myself. I looked at the glossy black hair, the high brow and cheekbones, small straight nose, the skin a little brown for elegance but warmly mixed with rose. I looked at the full red mouth, white neck, the bosom's lift above the top of my night-gown. I looked, and tried to see them through his eyes, wondering at the magic by which a face, a body, could inspire so strong a passion.

For passion it was he felt, and fiercely. It was nothing like either the coarse carnal urge of Edgar, or Michael's worshipful diffidence. It comprehended both but surpassed them, and centred on something else—a fineness, a trueness—which made it altogether different. Unlike Edgar's lust it was of a oneness with the man himself, compelling his heart and spirit. And unlike Michael's devotion, it evoked response.

I would not deny what had happened to me under the Arthur tree, nor belittle it. His kiss had aroused a feeling in me I had never known or imagined. I could vouch for my own effect on him by the strength of his on me. I had read of kisses and love-making in romances, but nothing I had read had prepared me for the reality. I had tried not to think of it, but it troubled me still.

Not because of the stirring of my senses. That had been strange enough, but not frightening. The fearful thing had happened not in my body, but to my inner self. It had been the longing—deep and blinding and growing, growing until it threatened to sweep away all resistance—to surrender everything, volition, will, identity even, to the man who held me in his arms.

I stared at the face in the glass—beautiful, men told me. Had that been me, and could it be again? I knew the first was true, and feared the second. If this was the love they wrote of, I rejected it. My will was my own: I valued it more than anything I had, or could hope to have. Far more than wealth or position, or even beauty.

And because I feared love, I would guard against it. What had happened that evening had happened unawares: warned now, I was forearmed. I thought of my commitment to Michael, and was grateful for it in quite a new way. Had I not been engaged it might have been more difficult. As it was, his love and my covenant protected me. I would not betray him or myself.

I finished brushing and turned down the lamp. The face that looked at me was darker, shadowed and mysterious, lit only by the second distant lamp beside my bed. But though a face might change, I would not. The time for indulgence was over: I would not think of him or that moment again. There were so many other things in the world to think of: safer things.

I went to bed, and did not let myself think of Andrew. But it was a long time before I slept.

'What should you like,' John asked, 'for a wedding present?'

We were on the croquet lawn, where he had set up hoops and peg and was teaching me to play. I said:

'A comb for my hair. I am always losing them.'

'A modest requirement. Or is it consideration for the meagre resources of a younger son? But I can do better than a comb, I fancy. I must start saving up, since the time is short. Within a month, is it not?'

'Yes, just. Three weeks from Saturday.'

He had the yellow and red balls, his yellow well placed for the third hoop. I aimed my black carefully and succeeded in knocking his yellow aside and taking the hoop. John rested his mallet against his leg and clapped.

'You need little instruction, but that seems true of everything you engage in. I had a letter from Edgar this morning.'

I concentrated on the ball. 'Oh?'

'His business, whatever it is, seems to be dragging out. He is vague about it, and vague as to the prospects of his return. He did not speak of the wedding, but it would not surprise me greatly if he did not return for it.'

I said carefully: 'I should be sorry if so, but doubtless he would have good reason.'

'Doubtless. And reason other than the business which engages him, maybe. I had a notion, before he went away, that he might be getting sweet on you.'

I shook my head. 'I did not notice it.'

'He put himself wrong with you at the start, of course.'

'That was over and forgotten.'

'Yes, you have a forgiving nature. But Michael is much the better choice, in any case.'

I looked at him but his expression was guileless. He said:

'A forgiving nature, and a caring heart. You are a woman who prefers to aid rather than cling. You are helping Michael already. He has not taken to his bed since your engagement was announced. And he looks twice the man he did. Where are you going for the honeymoon?'

'To Italy. The sunshine will do him good.'

'And you have planned it.' He laughed. 'Exactly. Michael is a fortunate man.'

I thought again of the difference between him and Edgar. I asked impulsively:

'John, why have you stayed here?'

He pretended hurt, saying ruefully: 'Would you have me gone, Jane? I thought you and I were friends.'

'No.' He had put on an expression of mock misery. 'Don't be silly. It was from your point of view I was considering it. Edgar ... it was different for him. But you are more intelligent—less concerned with cock-fighting and hunting and boxing matches.'

'I take pleasure in the hunt. And I am not sure about intelligence: perhaps I get on with books better, but Edgar is no fool. I cannot stand up to him either at backgammon or chess. But it is true he is more contented with country pursuits than I.'

'Then why...?'

'As the third son, I have my way to make. And I do not intend to look to England for my future. America is the place —the new world. And when I go there, I shall not soon come back; not until I am an old man, if ever. So I have given myself one last spring at Carmaliot, to remember when I am among the Yankees. Is that a wicked indulgence, do you think?'

Michael had been wrong about him, my own judgement surer. He had a purpose. I approved that: the rationality of his approach and the purpose itself. I said warmly:

'No indulgence. And I am glad you did not go to America as soon as you had got your degree, or I should not have met you.'

'Amen to that! I am happy to think I shall be leaving Carmaliot in good hands. You will write and keep me posted as to when the first daffodils flower?'

'Of course I will.'

'You are learning to love Carmaliot. I am glad of that. I know you were not happy here at first.'

I did not love it, and never would: its magnificence was of a dimension I knew I should never grow accustomed to. But he loved it, and must leave it. I nodded. I said, honest in this at least:

'I shall be glad when all the present fuss is over.'

'I can believe that. The wedding will be a taxing business. And before that there is the Betrothal Ball.'

'I did not want it.'

'Maybe not, but Father did. And as you know, he is not a man easily baulked of his desires. No, Janey, you must bear to be shown off to the county.'

I played my blue ball and it rebounded from the iron of the hoop, coming to rest a foot away, with my black a little further off. John aimed his red. It ricocheted from black to blue and neatly through the hoop. I said:

'Good shot. You have been toying with me, I suspect.'

He shook his head. 'A lucky hit—no more.'

I was determined, when Emily next came to see me, to make up for my failure on the previous occasion. The fault, I entirely acknowledged, had been mine, and it was up to me to set things right. She though was constrained in her manner. I paid no attention to that, except that I tried to be the warmer for it.

Gradually she thawed and we talked more naturally. She made no reference to Michael or the wedding, and I was quite happy to follow suit. I saw small signs of nervousness— she fidgeted with her gloves and later with her tea-spoon— but ignored them. I knew she was ill at ease still, but was surprised when she burst out:

'I am worried, Jane.'

'About what?'

'Andrew.'

I was silent. Once again, this was a topic I had no hankering for, and unlike the time of the tea-party by the lake, I truly meant it now. But she went on:

'He came to see you the other evening, after I visited you.'

It could have been either statement or question. I said reluctantly:

'He told you of it?'

'Not a word. But when I told him what you had said to me—that you were to marry Michael ... his face was white. I have never seen a man so shocked. And not long after I saw him on horseback and riding furiously to the west. I meant to ask him when he came back, but dared not. I have tried to speak to him since, but he will not let me. I cannot reach him.'

I was moved by her distress on his account, but glad she knew nothing of what had happened under the Arthur tree. That was something I wished to blot from my own memory. When I did not speak, she said:

'He loves you very deeply, Jane.'

'I am sorry, if so.' She looked at me. 'But as you told me, it is something that will cure itself. I recall you quoted Shakespeare to me—that men have died, but not from love.'

'I did not realize then how seriously he took it.' She shook her head. 'I was judging too much by my own character, maybe. I doubt if it is in my nature to be so engaged with another. I hope not, from what I see in him. For he suffers, Jane. He suffers greatly.'

I said slowly: 'I do not like to think of anyone suffering, least of all your brother. But what is there to do?'

She was silent for some moments; then said:

'You do not love Michael?'

I hesitated; but at least, unlike Andrew, she had put it as a question, not a rough assertion. And I wanted to keep her friendship. She deserved some frankness. I said:

'I do not love anyone.'

'Then why? Why marry him?'

'Might it not be for the reasons you yourself gave, the night of the ball? To be sure of a fortune—to secure the delights of being a rich young widow?'

'That was before I knew about Andrew.'

'Yes. But good advice is good advice, whatever happens. Is it not?'

She looked at me. 'And before I understood you as well as

I do now. One filly's pasture may not suit another. I might have found the reasons good, or imagined I would think so, but not you. That is not the explanation of your accepting him. I do not know what is.'

And I could not tell her—about what had happened in the chapel or what I felt for Michael because of it. I said nothing, and she went on:

'I know it is not my business. But I am fond of you, Jane. Perhaps that explains my interference even if it does not warrant it. I am unhappy to see you resolved on a course which seems wrong for you—which may bring you unhappiness.'

'It will not.'

She sighed. 'You are so sure of yourself. I admire your resolution, but I think there are times it may blind you. You set too high a standard for consistency, in yourself as well as others. A degree of fickleness is a part of human nature, but you deny it. You follow too straight a path.'

'Only the one I find before me.' I contemplated what I had said. 'How priggish I sound! I did not mean it like that.'

Emily laughed. 'I know you did not. My dear—you are determined on the marriage?'

'Yes.'

'Then I will hold my peace.' She got up from her chair, came round to mine, and hugged me. 'And wish you every joy. It may be I am blinded, too, by selfish wants. Poor Andrew. But I would not have you marry him without loving him, any more than Michael. And I have promised to hold my tongue. I must not try to tell you what your needs are.'

I was summoned to Lady Bedivere for a final inspection before the ball. Her expression was jovial as ever, but her eyes were critical. Her gaze took in every detail; then she nodded.

'I thought Mademoiselle did well by you last time, but she has surpassed herself.'

The mirror in my room had told me how I looked. The

195

tunic was of white gauze over blue satin, the bodice low and pointed with a white lace berthe. The pale blue crinoline skirt was trimmed with broad lace bands, set on in double rows of festoons, each row with a triple *bouillon* of white gauze, ornamented with bows of blue ribbon. I had blue satin slippers, and a bouquet of camellias pinned in the centre of my corsage. My hair had been set in rouleaux with clustering ringlets dropping over each ear, and a smaller bouquet of camellias fixed on one side. I had looked at myself again after Mademoiselle had gone—I was ashamed how long I had stared.

Lady Bedivere nodded again. 'You look beautiful, my child. I must call Sir Donald in. The dress was of his choosing.'

I snatched another glance, in her mirror, as she went to fetch him from the next room. Of his choosing? I could not imagine him concerning himself with dresses. It was lovely, though. I hastily moved away as I heard their footsteps approaching.

He bade me stand still, and looked at me a long time without speaking—so long that I grew nervous, thinking something must be wrong, and with me since I knew the gown was perfect. Then he said:

'It is not like hers, but the colours are the same. Blue and white. They were always her colours. I wanted you to wear them tonight.'

Lady Bedivere stood beside him, but she might not have existed. His eyes were on me, and the past. He said:

'She was very beautiful, more beautiful than you. You do not mind me saying that?'

I shook my head. 'No, I do not mind.'

'But where her beauty was fragile, yours is strong. Even when she was merry, there was sadness in her laughter. I had two years of her—no more. Before she died, she gave me Michael. And you, blooming where she was frail—you will give me Michael's son, will you not?'

I did not answer, but he did not seem to notice.

'She wore a dress in such colours to the ball we gave not long after she told me she was carrying my child. The dress, like she herself, has long since gone to dust. But something remains from that night. I have kept them till now, but I know she would want you to have them—to wear them on this occasion.'

From his pocket he took a small black velvet bag, tied with black cord. He undid the cord and opened it, tipping the contents into his free hand. Stones flashed in the lamplight. They were a pair of eardrops: of sapphire and pearl and little diamonds. He put his hand out, and I took them.

'They are very beautiful,' I said, 'but ...'

'Put them on. My hands are too clumsy for so delicate a manoeuvre.'

He watched while I did so, moving my ringlets so they could be seen. I had glanced at Lady Bedivere and seen her nodding and smiling. I could not argue over the gift. I said:

'It is too magnificent a present. But I thank you most sincerely.'

'They are from her—from Michael's mother. And this.'

He brought out a second bag from his pocket, and spilled its contents out in turn. I felt like gasping at the sight. Pearls and sapphires again, but more than fifty times the number of those in the eardrops, and of far greater size. They were studded on to a chain of gold, a choker necklace. And in the centre of the chain, half a dozen big sapphires framed a magnificent diamond.

Sir Donald put his hand out, holding it, but I drew back.

'I could not take it, sir. The eardrops, yes, but nothing so costly as that.'

'I had them made for her,' he said, 'as a set. For her, and now they come to you. But I will put this on for you myself. It is not too difficult a matter, even for an old man.'

Light dazzled from the diamond; then he stood at my back. I felt the necklace cool against my flesh, and bowed my head to let him fasten it. I could see Lady Bedivere, the broad face

197

smiling still. She had been Sir Donald's wife for more than a dozen times as long as his first lady—had borne him two healthy sons against one sickly one. What could she think of this resurrection of the past, and its linking with a future that was designed to see her son disinherited? Her broad neck carried a string of pearls, nothing like the necklace I wore.

She was smiling and nodding, and I felt abashed. I did not think I could have been so generous.

It was Michael this time who led me on to the floor, following Sir Donald and Lady Bedivere for the first waltz. He did not dance as well as Edgar, being stiff and awkward in his movements; but he did not hold me as close, either. I was glad of that and pleased by his happiness which was very evident. I told him he looked well, and he said:

'And feel it, Jenny. It is your doing.' I shook my head, smiling. 'It was a grey world I walked through, and you have transformed it. It gleams with light and hope.'

Emily had been by herself in the line. It had not surprised me that Andrew had not come, and there was no opportunity to discuss his absence. It was better, I thought, that he should stay away—not on my account but on his own. I was surprised when, as Michael relinquished me, he appeared out of the press. He asked the favour of a dance, and I awkwardly agreed. He too chose a waltz; then bowed and left me.

I looked for him during the time before he was to claim me, but did not see him dancing. I was uneasy. He had behaved correctly, but his face had a set unhappy look. When he took me on to the floor at last I wanted to say something which would lighten the atmosphere between us—any triviality would do—but could think of nothing. The fiddles scraped, the flute and clarionet were gay, there was the tap of feet and rustle of skirts, the murmur of voices—and silence like an iron thing between us.

He said at last: 'I have an apology to make to you.'

'It doesn't matter. Andrew ...'

198

'Two, in fact. For being late tonight is another. I could not bear to see him standing by your side and shake him by the hand.'

'You mustn't ...'

'And then for my behaviour that evening. I am truly sorry for it.' He managed a smile, though a poor one. 'I seem to be continually begging your forgiveness, do I not?'

'You have it, if you want it. All I should like to do now is forget it, and be friends.'

He did not answer right away, and I began to hope he had accepted and there could be a truce. He said, though:

'You can demand anything of me, so long as it lies in my power to give it. But you ask impossibilities. I could never forget holding you in my arms, and love is death to friendship.'

'You could pretend at least, in both instances. And I can ask you that.'

He was silent again as we whirled around the floor. He danced less well than Edgar, better than Michael. He did not hold me close, either, but his nearness, the touch of his hand on my skin, disturbed me. I looked past him and away, not liking what I felt.

He said: 'Let us have a last few moments of honesty, then, before the pretending starts. I expect nothing now for myself. You do not love me, and I am not fool enough to think you ever will. I cannot have you. But I beg you, as one who loves you, not to marry Bedivere.'

I forced myself to look at him so that he could not doubt my determination.

'Michael and I are to be married before the month's end. It is quite fixed and final.'

'You must not. It would be a desecration of yourself.'

I was angry suddenly. 'Would it be? I fancy I am the best judge of that. And what happened on the lawn—since you say it cannot be forgotten—had more of desecration in it than the love of a good and worthy man.'

I saw him wince, and was glad. The dance was nearly over,

199

and I was glad of that, too. He said, in a different, colder voice :

'Those are pretty eardrops you are wearing. And an even more handsome bauble about your neck.'

The music stopped.

'Think what you like,' I said, and turned away.

17

The days passed, each bringing the date of my wedding that much nearer. I did not dwell on the subject, and when it could not be avoided, thought of it chiefly with indifference. It was something I had set myself to do. I expected nothing pleasing from it, and would not anticipate miseries.

My main satisfaction, when I was free of the domestic requirements placed on me (not least among them submitting to Mademoiselle's labours of love in respect of my wedding gown), was to get out of the house. For fear of vagrant tinners I was not allowed to ride unaccompanied, but it was not felt there was any risk in walking in the immediate environs of Carmaliot, and I took advantage of that to gain some precious solitude.

There was one spot in particular to which I resorted. It was a grassy hollow beneath a spur of rock to the east. Boulders were scattered there, some of a size and shape to sit on, and one looked out across a fall of land to see on the left the trees above the village, while below and to the right the road to Lacdam ran like a thin twisting ribbon across the moor. I could watch carts and carriages go by from my vantage point, myself unseen. And far out I could see that distant line, grey or glinting blue, which was the sea. Best of all was what I could not view: the vast granite pile, turreted and spired and arrogant, which was Carmaliot.

I went there one morning when the line of sea was truly blue, but speckled silver by the sun. I thought of Harry as

I took my favourite perch on a long low boulder of blue granite, smoothed by long centuries of wind and weather. The *Belphoebe* was at Portsmouth still, but would soon be off, a dot in that flashing silver. Mama and the girls were to be at the wedding, but he would be on the high seas. I was not sorry for that. I longed to see him again, but on some different occasion.

He would have a wonderful career. He, I knew, would have preferred different days—days of battle against the French or Dutch or Spaniards. But I was happy that we lived in peaceful times. Napoleon was long dead and forgotten, and there was no fleet in the world to challenge the pre-eminence of our navy. It would not stop him making his way, and becoming an admiral in the end. I had no doubt of that. There was no need for wars.

I was so engrossed in my image of Harry as an admiral with lashings of gold braid and a great cocked hat, and smiling at it to myself, that I did not notice the approach of the horseman until he was only a few yards away—and then only when the horse snorted. I looked up, startled, and was more surprised still to see it was John. He had ridden off after breakfast, and I had thought he would be away all day. I rose to my feet as he swung out of the saddle.

He said, smiling: 'Well, Jane! I have found you out. It is here that you come to dream.'

My immediate nervousness at being taken unawares had gone. I said:

'It is a place I like. But what are you doing here? I thought you had business in Launceston.'

'The man I was to see had himself gone away, on other business. So I wasted a journey.'

'You did not travel back by the road?'

'I preferred to ride across the moor. I like it on a day such as this. And as it happened I chanced on something interesting on the way.'

'What?'

'I will keep the secret till I can show it you. And why not now? Can your dreaming wait for another day?'

My solitude was lost, and I could not regain it without seeming rude. But I would rather surrender it to John than any other at Carmaliot. I said:

'If you like. Shall we go back to the stables?'

'It does not lie that way.'

'I meant, so that I can get a horse.'

'There's no need. I can ride you there on my saddle bow.' I looked doubtful, and he laughed. 'Or would that offend your dignity?'

Although the chaffing was not unkindly, I took it as a reference to the enhanced status I was to enjoy and my own awareness of it. I said:

'My dignity is not easily offended. If you think your horse can bear it, I will too.'

He set me up and mounted himself behind me. As we jogged eastward on to the moor, he talked about the man he was to have seen in Launceston. He was an attorney who was supposed to have connections in America, and John hoped to take advantage of that. It was a nuisance he had been away from home, but could not be helped. And there was time enough.

Sitting close against him as I was, with his hands holding the reins on either side of me, I was conscious again of the innocence, the lack even of flirtatiousness, in our contacts. He would not, I was sure, have taken any liberty with a girl betrothed to his brother—his nature was in every way more refined than Edgar's—but I felt equally certain that there was no temptation there for him to resist. It might as well have been Harry sitting behind me, and while the thought made me reflect how greatly I should have preferred that, it was satisfying as well. Altogether I had had enough of the ways of men with maids.

He spoke of his future, of the prospect of life in America.

It dismayed him a little. Not so much on account of the Americans themselves—despite what Messrs Trollope and Dickens had had to say he was sure they were worthy enough in their way—as in regard to the vastness of the country, and the possibilities it presented. He had thought of the north-east—the attorney's contacts were in the city of Boston —but how did one choose, starting a new life and confronted with so many different avenues meriting exploration?

'Whereas you, Janey, will be settling down to your new life here at Carmaliot, where the only uncertainties are who is to give the next ball, and whether you should put on your blue bonnet or your cherry-red one when you go to pay a call. A very different range of problems, and yet most likely it is the change in life which is really the unsettling business. And that was as great for you probably, coming here, as it will be for me stepping ashore in New York harbour. I saw how much you had to contend with, and admired the resolution— yes, and the good sense and intelligence—with which you grappled with it all.'

'You helped me,' I said, 'more than anyone.'

'I was glad to do so, though you needed little help. Of course I did not know then the plans Father had for you, any more than you did.'

The horse jogged on. We were far out on the moor. The air was hot and still, the only other sign of movement a hawk circling far up in the blue. John said:

'We have always known he was a romantic at heart, with his talk of Arthur and Camelot and the last stronghold of Roman Britain, but I had not guessed how determined a romantic he would prove. I suppose as the truth about Michael's condition grew so plain that even he could no longer stay blind to it, desperation made his imagination yield still more exotic blooms. And one at least which he could pick and bring to Carmaliot. The poor girl, daughter of a widow with a large family and no means of supporting them, who is fallen in love with by her sadly ailing but

204

wealthy cousin. That is a romantic story, too, is it not?'

His tone was speculative and mild, but I did not care for the direction in which the conversation was being taken. I said, in an effort to change it:

'Are we not there yet? We seem to have been travelling a long time. We must be tiring your poor horse.'

'She's a sturdy creature and, being a mare, good at enduring loads. But her task is nearly at an end. Over there.'

He lifted a hand to point. I had already noticed a small hill rising out of the rolling contour of the moor, and now saw a building huddled beside it, or the ruin of one. It was low-lying, with a shattered slate roof that left much of its interior open to the heavens. I wondered, as we covered the remaining distance, what merit of interest it might have to justify his bringing me to see it. But at least there was no more talk of me and Michael: we rode in silence.

Close by the building John dismounted, and helped me down. The walls were of blue granite, solid still, but the window spaces held only the rotting remains of wooden frames. I looked inside and saw bareness: stone walls, a floor invaded by heather and grasses. I asked him:

'What was it used for? A dwelling—so far out on the moor?'

'Not a dwelling. It is an abandoned tin-mine. Or rather the surface part—the place where stores, picks and shovels and all that, were kept. The mine itself is on the other side.'

He led the way and I followed, puzzled still. The country hereabouts, I knew, was dotted with similar relics. It scarcely seemed worthwhile to come so far, riding double, to see one. John indicated the hill.

'That was the tip for waste material. The ore was taken away on pack-horses to be treated, but of course they were obliged to bring out a great deal of useless rubble as well. Hundreds of tons of it.'

'It must have been abandoned long ago—it is almost completely overgrown.'

'Nature has her kindnesses as well as cruelties. See, here is the shaft.'

It was surmounted by the remains of a superstructure. I saw a rusting iron wheel, weathered wood, and ropes dangling down into blackness. The shaft was square, about five feet across, the top of it rimmed with cracked granite paving stones. John picked up a loose chip, and tossed it in the hole.

'Listen.'

I strained my ears and heard a dull plop from the depths.

'Deep for these parts,' John said. 'A hundred feet I should say, at least.'

For all the warmth of the day, I found myself shivering. He said:

'And water at the bottom, as you can hear. It was probably flooding which made them abandon the working. There was one mine, over towards Bodmin, where a dozen tinners were drowned, following a cloud-burst. Think of it—scrabbling down there like a rat in the earth, and then dying like a rat in a drain. It is not a pretty picture.'

I shook my head. 'I don't know how they bore it.'

'They were used to it. Usage makes most things bearable. It is by its shocks that life drives us to rebellion, and desperate measures.'

I moved away from the mouth of the shaft, and he followed me. The horse was cropping nearby; the hawk still circled patiently in the blue. He indicated a place for me to sit, and sat beside me. He said:

'I like you, Jane.'

With another man and in such isolation I should have been on my guard, but I was not with John. I felt awkward, all the same. I said:

'I am glad of it. I like you, too.'

'I should have been happy, under better circumstances, to look forward to a long association, as relations and friends. I admire your character, and enjoy your presence. It is a pity it may not be.'

'There will be visits, surely. America is not so far away. Perhaps we shall come to visit you.'

'We?' He shrugged. 'Poor Michael.'

There was a silence. I watched the hawk, far above us. From one instant to the next the lazy circling was transformed into a dropping bolt from heaven. It went from sight beyond the hill, talons stretched to grip its unsuspecting prey. John said, in a tone of regret:

'I was so glad when you came. And angry with Edgar when he insulted you. He was a fool to think you were the kind of wench he uses and misuses.'

'It was good of you to defend me.'

'And then to compound the folly by making another attempt on you—this harebrained notion of violating you to prevent your marrying Michael.'

I said slowly: 'You knew of that?'

'He spoke of it before he went away.'

'You never hinted that you knew.'

'Why should I? If you and Michael said nothing.'

'That was on account of your father. We saw no sense in troubling him.'

'No. I was glad, too, on account of Mama.'

We were quiet for a time. I told myself it was understandable that John should have known, and also that he should have given no indication of it. Although his tone was mild, his words had been entirely critical of his brother. I did not know why it was I felt so uneasy. I wondered if I could propose returning: we had seen what little there was to see here. I was phrasing the suggestion in my mind, when John said:

'It is all such a pity. I like you, as I say. Who could imagine the old man would conceive of anything so unlikely—so absurd?'

It was Sir Donald he was speaking of. We were back on the subject of my marriage. I did not care for it, but I supposed he was talking of what it had provoked Edgar to. There was,

I knew, a closeness between the brothers, and although acknowledging his culpability he would be sorry at losing him. As I would with Harry, whatever he did—though I would not believe he could do anything so vile as Edgar had intended.

He put his hand out, and took mine, and I felt no alarm. The touch was gentle, with no trembling desire, no fierceness in it. His look was calm and I thought, as I had done that first time of meeting him, how much he resembled Sir Donald. He said:

'It was a hopeless scheme, that one of Edgar's. I think turbulence of blood prompted it more than policy. He wanted you, the more so since you had spurned him when he first tried you. He wanted the heirdom, but that as well. It was greedy in him, and short-sighted. The world is full of willing girls, and there can only be one heir to Carmaliot. And while you and Michael both lived, he stood to lose it.'

He still spoke quietly and reflectively, but the words struck cold. I said:

'I think I should like to be getting back. There are things to do before luncheon.'

He did not answer, did not seem to have heard me.

'I count myself fortunate, being spared that turbulence.' He looked at me in untroubled appraisal. 'You are pretty, but it does not touch me. Pleasant and entertaining as company, too, but that does not move me, either. I have sometimes wondered what it must be like to be concerned with people. I can see no advantage to match my own freedom of action.'

I started to get to my feet but his hand, no longer gentle, held me tightly, twisting my wrist so that with a gasp I submitted and sat still.

'While you and Michael both lived—as I've said. It did not matter which of you should go. Michael would seem the more reasonable choice, since he is dying anyway. But I like him, too, you see, and have done so for much longer than I have liked you. He is my brother—half-brother, any-way—and that makes a tie. There was only you. You see that, don't you?'

He spoke as though seeking my approbation for choosing one cravat rather than another. I did not know what to say. It was a joke, I told myself, and wished I could believe it. If he had shown some sign of passion, I would have felt less fearful.

'So I came to your room in the night, and saw you sleeping, in the lamplight. You were beautiful, and very peaceful. It was a touch of genius, I thought. You had been drugged by Father's orders, and it would seem that because of that you had choked yourself with your bedclothes. I arranged your linen and took a pillow before I blew out the lamp. Then I pressed down the pillow. I thought I had held it long enough for all to be over, but I had not. When I relaxed the pressing you struggled free, and I had to get away in case you raised the house.

'I thought you might speak of it next day, but you did not. Why was that, Janey?'

I stared at him in horror. The sensations of that night came back—the fear, the smothering blackness, blood pounding in my ears. I could not speak. He shrugged.

'It does not matter. I came to your door another time, and found it bolted. But I had already decided that it would not do. There was too much risk, there in the house. So the next time I tried for you in the open.'

I said involuntarily: 'The tinners.... The shot through the carriage window.'

'A shot that went wide. It was not my marksmanship that failed. The carriage wheel must have found a pothole—enough to throw my aim out an inch or two. I checked the window, and it could not have been more than that.'

He spoke for the first time with emotion—as though answering unwarranted criticism. I looked about us. The hill, the crumbling building, the stretching emptiness of the moor—nothing and no one else. Even the sky was empty now, while the hawk gorged on his prey.

'Father put guards on you after that, once they had scoured the moor and drawn a blank. It would have been amusing if they had come on some tinner with a gun, but on the whole I was glad they did not. I have nothing against the poor wretches, beyond the fact that they do not wash much. At any rate, I decided that though I had been unlucky the first couple of times, I had also been fortunate in arousing no suspicion close to home. And I resolved that the third time should be decisive. I would think and plan, long and hard, before I acted.'

His hand relaxed from mine to pluck a stem of heather. I was no longer held. I watched the hand, wondering if I dared run.

'Meanwhile, Edgar tried that foolish trick of his. I had been beginning to think that maybe there would be no wedding—that you would refuse Michael. It did not make sense that you should, but you are a strange girl in some ways. But Edgar was sent away, and then you let the engagement be announced.'

He looked at me with a little smile that was almost sad.

'You should not have done that, Jane. It meant I had no choice, and limited time. I had to think how to do it. Not in the house, and you were guarded out of it. Except on your walks and you did not go far abroad—not so far that a scream could not be heard. But I watched you, and found that spot you favoured. It suited my purpose well. It made it easy for me to set out on a day's business and return across the moor unobserved. After that, I had to persuade you to come with me. I did not think it would be difficult. You are a girl who rises to a challenge; and of course you had nothing to fear from me, or so you thought.'

I said, from a dry mouth: 'Why?'

He looked at me with a frown, but more of surprise than anything else.

'Why what?'

'Why do you talk like this—and threaten me? Because of marrying Michael? But what does that matter to you?'

He twisted the heather in his fingers, releasing its scent on the air.

'A great deal.'

'But if Michael dies—if there is no heir—it is Edgar who will inherit Carmaliot, not you! Or do you plan to murder him as well?'

I could no longer cling to the ghost of a belief that he was joking, and that meant he must be mad. But surely even madness had chinks through which reason might force a way?

He looked at me as though it were I who was being irrational.

'Edgar? He is my brother, in full blood. If I would not hurt Michael, how could you imagine I would lift a hand to him?'

'Then why?', I cried. 'To gain him an inheritance? Would you murder for *that*?'

He said simply: 'Not for Edgar. For Mama.' I stared at him. 'She has been slighted so long, and been patient under the slighting. That necklace Father gave you ... I will leave Carmaliot because I have my way to make in the world, but I could not leave knowing she must stay to see Michael's wife take her place as mistress and bear a child to usurp her son. The thought of it would be unbearable.'

His tone was patient. Mad, yes, but hideously resolved. I said, trying to keep fear out of my voice:

'I will go away. Tomorrow. Today, if you like.'

He shook his head. 'Father would go after you, and bring you back.'

'I promise you he will not find me!' He smiled, unmoved. 'If you like, I will go to Edgar—marry him as he asked. I will do whatever you say—anything ...'

His gaze convicted my protestations of absurdity. He said, his voice mild:

'It is no use, Jane. I have made my preparations. It will be better if no body is found. They will perhaps think a band of tinners have abducted you, or else that you have wandered on to the moor and met with an accident—fallen down an old shaft maybe. There are several close to the house, which they can search. It is better, too, that there should be uncertainty of what has happened.'

My breast was heaving, and he said: 'You are distressed, and I have no taste for cruelty. Since you know what must be, let us end it quickly.'

He moved towards me without haste. For an instant I was paralysed, a rabbit in front of a stoat; before fear changed and spurred me to action. I managed to get to my feet as his hand caught my dress, and heard the cloth rip. I ran, blindly, to be away from him. He had me within yards, his right arm hard against my throat, his left hand gripping my wrist. I screamed, my throat compressed against his arm.

He said, his own voice scarcely raised: 'It makes no difference. Scream, if you like.'

I struggled against his hold. Michael had saved me from Edgar, but here there was no one. He was forcing me forward. I had thought he meant to strangle me, but he did not even try to muffle my cries. Then I saw the shaft head in front, a few feet off, and knew his intention.

I struggled harder, in an effort not only to tear myself free but to avoid the gaping hole. He altered his position, dragging me. I tried to brace myself against the pull, but futilely. I heard my boots scrape against stone. We were beside the shaft, and he lifted me as easily as though I were a child. Emptiness was beneath me, and now I clung to him, holding on instead of pulling away. He pressed me back and down, and I still kept a grip on his coat. Then with a sudden sharp movement of his arm he forced me hard against the top edge of the shaft. The shock drove breath from my body: I let go and fell into blackness.

18

As I fell I cried out in fear—in the expectation of imminent death. And as I cried, I clawed with my hands at the blackness. I felt something, grasped at it, lost it and grasped it again. A rough abrasive surface rasped through my fingers, burning them. One of the ropes that still dangled from the shaft-head.... I found it with my other hand, seized it and hung on. I was suspended, swaying, bumping against the rough wall of the shaft.

I looked up. The square of light was broken by the outline of a head. I called, feebly, then more loudly:

'Help me.... For God's sake, help me!'

John's voice came down, echoing. 'Let go. You must, Jane.'

I cried again: 'Help me.' He said:

'You are only making yourself suffer. You will not be able to hold on for long. Let it happen now. Let go.'

My mind whirled in pain and despair. I could only repeat:

'Help me. For the love of God ...'

'I will help you.'

He paused, and hope cruelly rushed in. He said:

'I have no knife, but there is one on my saddle.'

The square of light was clear as he rose from kneeling by it. A knife.... He would slash the rope and let me drop into the depths. I wondered if I could climb the rope before he returned. I tried, but my arms lacked the strength. Harry might have managed it, but I could not. I attempted once more to pull myself up, but could only hang.

How long before he returned? A minute? It depended how far the horse had wandered in its cropping. And then.... I heard again the plop of the stone in water. Would I die at once, or drown more slowly? I did not want to, but could not help looking down.

My eyes had grown more accustomed to the dimness. I could see down the shaft—not to the bottom but a few yards at least. The wall was lined with crumbling stone. On one side it ran down, regular and unbroken. On the other ...

I strained to see: was that an opening, a ledge? If I could not climb the rope, I could let myself down by it. It was frightening to go down deeper into the blackness, but I forced myself. The hole was nearer and more plain: an adit leading off the vertical shaft. John would be back any second.... I was almost level with the adit, but nearer to the facing wall, unable to reach it. Desperately I kicked back, got my foot against the wall, shoved forward. I had a hazy glimpse of a level surface and let go the rope. I landed heavily, my arms and the upper part of my body inside the tunnel, the rest of me hanging in the shaft. I could feel myself slipping and scrabbled frantically to pull myself in. For a moment it hung in doubt; then with a last effort I heaved forward and inside.

I lay there, panting, too exhausted to move. My ears roared with the pulse of blood, but all round there was stillness. After a while, beyond the roaring and the silence, a distant voice:

'Jane....'

It came from above, from the top of the shaft. John's voice, distorted and echoing. I was on the point of calling back before I stopped myself. He spoke more loudly, and I could imagine him kneeling by the shaft-head, peering down into the darkness:

'Are you there, Jane?'

I crouched back but did not move for fear of making a

214

noise that would betray my presence. I could see the two ropes, to one of which I had clung, and watched them jiggle in the dim light as he tried them, and found them free of any weight except their own. His voice came down; gentle, melancholy.

'God rest you, Jane.'

After that, silence.

It was a long time before I moved. He might come back, to check again. I counted seconds into minutes, over and over. I could see the wall of the shaft, the hanging ropes, the rough-hewn sides and the uneven rocky floor of the gallery in which I sat. Gradually the conviction grew that he had gone. Across the moor, though not towards Carmaliot. He would want his presence vouched for a long way from home.

The conviction brought with it a small sense of victory. He thought me dead—smashed to pieces or drowned at the foot of the shaft. But I was alive, with no worse hurt than bruises, and hands smarting from the friction of the rope. And living, I had hope. It grew and blossomed. I found myself able to pray, and calmer for it. If I had been saved so far, might I not be saved altogether? I could believe it.

With a degree of composure regained, I could think more clearly. I reflected on what would happen at Carmaliot. Already someone might be wondering where I was, but it would not be until I failed to appear for luncheon that they would start looking for me in earnest. What time was it now? I felt for my fob-watch but found only a tear in my gown: it must have been ripped away in the struggle or the fall. But I had consulted it just before John's talk turned menacing and it had been a little after eleven. Luncheon was at one.

They would look in the house first, then in the immediate vicinity. How long before the search fanned out and took in the moor? An hour? Two? We had travelled more than half an hour on John's horse. It would be four or five hours before there would be a hope of a search party being near enough to hear a cry for help. It was a dispiriting thought, but at least rational. I could save my breath till then.

My eyes had grown increasingly more used to the dimness, my vision sharper. I could see a place in the wall where someone, a tinner doubtless, had started carving an inscription and not finished it. M A, it read. His sweetheart's name, or wife's? Mary, or Maud? But likely old and withered now, or dead, the pair of them. I thought of him crouching here, chiselling into the rock face. A lettered man, unusual in one of his condition. The thought, and the letters themselves, comforted me.

Behind me lay the darkness of the tunnel. As time went by I thought I detected, far off, a glimmer of light, no more than a trace, in the blackness. But I was not sure: it could be my eyes, confused by the shadows, playing tricks on me. Nor did it matter if there was light there. The light from the shaft was closer, and my hopes rested in it. I would not move from this spot. When my rescuers came, I would be ready for them.

Time passed; but I had no idea what o'clock it was. Hunger told me, hinting at first then naggingly, that it was likely to be luncheon time, then luncheon past. But how far past? I craned my neck and stared up the shaft. The square at the top was blue still, but that did not help much.

Two or three o'clock, I had thought, but it could be later. There might be men up there, searching for me. I called out, tentatively, then more firmly. My voice echoed in the shaft. I called and listened, called and listened again. The echoes of my voice died into a silence as complete and impenetrable as the black gulf beneath me.

The hope and confidence I had been feeling crashed suddenly. I found myself calling over and over, not listening to anything but the sound of it reverberating round me. As the echoes came back, I called more wildly; in the end I screamed. That too returned, distorted and magnified—

a shriek of the condemned. I sank back against the rock face, exhausted and shivering.

Little by little I recovered. Shame helped: I shivered with that instead of fear as I contemplated my own behaviour. I made a resolve: to call out each five minutes or so. I did so once, and waited. I tried counting seconds again, but could not keep to it. Was a minute gone by—or two, or three? A little longer and I called once more; and listened to the silence settle in its wake.

It became a routine—dull, and my thoughts duller still. Dusk crept on me unawares. I did not notice the diminution of what little light there was around me, but looked up, after some interval, to the top of the shaft, and was startled to see that the square was darker blue. The day was fading, night approaching. I had another fit of crying out, as senseless as the first. My throat was sore when fatigue put an end to it.

And the square was darkening fast. I told myself it made no difference—that they would go on hunting with lanterns—but that did little for me. All I knew was that night was falling and I was alone and trapped. I prayed again, but it was a prayer of desperation.

Gradually blackness gathered, a void of light to match the void of hope. I looked a last time up the shaft and saw only one bright star. Hunger returned, more urgently, a pain rather than a need; and was joined by thirst. My mouth was dry, my tongue felt swollen. I wondered, self-pityingly, if they had given up the search—were perhaps all seated round the long dining table, eating and drinking wine. John, too, no doubt: he would have made his way back by now.

I could no longer see my hand before my face: I might as well have been blind. I thought of the miners, who had worked down here. At least they had had lanterns. But even with lanterns they had feared the darkness of the tunnels. The knackers.... On a pleasant afternoon, picnicking beside the lake, the notion had been something to shiver at and forget. It was different now. Little old wrinkled men, evil and malicious, who could take on monstrous shapes, appearing and vanishing at will. I was being silly, I told myself: it was an absurd country tale. But fear would not be subdued by common sense. If such things did exist, with the under-earth their domain ... would they not, with the powers they possessed, know of this intruder into their kingdom? Might they not even now be travelling, silent and malevolent, along this tunnel in whose mouth I lay? I shrank back. Or climbing the shaft from recesses deeper still...? My heart leapt with fear.

With hunger, thirst and terror, I did not believe I could ever sleep. Even without those tormentors, a rocky floor was the only bed I had. But in the end I slept, and dreamt wild dreams. I was with Harry on a ship and he, though no older, wore an admiral's hat. The sea was blue, a salt breeze blew, and I was happy. Then the ship was no longer sailing, but berthed in a gloomy port, and I was aware of others—menacing figures, ugly faces. One in particular, whom I feared and hated. And the ship turned into the chapel at Carmaliot, and strong arms held me powerless. The loathed one stood before me, and it was Edgar, but with my father's face.

I awoke, trembling, cramped and cold and wretched with fright. Blackness—no candle by my bed. No bed but rock, no sound but the sound of my own panting breath. I wept; then tried to check my weeping for fear the knackers would hear it.

Later, after lying huddled in misery for what seemed an age, I drifted into sleep again, and dreamt again. In this dream there was no horror. I was back in Portsmouth, in the house at Pratt Street, and all the family were there except Papa. I did not know why he was absent and did not care. It was Christmas and we were feasting—on goose with sage and apple stuffing, roast potatoes and peas and cabbage. Everyone was noisy and cheerful—a fire blazed in the hearth. I told Harry I was thirsty and he poured me a glass of sarsaparilla. I drank it, and asked him for another and another

218

after that, and he poured them for me, laughing at my having a thirst that could not be satisfied. Then I awoke. The thirst was there, but nothing else: no blazing fire but blackness.

So the night interminably passed. At last there was faint light in the shaft, which grew and hope once more grew with it. Whether or not the search had continued through the night, they would start again with the dawn. I called for help, and though only silence answered my cry was not too despondent. The light kept up my spirits.

The weather had changed. The square above did not turn blue but grey, and raindrops pattered down the shaft. I put my hand out and tried to catch them, but they were scant: one landed on my palm and I licked it off. I thought the rain must be slight, until I realized that even in a downpour few drops would fall so far without striking the wall of the shaft. Later I heard something drip on to the ledge. I reached up and found the wall wet above. I cupped my hands for the drips, but they were maddeningly slow. In the end I reached up and tried to scrape moisture from the rock with my palm. The little I got gave my dry mouth more torment than relief.

Time went by. I called, though less strongly, and listened for an answer. There was nothing. I suddenly realized, with bleak conviction, that I had been wasting my breath all along. From so far down the shaft I would not be heard on the surface except by someone directly above the hole. And if anyone took that post he would call down, to see if I still lived.

Nor was there reason to believe anyone would call—would even come to this place. I had been on foot, and they would have no reason for suspecting I had strayed so far. They would search the area around Carmaliot, within a mile or two of the house, over and over again maybe, but they would not come here.

I stared out at the wall of the shaft. No one would come here, except some idle sightseer, months or years hence, to peer into the blank windows of the buildings as I had done yesterday and idly throw a stone down to hear it strike water. Long before that I would be dead, but the dying could be long, too. There was no point in praying, except to pray my end might be soon.

John had been right in that, at least. It would have been better for me not to have gripped the rope, or for him to have slashed it. I looked at the two ropes dangling in the shaft. I had tried to swarm up the one to which I clung, and failed, but I had been weak from shock and the fear of John's return. Was it worth trying again? I did not think I could do it, but did it matter if I failed, and crashed to the foot of the shaft? It would end things.

I resolved to tackle it, and without delay. I knelt at the tunnel's lip and stretched my arm out to the nearer rope. It was no good. The ropes hung closer to the opposite side; at my furthest stretch I was inches short of touching it. I sat back against the tunnel wall, and wept tears of frustration. The tears fell on my hands, and I licked where they had fallen, feeling their saltness on my tongue.

For a long time after I sat in mindless despair. There was no point in doing anything, thinking anything: the only thing to look for was death, the only hope that it would come quickly and not too painfully—a poor hope that, with thirst raking me again. I had turned away from the shaft and was gazing, blindly though with open eyes, into the tunnel's darkness. A black void, yet not absolutely black. The hint of a glimmer of light, which I had noticed yesterday afternoon. It was there again—but real, or an illusion?

I struggled to my feet: one could stand upright in the tunnel though only by stooping. I started walking forward, away from the shaft. My head bumped painfully against a bump of rock in the roof, but I kept going. I had an impression of the tunnel bending to the left, and realized it must be true when I looked back and saw no sign of the shaft entrance. It was dark all about me, but the glimmer ahead was stronger.

I walked on, feeling along the tunnel wall with my out-stretched hand.

The light *was* stronger. I struggled towards it with the clumsy determination of a moth. I could just make out the line of the tunnel wall in front, and further off an opening. I scrambled on more quickly. It was pale and indirect, but it must be daylight. Then I came out into an open space.

It was very small, the bottom of another shaft. I could tilt my head back and look up at the sky, though the hole at the top was more ragged in outline—overgrown, I guessed, by vegetation. The walls, a single glance told me, were un-scaleable—smooth and vertical. And there were no ropes here, even if I had the strength to climb.

From looking up, I turned to look about me. This was a junction of tunnels: two others, apart from the one I had come through, led away from it. The floor was littered with loose stones and at one point, partly blocking the mouth of a tunnel there was what I took to be a jumbled heap of white sticks; until I looked more closely, and saw they were not sticks but bones.

It was the shattered skeleton of some quite large animal—a sheep, probably. It must have fallen down the shaft, and rotted here. I turned from it in distaste, and noticed some-thing else. On the far side there was a depression in the rocky floor; and water had collected in it from the rain whose residue still seeped down the chimney above. In a moment I had dropped to my knees and was drinking from it, greedily, like an animal.

Afterwards, I considered my situation. Essentially it was unchanged: I was just as deep underground, with no better prospect of rescue. But at least I had slaked my thirst, and could again: there was still water in the little pool. And I had the light of day directly over me. A drop of rain landed on my face.

Hope, or rather its pale shadow, came back. I had water—enough, perhaps, if I used it sparingly or the rains continued, to last a few days. It would give them more chance to find me. If they did not ... I looked at the sheep's skeleton. If not, in due course there would be another heap of bones, to keep it company.

The day passed slowly. I sat, getting to my feet occasionally to stretch my legs, and sometimes thought of things and people I remembered, and at others let my mind drift aimlessly. Hunger brought food constantly to my mind, with visions of steaks and pies and puddings—tantalizing recollections of sight and smell and taste.

I thought of Andrew, and the kiss he had taken. Suddenly, even more than the longing for food I had a longing for that, to have him hold me warmly in his arms. I felt again the urge to surrender to his strength, and this time did not resent it. I shook my head. It made no difference, anyway. Both surrender and resistance belonged to another world. The realities here were sterner and past challenging.

Night came again. The square of light above turned from grey to black. No star: there would be cloud covering the sky. I wondered if the wind was sweeping across the moor. There was no way of knowing: no breath or sound of a gale could penetrate down here. I did not even know if it were still raining. I heard the faint occasional drip of water into the little pool, but that would continue for some time after the rain had stopped.

The second night was like the first, nightmarish spells of sleep alternating with cramped and wretched wakefulness. I had panicky fears again about knackers, and once imagined I heard something coming towards me along one of the tunnels. I listened, petrified, but all was silent.

I had a dream, interrupted by periods of half-wakefulness but continuing, about my childhood. It was a happy dream, set in a day of sunshine, and I wanted it to go on. When a full waking drove it from me I was miserable, and would have sunk back into it if I could. I thought about it, hugging what details I could remember, to hold onto it. A dream of happiness, in every respect but one: it was of my childhood, yet Harry had not been there.

But he could not be, I reasoned: I had been only three or four myself, so he would not have been born. Or be only a baby.

I sat sharply upright as into my mind a scene came sharply: not from the dream but from the reality of the past. A memory and, I knew it to be true. As on that time when I had lain awake in bed after being given Dr Roberts' Black Drops, my father was with me, and I was happy with him, loving not hating. We were in the garden of the little cottage we had lived in before we moved to Pratt Street, on the outskirts of the city. Recalling it now, and the happiness I had known there, I was astonished that I should otherwise have forgotten it so completely—forgotten the grass and the butterflies, the dazzling daisy-tree, the red and blue of peonies and asters, sweetpeas scenting the air, the musk-roses round the arbour my father had built for us to sit in of a summer afternoon.... And the little rustic bench he had built for me, on which I now sat while he told me a story.

I had forgotten what good stories he told, as well: long and involved but so engrossing that I never wanted them to stop. This was one of my favourites, about a dog we had lost some months before. He had been called Bosun, and in my father's tale he had been so taken up with his nautical name that he decided to go to sea. So he had signed on (my father gravely said) as a Ship's Dog. All sorts of adventures came his way, many familiar from previous tellings but some new, or newly embroidered. But the end was always the same: the ship was wrecked in the South Seas and Bosun, clinging to a spar, was washed up on the shores of the Fiji Islands. And the islanders, finding him on the sands and being amazed by this creature who was black like themselves but so strange in shape (they had never seen a dog before, my father said), made him their King, so that now he sat on a golden throne, with a golden bowl to eat from, in a land of perpetual sunshine.

That was the bit I loved most, and we were still some way from it when my mother called me from the back door. She had to go out, she said, and I must come in and look after Baby. I protested that I was listening, but she simply repeated it more sharply, and my father said I had better do as I was told—we would finish the story another time. And I whispered to him fiercely:

'I hate him. I *hate* him!'

He patted me on the shoulder, not unkindly but his voice was firm:

'Nay, lass, you mustn't hate your little brother. That will never do.'

So I went into the house with dragging feet. He was lying in his cot, and I thought how happy I had been before he came to spoil it all. I stared at his round fat face. Babies often died, didn't they? Why could not he?

That was where the scene ended. I could remember nothing after, but remembered those few minutes with the sharpness of yesterday. Could it be true—had it happened like that? Had there been a time when it was my father I loved, Harry whom I hated? Wretchedly I was forced to acknowledge it. My hatred was not so pure and simple as I had thought it; but neither was my love. I looked at myself, and did not like what I saw.

Tiredness put an end to self-reproach, and I slept again. My dream this time was not a cheerful one, and not far removed either in time or space. I was here, trapped underground. Something was approaching me, a tramp of feet that sounded like a giant. I waited, unable to move, watching one of the tunnel mouths. The tramp was heavier and nearer. I thought of running away along one of the other tunnels (it was black night in my dream, too, but somehow I could see); then realized I was not sure down which tunnel the feet were coming. But I chose one at last, and ran towards it. And as

224

I did the figure, small but squat, immensely powerful, hideously grinning, was in front of me.

My own screams woke me. All round there was blackness, impenetrable, but in my mind I could see him still. I shook as though in a fever. Only gradually, over minutes, did some sort of composure return.

And that was when I heard it: a sound faint at first but growing, loud in the embracing silence: the sound of footsteps. Like those others, they were coming nearer, coming along one of the tunnels which led to where I lay. And I was wide awake. I struggled to my feet in terror. The knackers ... I had roused them by my screaming. I wanted to cry out, but knew there was no one to help. I stared into the blackness: the footsteps were very loud.

Then I saw light in the blackness, for a moment before I fainted.

19

Something touched my face. I was aware of light through my eyelids but would not open my eyes for fear of what I should see. A hand was lifting me. I could visualize it—gnarled and black, more beast-like than human—and screamed again. Then a voice quietening me, calling my name:

'Jane . . . are you all right? There's nothing to be frightened of. I promise you.'

Andrew's voice. I opened my eyes. In the light of the miner's lantern I saw him bending over me. I whispered:

'Another dream?'

He shook his head. 'No dream. You are safe now.'

He helped me to my feet, and as he did I clung to him, putting my head against his chest. I still could not believe it. He would vanish and I would be left in blackness. I wanted one thing, but desperately—that before that happened he would kiss me. It was all I needed, but the need was an agony.

Gently he disengaged me from him. I hated that, but knew anything he did was right. And I knew at last he was really beside me, and no ghost. He said:

'Here.'

He took a flask from his pocket, and put it to my lips. I drank obediently, choking on the fiery liquor. My eyes were streaming, and he gave me a handkerchief to wipe them.

'Now water.' He produced another flask, and I drank from it greedily. 'And food, of a kind. Only a couple of cold pasties, but better than nothing.'

The cook at Carmaliot made Cornish pasties for the men when they were working away from home. They were a labourer's diet, originally a frugal preparation for the miners to take underground with them. I had never eaten one before: one did not find them in Portsmouth and it was unthinkable in Cornwall to serve them to the gentry. But I never recalled tasting anything in my life as good. While I ate Andrew watched me. His face, shadowed in the lamplight, was much like I had seen it that first day on the moor, with a stubble of beard, dark brown glinting coppery red. And yet it was so different. How could I have thought those blue eyes hard?

I finished eating and asked, not really curious because now it seemed something inevitable:

'How did you find me?'

'The others were searching above ground. Dozens of them, scouring the moors. This is the part I know best. I know the old shafts and the tunnels that lead to them.'

'But what made you think I would be here?'

'It is easy enough to fall down a shaft—many of them are overgrown and one false step is enough. I have lost more sheep that way than I care to remember. I went to Carmaliot as soon as the news came that you were missing—the evening before last. I wanted them to concentrate on exploring the shafts. John Bedivere opposed it. He said you must be near home, unless tinners had made off with you, and that was where the search should be. They listened to him, not me.'

I said: 'He had reason on his side.'

'Reason?'

'Since he knew where I was.'

He looked at me; then said:

'Tell me.'

I told him all, about Edgar as well as John. He quietly listened and nodded at the end; but the nod was fearsome, the blue eyes savage. He spoke to me gently, though.

'Listen, Jane, it is getting towards day.' He gestured upwards, beyond the circle of lamplight, and I looked and saw

the top of the shaft pale grey with dawn. 'I can take you out
with me the way I came, but it is hard going in places—very
hard. Or I can leave you here ...'

'No!'

'Until I can get a ladder down to you from above. That
would be the easier thing, as far as you are concerned. You
are weak from what you have endured, and the journey out
through the tunnels would try you heavily.'

'I want to go with you.' Any other idea was unthinkable.
'Andrew, please.'

He looked at me; then smiled and I was happy.

'All right. Are you ready now, or do you want to rest a
while?'

I looked at the rocky earth all round me, at the skeleton
of the sheep, the shallow pool from which I had drunk.

'Now,' I said. 'I'm not tired.'

I had not been lying when I said that, but weariness came
on me before long. He had not exaggerated when he said
the going would be hard. At best one had to stoop continually,
and generally far more than in the stretch I had traversed
from my original position; but there were many places where
the roof was so low that one had no choice but to crawl on
hands and knees, and even then find one's head banging
painfully against stone.

There were parts where the tunnels had been reinforced
with wooden props which sometimes creaked alarmingly;
and others where there had been a caving in, and we were
forced to crawl through narrow channels over rubble. I
thought of the weight of earth over our heads and the risk
that at any moment there might be another fall, pinning us
down. But I did not feel afraid. Andrew was ahead of me
with the lamp. I did not believe anything could go wrong
now.

All the same, I soon tired, my muscles more and more
weakened by the unaccustomed strains this crawling and

228

stooping progress put on them. I determined I would not give in and beg for a rest, so gritted my teeth and forced my aching legs to new efforts. The ache there was matched by another in my back, a conflict of agonies. Andrew now and then called back to ask how I was getting on, and I managed to mumble some sort of reassurance through clenched teeth.

We came to another junction of galleries. There was no shaft to the surface, but the roof was higher. It was possible to stand upright. I tried to do so, and almost fainted with pain. I bent my back again, but that was torture, too. I thought I could totter forward, stooping, but my legs would not carry me. I found myself falling forward quite helplessly. I would have crashed to the ground had not Andrew, turning at the sound of the small moan that had escaped me, put out an arm and held me.

He eased me to the ground, and knelt beside me. His hands massaged me: my back first until I could straighten it and look at him, then my legs. His fingers, strongly kneading, were no hostile invaders but brought relief from burning pain, a comfort that made me want to swoon. And more than that: a tingling joy which went out to the extremities of my body.

He asked: 'Better?'

I nodded. 'Yes.' He stared at me.

'You're a fool.'

'Am I?'

I did not mind him chiding me if he would stroke me still. But he did not. He shook his head, in wonder almost.

'I blame myself. I should have realized, and made you rest. My muscles are accustomed to this work, and yours are not. But you said you were all right, and I was fool enough to believe you.'

'I'm all right now.'

'When you set yourself a course you look neither left nor right, but gallop a straight line like a blinkered horse. And you will not give in, even though the advantage of doing so is enormous, and the cost trivial. Except that nothing is trivial, is it, where your pride is concerned?'

I said meekly: 'I'm sorry.'

'Are you? I wonder. You would do the same again.'

I listened, enjoying the sound of his voice and not particularly concerned with what he said. He insisted that I should rest for quite a long time, and I had no objection to that, either: I wanted to be free of this confinement, enjoying the liberty of fresh air, the sight of sky, but the need was less urgent. I was almost sorry when he decided I was once more fit to travel.

He had explained that this part of the mine was relatively unfamiliar to him—the workings themselves stretched many miles, a product of centuries of tunnelling—but that he had left markers by which he could retrace a path to the main entrance. At one point, though, his tracking went adrift, and we were obliged to cast about. We traversed, in doing so, a tunnel whose side had caved in badly, forcing us once more to crawl over rubble. I saw the golden gleam in the lamplight and called to him, my voice echoing:

'Andrew!'

He stopped, and looked back. 'What is it?'

'Look ... gold!'

The rock face which had been exposed was full of little specks that shone in the light as he brought the lantern closer. There must be enough gold there, I thought, to make him a wealthy man. I watched his face, as he studied the rock, but no excitement appeared. He shook his head.

'Pyrites. Fairy gold, they call it.'

'I'm sorry.'

It was a pity he would not be rich, but it did not matter. He looked at me, and shrugged.

'Are you all right to go on?'

I nodded. 'Yes.'

The going grew easier as the tunnels became broader and higher. We reached a gallery in which rails had been laid, and there were one or two abandoned small trucks which had been used to transport ore. The gallery widened, and in the distance the blackness turned grey with a promise of daylight. We could walk upright, and side by side. I said suddenly:

'When we get out ...'

'Yes?'

'Will you take me to Carmaliot?'

I was asking, not requiring. Whatever he decided was right. He said:

'Not until I have dealt with John Bedivere. You shall come back home and Emily will look after you.'

I was pleased by that. I had no fear of John with Andrew beside me, but I did not want to go back to Carmaliot. The light was much stronger and as the tunnel curved I could see the tunnel mouth and a patch of blue sky. It would be nice to see Emily again. The inadequacy of the thought appalled me as I recalled the fate from which I had escaped. To see Emily—breathe fresh air, feel the sun's warmth, eat and drink and sleep in a bed: all the things I had taken for granted were wonders beyond reckoning. To live. . . .

I started trying to say something to Andrew—to express, however inadequately, my gratitude. We came out into the open as I was talking, and I blinked at the sunlight: the weather had changed again and it was a radiant morning.

Then he stopped, and put a hand on my arm. I wondered if I had said something foolish, and my words trailed off. Only after that did I follow his gaze. Just outside the mine entrance stood an old stone drinking trough. A horse was tethered nearby. Sitting on the edge of the trough was John Bedivere.

He had not noticed us at that point—he was whistling a tune as he inspected the side of one of his boots. The confidence I had felt a few minutes before evaporated. I remembered the horrors and even with Andrew by me felt monstrously afraid. And at that instant he looked up, and the whistling stopped.

For a long moment he stared at us, as though unwilling to accept the evidence of his eyes. Perhaps he would take to his heels, I thought; our appearance must have shaken him, too. I desperately hoped for it, for anything which would put off a confrontation. He stood up and half turned away, fiddling with the pocket of his coat. But instead of retreating, he walked towards us. He said:

'I should always trust the prickle in my thumbs. I was unhappy, Andy, when I heard you were poking around in your warren underground. There seemed no good ground for uneasiness. She was dead, I was certain. The chances of your finding her body were tiny, the possibility of connecting her death with me non-existent. But I was unhappy about it all the same. I thought it worth a journey, and the tedium of waiting for the mole to break ground, to have a word with you. I thought I might keep an eye on your activities—perhaps steer them in the right direction. I must say, I did not expect anything like this.'

Andrew said: 'I am taking Jane home. I will deal with you afterwards. Do not imagine you can lie your way out of it.'

John smiled. It disconcerted me that he seemed so unperturbed. He said:

'Quite impossible, I agree.' He turned his gaze, apparently amiable, on me. 'How are you, coz? A little dishevelled, I see. Not quite the glass of fashion. But in robust health, it appears. I should quite enjoy hearing the tale of how you escaped from that fall, but it would be wasting time that might be of the essence. So I fear I must forgo the satisfaction of curiosity.'

Andrew said quietly: 'Get back, Jane. Away from here.'

'No.' John's voice was colder. 'She must stay where she is.'

He was standing perhaps ten paces from us. Andrew took a step forward, and John said:

'Both stay.'

One hand was in that pocket with which he had fiddled

before approaching us. He brought it out, and it held a pistol. Andrew stopped. He was in front and trying to cover me. John levelled the gun.

'It is cocked,' he said. 'Both barrels are cocked, in fact. And fortunately I am a tolerably good shot, so there should be no messy business of merely winging you. Fortunately, too, it should not be difficult disposing of the bodies in your beloved mine.'

Andrew said: 'Let her go. If you do ...'

'Don't be absurd. And don't think me fool enough to let you waste time. Now, I think.'

Fear had me rooted. Then I saw him sighting the pistol, with Andrew as his target. I broke away, running towards him and the gun. The bang was very loud and I felt something tear hotly into my side: I cried, and fell.

Andrew had started running immediately I did, calling out something which I could not distinguish. He was past me as I went down and had flung himself on to John, grappling with him for the pistol. Shocked and dazed, I watched them struggle, and tried to get to my feet—I started to rise but collapsed again. Sunlight flashed from the metal of the gun as they fought for it.

The second explosion, lying helpless as I was, shocked me more than the first. I saw the two figures collapse in a heap on the ground. Slowly one of them freed himself and stood up. I saw it was Andrew. It did not matter if I fainted now, I thought; and did.

20

Dr Roberts was a small plump hairy man: not only was he full and curly of beard and head, but black and silver hairs grew out of his ears and his eyebrows were bushy and tufted. Hair was also thick on the backs of the small delicate fingers with which he had just been replacing the dressing on my wound. He rinsed his hands in the bowl and dried them on his handkerchief; then gestured to my nurse to take the bowl out. She was a woman from the village, a tall gaunt silent creature but said to be skilled in nursing. He said, in his surprisingly deep and rustic voice:

'It looks clean enough. There is no sign of an inflammation developing.'

'Thank you,' I said.

He shrugged. 'It is due more, I fancy, to your having healing flesh than to any skill of mine. You were fortunate, young lady, that the bullet passed through your side and did not lodge; and even more fortunate in that it did so little damage in its passage. An inch to the right, and there would have been two coffins to find room for in the family vault, instead of one.'

He spoke in a grimly jesting tone: the reference was to John, who was to be buried the following afternoon. When I made no comment, he went on:

'Lucky in every respect: the scar will not show, even in such décolletage as is favoured for ball dresses these days. How do you feel in yourself?'

'Very well.'

'You are a sturdy creature.' His look was dispassionate. 'I was impressed when you made no outcry while I was treating your wound yesterday. Sir Donald had the right of it in looking for healthy new stock to graft into the Bedivere line.' He shook his head. 'Though I doubt he will live to see the fruit.'

'How is he today?'

'No worse, no better. It does not promise well.'

The news of my recovery after being almost given up for lost, coupled with the news of his youngest son's villainy and death, had brought on a seizure. He too had been put to bed, with one side of his body paralysed, and the power of speech lost. I asked:

'And ... Lady Bedivere?'

'There is no change in her, except for one thing. She has ceased her smiling.' He peered at me from under the tufted brows. 'Your coming to Carmaliot has been a cause of much tumult, has it not?'

'I did not ask to be brought here.'

'True. And if you had I do not see you would have been blameworthy. One can be a cause without being a responsible cause. Not that I feel inclined to make any judgement on matters touching responsibility. The physician's province is the body—thank God our profession has never been tempted to meddle with the soul.'

He drew on his gloves and picked up his black bag, while I watched him from the bed. He said abruptly:

'I saw Michael downstairs. He asked me to ascertain if you were fit to receive visitors, and also if you were so inclined. As to the first, my answer is affirmative. The second, of course, is related to your opinion, not mine. What message shall I take?'

I felt tired suddenly, and was glad of the heaped pillows at my back, supporting me. I said:

'If he wishes to visit me, of course I shall be happy to see him.'

He nodded. 'Till tomorrow, then. I have left a draught with Mrs Wherry, to give you if you are restless in the night.'

When Michael did not come in the next half hour, I thought he had changed his mind or that something had occurred to occupy him, and was glad of it. It was not that I had a distaste for seeing him, but rather that I did not feel equal to contending with any company except my own. I felt a dull disappointment when he knocked at last and I was obliged to bid him enter.

'I waited for the post,' he said. 'I hoped there might be something in it that would cheer you. And I believe there is.'

He passed me an envelope in Harry's hand, and I thanked him. He said:

'How do you feel today? Dr Roberts says you are p-progressing well.'

I said I was. I was aware of constraint in my manner, a failure in response, but could do nothing about it. My wound was an excuse: no one would expect me to be lively. Michael did his best to make up for my deficiency, talking cheerfully and on neutral topics. I was grateful for that. Only at the end did he say:

'My father is not likely to recover fully, it seems. I am not sure if he understands much, or anything, of the things around him.'

'I am sorry.'

His thin pale face was fixed on me. He blinked.

'Since one c-cannot communicate with him, I suppose it is best to act in accordance with the wishes one knew him to have. Our marriage. Despite all that has happened—his own seizure as well—I b-believe he would not want it delayed. What do you think?'

I said, trying to dispel listlessness from my tone but only

doubtfully succeeding: 'I am sure you're right.'

He nodded, smiling. 'You are tired, my dear. I will go, and let you rest.'

Outside it was blowing half a gale: from my window I could see clouds scudding past, grey-black, with fugitive patches of blue. In my room there was warmth and peace, a fire stoked up and crackling. I lay in clean sweet-smelling linen, with every comfort I could require within call. How different a situation from that of the girl, cold and frightened and dirty, suffering from hunger and thirst, who only two days since had huddled underground in the lonely recesses of the earth.

Between her and me there was no link except identity, and even that was tenuous. I remembered times when I had been ill with a fever, and how the landscape of delirium with its bright ballooning spaces and high echoing sounds had been so inaccessible and alien to my later saner self. The time underground was something like that. Especially, I reflected, forcing myself to the thought—especially the time with Andrew.

I did not deny it, nor the feelings I had had. It had been ravishing, an experience I had never known nor dreamt existed, and real, then. But a dream is always real to the dreamer: afterwards the more basic reality of everyday life, with its duties and obligations, takes shape again, and the dream bursts into bubbles that float away on the river of living. It was precious, and always would be, but I did not wish to keep it nor pursue the fleeting fragments. It had been an idyll, a surrender, to put behind one and forget.

From the standpoint of obligations, priorities were clear. I owed my life to Andrew, but so I did to Michael—my life and my escape from a beastly degradation far worse than anything that could have happened to me when I was trapped underground. And the obligation to Michael came first, and had been sealed by my decision. I had hesitated

237

before I promised myself to him, and the hesitation made the contract that much more binding.

All that stood against it were my own desires. In the mine, miraculously saved and dazzled by my rescuer, I had succumbed to them. But that had been an interspace, a time outside time. Now I was myself again, and knew that desires were things to be subjected to will. And will must follow conscience.

While I had been brooding, the letter from Harry had lain unopened on the bed. I shook my head: my lethargy must be more deeply rooted than I had thought.

I opened it, and read it.

It was a cheerful letter, saying little except that while life had its hardships he did not mind them: he spoke of unfamiliar names, other midshipmen—new friends who would accompany him in his new life.

My duties to him, at least, were at an end, and I could rejoice freely in his happiness. He could no longer, probably, look to Sir Donald for particular favours, but that had never mattered compared with my need not to be responsible for depriving him of them. With or without a sister married to or widow of a wealthy baronet, Harry would make his way.

Compared with my need ... I considered myself with tired contempt. The least such a person could do was to turn her back on selfish considerations, and honestly pay her debts.

Andrew came while John's funeral was being held. I had known this must happen and thought I was prepared, but felt my heart beating faster, a hurtful traitor in my breast, when Mrs Wherry showed him in. I forced myself to look at him as I smiled a greeting, and examine him coldly. His was not, compared with John's, a handsome face. There were lines of stubbornness and wilfulness, too, marks of a stiffness of nature which were unlikely to change. None of that mattered.

And it did not matter that it did not matter. Through my open window came the scents of growing things, and the tolling of the chapel bell. The sun escaped his racing cloudy guards and threw a golden spear. What had happened was behind me.

He asked after my health, soberly, and I answered in the same fashion. It might be easier than I had thought. He had taken a chair, and sat beside my bed, but not so close that it disturbed me. There was a silence, but even that was not awkward. The bell tolled on, and stopped at last. He said abruptly:

'I owe you my life. He could not have missed me at that range.'

'I do not know, but if you do I owe you mine. It makes us quits.'

He stared at me. 'You were a fool. He might have killed you. He almost did.'

I did not mind him calling me a fool. It was scarcely lover-like, but that was no misfortune. I said:

'It is over and done with. Let us forget it.'

'No, we shall not. And we are not quits. There is no accounting between us, and nothing final. There never can be.'

I heard the emotion in his voice, and was conscious of an answering tremor. I steeled myself to master it. He said:

'I want you, Jenny, and I claim you. Not for anything I did, but because I love you.'

'No.' I heard my own voice, small but resolute. 'I am engaged to Michael, and we are to be married. Quite soon.' I looked at him. 'I wish you every happiness, Andrew.'

'Without you?' I did not answer it. 'And you, without me—shall you be happy?'

'Yes. I shall.'

He put his hand out, resting it on the counterpane close to mine. I did not touch it. He said:

'You could have persuaded me of that once. Even after I had first kissed you, that evening under the tree. But not after

239

what happened in the mine. It is not my love that makes the claim: that never could. It is yours, replying to it.'

'You are mistaken.'

'I know I am not!'

He spoke with the old arrogance, rousing the old resentment. I did not mind that, either, but clutched at it. I would protect myself with anger if no other defence was possible. I said, with deliberate indifference:

'If it suits you to deceive yourself, there is nothing I can do. Nor do I need to. I am concerned only with what I know, and what I intend.'

As I said that, unexpectedly and piercingly, the memory of a memory assailed me. I was back at the foot of the shaft, waking from sleep, and then further back in the summer-scented garden of my childhood. My hatred of my father had been born in love: my love for Harry stemmed from a child's fierce hate. What good did will serve, when our selves were treacherous? I looked at Andrew, and wanted him to plead with me, to renew the claim of love I had rejected. What else was there?

But he did not plead. For a moment he was silent; then said:

'I went back into the mine yesterday.'

I was surprised. I murmured something in a show of interest, and he said:

'The place you pointed out to me—where the wall had collapsed.... Those bright specks you saw—as I said, they were not gold but pyrites. But not worthless iron pyrites, as I judged them. They are pyrites of copper. It is a copper lode, a rich one and a wide one. I worked ten hours on it—long enough to be sure.'

I shook my head. 'I know nothing of copper or mining.'

'I had nothing to offer you before. Now I have. You shall not be poor.'

I felt suddenly drained of strength—tired and unhappy. I said:

'If it means you will recover your fortunes, I am very

glad. Glad for you, and your mother, and Emily. But how could you think it would make any difference to me?'

He was silent again, and for longer. When he spoke, it was with bitterness:

'Things have changed, have they not? I had forgotten.'

'Changed?'

'There are other things than money.' I looked at him. 'They say Sir Donald will not last a month—for a certainty cannot outlive his son. Michael will come into his baronetcy. He may not keep it long, but that does not matter does it? You will be Lady Bedivere, anyway.'

My own feelings were more sick than bitter. I had told myself it was an illusion, and vowed I should not pursue it, but however little I thought I valued it I had not wanted to see it so demeaned and soiled. I said:

'Go, Andrew. And do not come back.'

He stood up. 'If you mean it . . .'

'Yes,' I said. 'I mean it.'

21

It was in the early evening that I first came down again: Dr Roberts had advised that I might get up for dinner. Michael insisted on assisting me down the staircase. Mrs Wherry, who had helped me dress, walked behind us, ready, I thought, to catch either or both of us if we should falter.

She accompanied us to the gold drawing-room, but left us there. Michael made me comfortable in a chair; then went to the sideboard. He asked me:

'Which will you have, Jenny? Sherry wine, or madeira?'

'I don't think ...'

'It will do you good. Dr Roberts said you need fortifying.' He smiled. 'The madeira is the sweeter, and that suits you b-best.'

He spoke firmly for him, and did not wait for my consent but poured a glassful from the decanter. I looked about the room as he did so. Although it was only a matter of days since I had last been here, it had an air of strangeness that made me recall my feelings that first evening at Carmaliot. All the gold and glitter—the dazzle of light from mirrors and the big brass fender: it was as though I looked at it with the same timid and uncomprehending eyes. From the distorting mirror with its guardian eagle the room was thrown back, small and bright and twisted. But there was a difference between that night and this. Then it had shown a family assembled; now there were only two of us.

I took the glass Michael proffered me, and sipped it. The

vague depression which I had lately felt had settled more positively on me since I left my room, and I hoped the wine might free me of it. The room was so vast, so empty. I said to Michael:

'Lady Bedivere ... is she not joining us?'

He shook his head. 'She remains with my father constantly.'

'It has been a terrible time for her.'

'Yes.' He paused. 'I spoke with her this morning. She told me that when ... that if my father dies, she will not stay here. She has heard from Edgar that he is remaining for the present in London, and plans to join him there.'

So, two of us; and then, in due course, one. But if the flesh had done its work, two still. Michael, I knew, would see to all that was needed to make my position here secure. Lawyers would take instructions, and I would be guarded from all possible harm—I, and Carmaliot's heir.

I would be mistress of Carmaliot, and Lady Bedivere. I would own this house, in my son's name, and the great estates surrounding it. Hundreds of people would depend on my favour and my patronage. I would be rich, and wealth would bring power. I could lead, if I chose, the life of a merry widow —could have my pick, probably of a dozen suitors if I decided to marry again.

But not Andrew. I knew him well enough to be sure of that. He might lift up a woman ruined: he would have no truck with one who had sold herself, as he must see it. Nor would I want him to. And did it matter, when one had so much else?

I knew I was silent, but Michael did his best to talk for both of us. He spoke of unimportant things—for my comfort, I guessed—then said:

'My father ... may I take you to see him before we dine?'

I nodded. 'Of course.'

He had been downstairs, Michael told me, when he had his seizure, and they had not taken him to his room but made up a bed for him in his study. He was a man who had enjoyed the exercise of authority, and he would feel his powerlessness less keenly there than if he were relegated to the remoteness of a bedroom. That was true, I realized, as we made our way to the study; and it was characteristic of Michael that he should see and act on it.

The day-bed had been set up with its head against the wall, between the two high windows. Sir Donald lay with cushions propping him; beyond his bed on one side he could see his leather-topped desk, on the other a cheerful blaze in the hearth. On a chair at the foot of the bed sat Lady Bedivere.

Of their two faces I saw the greater alteration in hers. The paralysis which had seized on Sir Donald had only graven more deeply the lines of immobile calm which had been his usual expression. Now her face, which had smiled so constantly, was as fixed and blank as his, the more solemn for the heaviness of her features. She glanced up as we came in: no more than that. Michael spoke to her, saying he had brought me to see his father. She nodded, but made no reply.

I did not know, and never would, if she had been privy to the plots her sons had laid against me. It did not matter. A mother in the chief degree makes her sons, and she had fashioned hers badly, either by intent or indifference. Now one was banished, one dead. Whatever blame was attributable to her, her state was pitiable.

Sir Donald, even in his helplessness, was luckier. Whatever bitterness he might know, it was not like hers. He had lived for his dream, and his dream remained, embodied in the two figures who stood beside his bed.

'She is well, Father,' Michael said, 'as you c-can see. Quite well.'

The still face looked at me, unable to make response. Michael had brought me here, I saw, as reassurance; in case the old man, not seeing me, might think me lost still, or dead. He would not have him tormented by uncertainty. He went on:

'All is well. We shall be married, as you wished, and Carmaliot will have an heir.'

We faced each other down the long table. The servants had cleared away, and the butler had brought the decanter of port and set it before Michael. I had made as though to retire then, but he had stopped me, asking me to stay. I would have preferred my own company, but did not really mind. This mattered no more than anything else did.

Michael raised his glass.

'A toast,' he said. 'To you.'

I shook my head. 'I am not worth it.'

He smiled. 'I know you are. For what you did tonight alone.'

'Tonight?'

'In letting him go on b-believing we are to be married. It was a kindness.'

I was silent, puzzled. He looked steadily at me. I said slowly:

'I do not understand you, Michael.'

'Do you not? It is simple. He has not long to live: Roberts is sure of it. It would be t-torture for him to die with his hopes destroyed, and it does no harm to anyone if he is deceived.'

'But there is no deception. We are to be married.'

'No.'

'Why not?'

'Because of what you are. Because it would degrade you to be yoked to such as me, and I will not have it.'

'It was my choice! It was I who asked.'

'I know.'

'And you accepted.' My mind was in a tumult. 'You will not go back on that.'

'To make you s-safe, you said. You are safe now, and will be hereafter. All that is over.'

He was offering me freedom, and I could not take it. I said:

245

'It was what I chose, and choose still. You believed me then. Will you not believe me now?'

He did not reply. He loved me, and wanted to be persuaded; and I had persuaded him. I was sick at heart. He had opened the door for me, and I had slammed it shut. But I could do no other.

He said at last: 'That day, in the sunken garden, I told you I would never doubt your honesty. I ask you again, to tell me truthfully: do you love me?'

'Yes.' I looked at him. 'Yes, Michael.'

'As a woman should love a husband?'

It ought to be easy to say yes: so small a lie. But his eyes were on me, and I could not. He smiled, and said:

'You have changed, Jenny. Had I put that question to you then, I think you would have said yes, and quickly, n-not knowing what it meant. But now you know. I saw your eyes on Pellinser when he brought you back. I know he loves you, and is a fitter man for you to love.'

I said in a choked voice: 'I have refused him.'

'Yes. You are hard on yourself, and would be hard on him b-because you love him. It makes no difference. We are both of us free to choose, and I choose to release you.'

'And if I beg you not to?'

He said gently: 'You have a great d-deal of pride, Jenny, and even if it is sinful I admire it in you. But I have some, too. I love you, as you know, but you can offer me nothing more that I will take.'

I rode to Lacdam on a blowy morning, with the wind behind me. It had rained in the night and was likely to rain again— the scudding clouds were heavy with it—but the air was mild, and rich and juicy with spring.

Emily saw me coming, and ran out of the house to meet me. She cried:

'Jane! Are you well enough to ride out yet, and alone?'

246

'Yes. Quite well. The wound is almost healed.' I had made no move to dismount. 'Is Andrew in?'

She shook her head. 'He is up at the mine. He spends more time there than ever.'

I checked my horse from browsing on her hedge.

'I'll find him.'

'Do you want me to come with you?' She looked at me, and laughed. 'I perceive you don't! But you'll come back afterwards—both of you?'

I rode to the mine entrance and dismounted. I waited beside the horse-trough, where John had been, but felt no tremor at the memory. It was all past and over, like so many things. Ghosts did not walk; it was rather our fretful minds that made them restless.

I was a long time waiting, but was not impatient. Content with solitariness, I thought of people. Of Harry, proud in his navy dress, sailing the turbulent seas. Of my mother, and the girls. Of my father, forgetting all else except that I had loved him.

I thought of Michael. I had judged him weak but knew he was stronger than I—braver and more generous. What I could not take he had given me, knowing it left him penniless. From pride, he had said; but it was a finer pride than mine. Whatever the Bediveres had been, or had not been, Carmaliot's last heir had true nobility. My first son, I resolved in that moment, should be named Michael.

Content with solitariness—because the term was short. I saw him at last coming up; out of the earth as he had done that first day. He was tousled and dirty now, as he had been then. I did not call, but waited for him to see me.

For a long moment he stared; then, as he took a step forward, I ran to him. Nothing needed saying. I went into his arms and he held me, and I winced from the pain of my wound.

He noticed it and drew back, but I would not let him.

247

I tightened my own arms round him, glad of the hurt.

Andrew would not let me ride back, but drove me in the dog-cart. We talked easily and lightly, nonsensically I suppose, as lovers always do. The wind blew in our faces, damp and heavy still with unshed rain. Then, as we neared our journey's end, the wind brought something else, which stopped our chatter.

It came from the spire of Carmaliot, perched high and far above us: the deep tolling of a bell. A dream ended as a dream began.